BOOKS BY J. C. MCKENZIE

The Lark Morgan Series

Death Stealer *(prequel)*

Death Maker

Death Raiser

Death Taker

Isle and Eyrie Series

Cormorant Run

Heir of the Eyrie

House of Moon and Stars

The Night House

House of Chaos

Crawford Investigations

Conspiracy of Ravens

Nevermore

Queen of Corvids

The Call of Corvids

From the Shadows

Into the Fire

Dark Legacy

Embrace the Flame

BEAST

J. C. MCKENZIE

COPYRIGHT INFORMATION

Beast

Contact Information: jcmckenzie@jcmckenzie.ca

Cover Art: Olga Sauchenia

Publishing History:

First JCM Publications Edition, 2024

First Black Rose Edition, 2014 (*Beast Coast*, Wild Rose Press)

ISBN: 978-1-990143-55-7 (print)

ISBN: 978-1-990143-56-4 (ebook)

To my mom and dad,
for reading all those bedtime stories to me and encouraging
my imagination.

You're entering the creative domain of a Canadian author. There will be a combination of British and American spellings, a combination of measurement systems, and maybe even a little French thrown in to spice things up.

This series contains explicit language, open-door spicy scenes, ghosts, violence, gore, torture, PTSD from past SA, threat of SA, murder, assassinations, sociopaths and narcissists. This series also contains death, grief, and loss.

Please read with care.

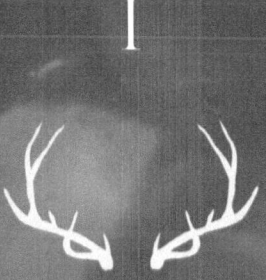

Stomach acid bubbled up my throat and settled at the back of my mouth. I stood a yard away from Lucien, the Master Vampire of the British Columbia Lower Mainland, while my feet grew roots into the palace-worthy tiles beneath me. My gut twisted into a hard rock and it took every ounce of willpower not to shriek in defiance. The first time I'd been here, Lucien's goon squad had dragged me down the red carpet of his receiving room, while I expected to lose my head. The consequent visits hadn't gone much better, but this time, things would be different. I planned to have my debt expunged tonight, and I refused to run away like a scared little girl.

Lucien sat in his big throne chair wearing a dress shirt with the first few buttons unfastened, under an open, pinstriped jacket. Rich black hair fell in shiny waves across Italian good looks as he leaned forward and steepled his hands together like a maniacal priest. The cool night air carried his Vampire scent to me along with the beginning hints of summer, but it contained none of Lucien's emotions—only death and blood.

His crystalline voice shattered the heavy silence in the large sterile room. "Andrea. It is a pleasure to see you have recovered from your most recent endeavours." Clint, his human servant who stood beside me, chuckled at the Vampire's choice of words. The sound rumbled from his broad chest and shook his massive shoulders. My recent endeavours involved getting my ass handed to me by a rival master. I might be badass and able to shift into multiple animal forms, but if Clint hadn't stepped in, I'd have been sucked dry. It almost made me like the guy. Almost. Right now, I wanted to punch him in the throat.

Wick flanked my other side and essentially made me the bologna of a beefcake sandwich. Standing tall, with blond hair and chocolate brown eyes, his sugar and rosemary scent bolstered my confidence. The Alpha Werewolf of the local pack might have to obey Lucien's every command, but he had a little thing for me, so he didn't pose as big a problem. Okay, more like a huge thing— potential mate, huge. We'd spent the last week making out like horny teenagers on his living room couch.

We were taking things slow because I refused to let my wolf lead. I might've used my body to get close to targets for assassinations, but that didn't mean I was comfortable jumping in bed with someone I actually liked, nor did it mean I could undo decades of pain and simply trust my heart again.

Lucien reached out and curled his index finger in a

come hither gesture. I stepped forward, which put Lucien uncomfortably within my personal space. The animals cohabitating in my head space screamed at the vulnerability of my exposed back, but I couldn't turn around and snap at either Clint or Wick. That would mean taking my eyes off two bigger threats.

Lucien's second in command and the largest Japanese Vampire I'd ever encountered, stood at Lucien's side. Allan could read every thought running around in my head but for now, he chose to keep the information to himself. A little red blotch stained his crisp white collar.

"You spilled." I nodded at his shirt.

Allan's eyes shuttered for a second, and then he licked his lips. "A little blood spatter. Does it frighten you?"

I snorted. "No."

Not food, my mountain lion hissed. *Not prey.*

Allan shrugged.

A long silence stretched into the awkward zone. Lucien puckered his lips and waited, losing a little of the scary factor by looking like a runway model—all chiseled cheekbones and full lips. He seemed to enjoy tormenting me, using silence to force me to speak and reveal my thoughts. It worked.

"My debt is paid in full," I said.

"I disagree, Andy," he answered without hesitation.

Anger coiled up my neck and settled behind my eyes as I tensed. This was not how I wanted things to go. "I did as you asked. You got Ethan's head."

"Ah, but I requested *you* deliver Ethan's head. You weren't the one to present the item, now were you?" He flipped his hand in the air as if what he said held little consequence, as if still owing him was no big deal. I stared at his hands, wanting to rip them off with my teeth. *I hated owing anyone anything.*

Taking a deep breath, I tried reason. "I cut off his head and delivered it to your second in command. That's good enough considering the circumstances."

Lucien tapped his chin, feigning deep thought, but I knew he was toying with me. Not nice.

"It's semantics, Lucien. Stop pissing around," I said.

Lucien's finger stopped tapping. His face blanked and his eyes vamped out, the irises receding until only the pupil remained. "Not many would dare speak to me so."

I jutted my hip out and placed my hand on it. "Well, it's not going to change your verdict, is it?"

He shook his head.

"Thought not." My heart hammered in my chest despite my bold words.

Lucien relaxed into his chair. "I will consider your debt paid in full if you stay the rest of the night and partake in our *activities*."

"Absolutely not."

"No?"

"No fucking way. I will not stay so you can serve me as an entrée or fob me off to one of your minions. There's a lot of night left for you to make my life miserable."

Lucien laughed. "I will amend. I would like you to

stay and no harm will befall you. You will walk out of here as healthy as you already are, or better."

"Why?"

Lucien's seat creaked as he shifted his weight. "I wish to discuss your future, after I have a quick word with Wick."

The Alpha Werewolf shuffled his feet behind me at the mention of his name, probably bracing for whatever sadistic thing Lucien planned.

"My future is my business," I said, wanting Lucien's attention away from my Werewolf. He couldn't control me, but the same couldn't be said for Wick.

"You'll want to hang around and hear what I have to say, *Carus*."

My eyes narrowed as my heartbeat quickened.

I'd been called a lot of things in my lifetime—shifter, beast, demon... But the one name that gave me pause was the one I didn't understand—Carus.

Lucien knew my Shifter name. Of course Allan would've told him about my abilities weeks ago, but it was more than that. I hadn't told anyone about being called "Carus." Only two others had spoken that name to me—one was dead at my own hands, and the other probably sat in his rocking chair right now minding his own business.

Lucien called me *Carus*. The twinkle of his eyes and smug smile said he probably knew more about my nature. After all these years of searching, I might learn something valuable. It didn't matter if the information came from him.

"Fine," I said.

Lucien nodded and I sensed more than saw Clint and Allan move into position behind me. Part of me instantly regretted my hasty decision. There would be a cost for the knowledge Lucien offered, but I'd agreed and the price couldn't be too high. He'd said no harm. I'd walk away from this deal all the way to Wick's place.

Lucien flicked his dead, empty gaze to Wick. "Come forward."

Wick's body jerked as the power of Lucien's order wrapped around him. He walked past me to stand before the Vampire.

"Kneel," Lucien said.

My scalp prickled at the sight of powerful, dominant Wick forced to follow the demands of someone else. Had Lucien's animal to call been anything other than a wolf, Wick wouldn't be here.

"What is Andy?" Lucien asked, his voice low and quiet.

My head snapped up and my eyes narrowed. Why ask Wick? Lucien already knew, didn't he? I stepped forward a little, to give Wick some sort of signal to dish all the goods, only to falter when a strong hand clamped down on my shoulder. I looked behind me to see Allan shake his head. *Mind speech is out then.* Able to read my mind, Allan would report me and I didn't want to find out Lucien's punishment for that.

"A Shifter," Wick answered Lucien's question.

"What type of Shifter? What animal does she turn into?"

"A mountain lion."

My skin itched. I'd never told Wick about my Shifter name. I hadn't trusted him at first, and then there'd been no time. We'd spent the last week building up trust while I worked through my emotional baggage. Wick might be a dominant Alpha, but he knew patience was more important than pushing too hard, or using his dominance to fix me. He respected my boundaries.

"Anything else you wish to tell me?" Lucien asked Wick.

"No."

Lucien laughed. "I have no doubt you don't want to tell me anything. Yet, I know you haven't been a good, faithful dog." The Vampire stood and glided closer to Wick. "Tell me everything you know and suspect about Andy's nature. Leave nothing out."

I cringed in unison with Wick. The words tumbled out of the Alpha's mouth despite the sweat running down his forehead. "She's not like any Shifter I know. She has three forms, instead of one—a mountain lion, a wolf, and a peregrine falcon—maybe more. Her animal familiars, her feras, seem to be inside her somehow, which is not something I've ever heard of. They aren't physical animals like other familiars. She also..." Wick hesitated.

"Out with it!"

"She also talks about a beast in her sleep. She has nightmares about it. I think she has another form, a dangerous one, and it scares her. Whatever it is, the beast has something to do with how she escaped Dylan's pack."

I stiffened. Wick suspected *a lot*.

Lucien's lips curled up into a smarmy smile while he tapped his chin and listened. When Wick finished, Lucien leaned down to him. "I already knew."

"Then why ask me?" Wick bit out.

"To test your allegiance," Lucien said, flipping another noncommittal hand in the air. His usually blank face twisted into something unpleasant. "I am not impressed."

Wick looked back at the ground. His body tensed. He knelt, frozen in place, and waited for his punishment. Dread shimmered down my body along with the uncomfortable sting of guilt. My need for secrecy and Wick's need to protect me would cost him. A good servant would've told his Master Vampire everything right away.

"I have the perfect punishment for your disobedience." Lucien looked up and his gaze slid to me. I caught the gleam in them too late. Hands clasped my arms, holding me in place before I could run. Even shifting wouldn't make me fast enough to escape Allan's Vampire hold. My skin tingled at the contact, and my chest felt like a stampede of horses ran around inside.

"You said no harm!" I shrieked.

Lucien turned away from me. "And no lasting harm shall befall you."

The beast deep within settled in confusion. I took control and hugged my mountain lion close with my mind. Whatever Lucien dished out, it wouldn't be as bad as losing myself to the beast inside me. It couldn't be, could it? Whatever happened tonight, I wouldn't lose control. I didn't want to hurt Wick.

Twisting my head around, I gave Allan and Clint death stares. Allan, staring straight ahead, gave nothing away. Did that mean something? Part of me hoped he felt some sort of remorse for his actions. Clint in comparison vibrated with excitement, arousal, and anticipation—the scents sprung up from him and danced around me.

"Wick." Lucien's voice cut through my thoughts. "Bring Andy before me and hold her still."

I watched in horror as Wick, the man I wanted to open my heart to, staggered toward me. A whole new slew of raw emotions erupted, but none of them pleasant. Wick's yellow irises bore into mine. His face strained with effort, fighting Lucien's control and failing with each step. "Don't make me do this, Lucien," Wick choked out.

The Vampire smiled and leaned forward. "The sooner you accept my complete dominion over you, my little pup, the easier your life will become. Now, *bring her to me*."

Wick lurched to where I stood. When his big calloused hands closed around my arms—his touch warm, but firm—Allan and Clint let go. Wick gave a gentle tug for me to step forward. My legs stiffened. His brow creased when I resisted.

My wolf paced in my head, confused. *Mate,* she repeated over and over again, sounding less sure with each frantic breath. My mountain lion yowled, yearning to break free and my falcon flapped her wings.

Wick led me to face Lucien, leaving Allan and Clint somewhere behind us—their presence, a discomforting pressure at my back.

"Make her kneel before me." Lucien's half-hooded eyes watched me.

Wick tugged down on my arms, but my knees locked.

"Please," Wick whispered. He switched to mind speech. *Don't fight me. I don't want to hurt you.*

Screw you, Wick, I flung back.

"Now," Lucien demanded.

Wick forced me down. Pain lanced through my muscles as my knees buckled under the pressure and slammed against the hard stone.

I'm so sorry, Andy, Wick said.

Lucien's smile widened as he stepped forward. "Hold her still," he said to the Alpha. "We don't want her to flinch and scar badly. I like my marks clean."

For a moment I remained frozen, trying to figure out another way to interpret Lucien's words.

No, he couldn't mean—

My arms shook, the skin where Wick held me felt encased in molten-hot shackles. The beast stirred, flowing fast to rise up to take control. She would teach them all.

Wick's eyes met mine and cold numbness swept through my body as a stronger fear replaced the old. I couldn't let the beast out. The one and only time I had...I destroyed a whole pack. I couldn't risk hurting Wick.

The beast surged within my skin, and I pushed her

down. The only thing that scared me more than Lucien was a world without Wick.

"How is this even possible?" I asked, hating the quiver in my voice. "You already have a human servant."

Lucien smiled. "Master Vampires develop unique skills as the centuries roll by and they amass power."

"Yes, but—"

"Just as some Vampires acquire the skill to call and control one specific type of animal, like wolves or leopards, some, like myself, are able to blood bond more than one servant."

"Don't do this, Lucien," I said.

Lucien shook his head before bending to the soft tissue of my neck.

I'm so sorry, Andy, Wick said with a raw voice that scratched my heart. His fingers gently brushed back my hair, while his palms squished my cheeks and jaw. Tears streaked down his cheeks and splattered against my face, hot against my skin.

"Don't!" I lurched my body forward in an attempt to twist away, but my head, clamped between Wick's hands stayed immobile as my lower half flailed around. "Fuck you, Lucien. Don't you da—"

The sharp pain of Lucien's fangs piercing my neck cut me off. His embedded teeth, foreign and wrong, violated my body. A cold numbing wave started at my toes and flowed up my body. My skin tingled as if I'd opened the door to a walk-in freezer.

The acrid scent of blood sprung from my neck and flooded the air, tinged with pine and fear. Lucien patted my hair and despite his sophisticated air, ate like a messy two-year-old. The sounds of him slurping filled the room. His wet tongue licked my skin. Blood trailed down my neck and seeped into the neckline of my shirt.

I dropped my head back, using the only control I had left to keep the beast locked down.

Wick no longer had to hold me, but he didn't let go. My face looked serene, as if I slept.

What the fuck? How can I see my own face?

I looked down at my body, floating while observing the scene through fuzzy glasses, like I had many times with Dylan to escape the pain and humiliation he inflicted on my body all those years ago. But something made this time different, something worse.

Where are my feras?

For the first time since pubescence, I couldn't feel or hear them.

Guys? Wolf? You there?

No one answered. My security blanket had been ripped away.

Lucien's head snapped up—his mouth ringed with my blood, a dazed but pleased expression on his face. He licked his lips.

I slammed back into my body and forced my eyes open, the small movement difficult, as though I'd been woken up at three in the morning and hadn't gained control of all my limbs yet. Everything felt heavy, as if drugged.

My eyes fixated on Lucien's fangs and smiling lips.

That's my blood. He drank way more than he had to for a blood bond. Disturbing that I knew that.

"I like the taste of you, Shifter." He licked his lips again, and stroked my cheek. The skin around his mouth stained pink. "You taste like a cold mountain spring. And remind me of running through the forest during the summertime of my youth." He leaned down and took a deep breath in, smelling me, scenting my blood. "Ahh…" He smiled and rubbed his thumb on my bottom lip. "So fresh."

Icy fingers curled around my fast-beating heart and squeezed. *Breathe woman!*

Lucien looked over my head. Wick still stood there holding me. I'd forgotten about him.

"Hold her mouth open," Lucien ordered.

No!

My silent protest did nothing to prevent Wick's strong hands from clamping on my jaw and head, and prying my mouth open. The same hands that had caressed and embraced me in a lover's hold. They would never be the same again.

Lucien withdrew a knife and slashed his wrist open in one stroke. The sight of his ceremonial blade blurred with speckles of black dots and my breath came in and out in short huffs of air. My heartbeat pumped hard in my eardrums, drowning out all other sounds. *This is happening. I can't stop this.* He held his wrist over my mouth and let his blood spill into it. Then, he pressed his arm forcibly against my mouth.

The lukewarm blood hit the back of my mouth,

gagging me. I tried to cough and spit it out, but Wick's unrelenting grasp prevented it. Squirming and writhing around in Wick's embrace did little to deter anyone.

I'm so sorry, Wick said. *Forgive me. I'd kill him for this if I could.*

My mouth filled up with the viscous slew of filth; warm, from my own blood's heat.

Lucien withdrew and nodded at Wick. He held my mouth shut. I tried to spit it out, but his hand covered my lips. I choked on the backlash of blood and swallowed involuntarily. The liquid heated as it travelled down my throat, and slithered into my stomach. It hit my core and pain radiated out. My muscles spasmed and shook as my body fought the link. Lucien touched his forehead to mine. He mumbled something in a foreign language, maybe Latin. Intense fire flared up inside and flashed to my fingers and toes.

When it faded, it left me cold and shivering.

I sank to the floor, pulling Wick down with me.

"You said no harm," I gasped.

"And no lasting physical harm has befallen you. In fact, some would argue, you're better off now than you were before. I've kept my word."

"We have a different definition of harm." I curled my body into a small ball. "You promised answers about being the Carus."

"I never promised answers. I wished to discuss your future, and now it's been determined." Lucien's voice reflected the smug look on his face. "You're mine."

2

I should never be woken up at three in the morning by a troop of drunken lunatics belting out off-key versions of 80s remix songs. Normally, I'd correct my neighbours with a fist in the face, but in this case, I made an exception—I didn't like the dream they interrupted anyway. Instead of my usual nightmares filled with memories of the sadistic man who ruined eleven years of my life and all the horrible things he did to me, I dreamt of Wick.

The bonding happened over a week ago, but time did little to dull the pain. As the memory of the Werewolf Alpha flickered through my mind, my gut clenched, and a sharp jab punched my chest as if a pissed off Harry Potter stabbed my heart instead of Tom Riddle's diary.

The neighbours rattled off a few more songs while I lay in bed and tried to ignore the images of Wick's anguished expression when he held me down for Lucien to blood bond me, but then the opening music to another 80s hit drifted through my condo.

Enough.

I stumbled out of bed and into my office. The sight of my empty living room sent another series of stabbing pains to my heart, but this time, ones of loneliness. If I'd been born a normal Shifter, I'd have an animal familiar to keep me company. But instead of a warm and fuzzy fera, I had voices in my head.

My neighbours reached the chorus, chanting about the final countdown.

Gah! At least three inept males threw me a pity party and didn't even know it.

Storming to my desk I grabbed a black marker and a sheet of paper from the feed of my printer. Like a mad scientist, I scribbled down a message with a gem-encrusted pen:

Dear Morons,

Thank you for keeping me up all night. Had I been able to sleep through a stampede of screaming elephants, I would've missed your mediocre rendition of songs from over three decades ago. Your singing is the worst thing I've heard since the latest reality show's blooper reel.

Please stop or I'll silence you myself.

Your sleep deprived and deeply pissed-off neighbour

I sat back to take a look at my handiwork before flinging myself out of the desk chair, and marching into the hallway. I glared at the neighbours' door. I hadn't met them yet. They moved in while I was busy running around like a headless chicken trying to pay my debt to Lucien.

And look where that got me. Blood bonded. Now the Master Vampire haunted my head like another animal, influencing my thoughts and pulling my attention in yet another direction. Theoretically, at least. He'd been pretty quiet so far, which made me wonder what he was up to. I didn't know what he wanted with me, aside from my value as a collector's item, and I didn't really want to find out. Ignorance was bliss, or at least it had been for the last week.

I should've used the time to find out more about my neighbours, but instead, I'd moped around my place and spent hours feeling sorry for myself. It was an occupational hazard not to be aware of everything in my vicinity. *Know all and be known by none.* Ever since I got involved with Lucien, things went to hell, including my professional integrity. If the Supernatural Regulatory Division found out about the blood bond, I'd be out of a job. *Badass SRD assassin, my ass.*

Sniffing the air immediately made me recoil. Pine-scented cleaner—so strong it stung my eyes. I backed away from the door in a sneezing fit.

Whatever.

With my shirt pulled up over my nose, I folded my ranting letter and slipped it under their door. They were so drunk, they probably wouldn't see it until the morning, but at least the letter might put a stop to future karaoke sessions.

I marched back to my apartment and slammed the door behind me.

Their song ended, and I held my breath in the silence that followed. Maybe they wanted applause? They wouldn't get any. If the other owners in the building were anything like me, they'd more likely band together to tar and feather my neighbours than support their inept nocturnal habits.

The silence stretched. *Please, let it be over*.

The crickets, stupefied by the earlier noise competition, gained confidence and started to pick up their usual tune. No singing. Finally!

Flopping onto my bed, I shut my eyes and enjoyed the feeling of sinking into the mattress.

The beeping of my phone fractured the stillness—cutting my relaxation to shreds.

Text message.

Groaning, I rolled over and grabbed the phone. A text from Clint:

Your presence is required.

When?

Now.

I glanced at my clock.

It's four in the morning.

Then you better hurry.

Cursing, I flung back the blankets and marched to the living room, tearing off my clothes with each step. I threw open the window and willed the change. Sharp flash of pain, muscles condensed, skin folded inward and feathers sprouted. The fastest way to Lucien's was to fly.

THERE WAS NOTHING WORSE THAN STARING down a Master Vampire in the buff. The cool air made goose bumps prickle up on my naked skin, dashing my hopes they'd provide warmth and modest coverage. Lucien glowered at me, sprawled like an errant prince on a throne-like chair in the middle of his otherwise empty grand ballroom.

He wore a solid gray suit with a crisp white shirt underneath, collar popped. It seemed like the house uniform, and being naked, I was definitely underdressed.

"Could you get me a robe or something?" I hissed out of the side of my mouth at Clint, who stood beside me. Tall and built like a dense forest, Clint's broad shoulders made a girl want to learn how to scale trees. Except me. I wanted to start a forest fire.

A few weeks ago, I'd tried to kill him under what I thought were government orders. Turned out my handler was on the payroll of another master who wanted the Lower Mainland territory, and I'd unwittingly attempted an unsanctioned hit. A mistake I still paid for, despite having my debt expunged.

Clint leaned in, his gelled black hair unmoving. "Where would the fun be in that?" The human servant knew how to hold a grudge. I successfully tore his throat out, which he miraculously survived, but having him request me as a play toy for all eternity from Lucien—a fate I narrowly escaped—made us even in my books.

"I don't think clothing is your biggest concern." Lucien's smooth voice interrupted whatever insult I would've come up with to fling at his human servant.

I narrowed my eyes. "What should I be concerned with?"

Lucien's lips twitched into a slow smile. He laced his fingers together. "You're not the least bit curious about my plans for you?"

Part of me didn't want to know. Part of me did. And part of me wanted to shred his stomach apart so his guts fell out. The idea he had any control over me made my blood boil. I forced my fingers to unclench and examined my cuticles in an attempt to look nonchalant—attempt being the key word. The smirks around the room told me I didn't fool anyone. "You can plot and scheme to use me all you want, but the blood bond gives your power *to* me. Extended life, faster healing, et cetera." I left out our bond also gave him the ability to sense my location, and read my emotions. He didn't need to be reminded.

"If that's what you need to tell yourself, Carus." Lucien smirked. *Kneel before me.*

Oh, and he had the ability of mind speech that made

me do his bidding like a good little girl. I'd avoided thinking about that one, since I already had enough nightmares to fill up my sleeping dance card. I hoped to evade this hard truth altogether, but the tug of Lucien's command made me stagger. Beads of sweat pebbled on my nose as my legs started to bend. I fought the compulsion. *No.*

Lucien's head dropped back as he bellowed a laugh. "Fight me all you want, Shifter. I can make your life miserable and you know it."

The weight of his order lifted and I straightened up. If Lucien wished to force the issue, I would've been kneeling and licking his boots. I glanced down at the snakeskin ones he wore tonight and shivered.

"I suggest you make it easy on the both of us and comply. You'll find I'm very reasonable."

For a Vampire. The words didn't need to be spoken. Fine. I'd play his game. At least he didn't seem inclined to suck on my neck like a juice box. "What do you want?"

Lucien's eyes gleamed. If Vampires weren't impervious to diseases, I would've said feverish. He moved forward on his seat as if preparing to open birthday presents. I didn't like his expression at all. Anticipation.

"There's an important Vampire Summit in Portland this weekend. I am not attending, but Clint will go as my representative."

In his pause, dread flittered through my body. This led nowhere good and I didn't like it one bit.

"I want you to accompany him."

Fuck that. "Why?"

Lucien's eyebrow arched. Not many would dare to openly question a Vampire of his power. I tested his tolerance, a little, maybe a lot, but rolling over had never been my thing. A deafening silence stretched as I forced myself not to fidget or drop my gaze.

Not submissive, my mountain lion hissed in my head.

I cleared my throat. "I mean, why me? Surely Allan would be a better option. A loyal subject with your best interests at heart."

Lucien's forehead relaxed, and a slow smile spread across his face. "You better have my *best interests* at heart. Need I remind you? If I die, so do you."

I looked away. My life force bound to Lucien's was the only thing stopping me from trying to rip off his head with my teeth. My good health depended on keeping this Vampire alive. Shouldn't be too hard—he'd managed to do a fine job without me for the last, what, three, four hundred years, give or take a few centuries? I sucked at guessing vamp ages, but I knew Lucien was *old*. He had enough power to call wolves and bond two servants.

"Think of me as another fera in your head, dear *Carus*. A blood sucking one."

I had nothing to say. He said exactly what I thought. *Gah, Carus!* Why did random supes know more about me than I did? Lucien sure as fuck wouldn't call me *beloved* in Latin.

"To answer your unrequested *why me?*" Lucien interrupted my thoughts using a high-pitched girly voice to mock me. "Allan is already pursuing another interest of mine. Besides, what is the saying? Don't put all your eggs in one basket?"

Well, at least he didn't plan to suck me dry, yet. Escorting Clint to some Vampire powwow was better than hooked up to Lucien's face as his eternal blood donor. Thank Feradea, the beast goddess, he had no interest in me as a woman. "Am I arm candy or is there something you'd like me to accomplish?"

"With Allan absent, Clint will need someone capable of mind speech who can distinguish lies from truths." All Weres and Shifters could use their noses to detect the truth of a statement, but Weres could only mind speak to other members in their pack, pride or prowl, and Shifters could only mind speak to their fera.

And then there was me.

"How did you..." I let my voice trail off, figuring it out. Wick would have told him I was capable of mind speech. "I don't think it extends to anyone other than Shifters and Weres." I didn't mention I tried to mind speak to Allan during our takedown of Ethan and was pretty sure he heard me.

"Try." Lucien sat back and relaxed.

I think you're a disgusting pig, I thought at Clint.

Clint laughed and then shook his head. "I think I will have plenty of time, kitten, to convince you otherwise."

I batted his hand away before he got the chance to caress me. "You don't get to call me that." Despite the pissy tone, my mind reeled. *Clint could hear me too?* And Lucien knew he could. What else did he know about my abilities? That made me valuable. More than a mere collector's item.

"How did you know I could do that?" I asked.

"See? You're learning already." Lucien's gaze flicked to the window and the light blue sky of predawn. He yawned, and his eyes vamped-out, like all bloodsuckers before bedtime. "Clint will fill in the rest of the details. You are dismissed."

Needing no encouragement before Lucien gorged himself on whatever willing blood donor waited in the next room—the one who smelled of olives, wine, and excitement—I spun on my heel and stalked out with Clint close behind. And naked as naked could be, he'd see every bounce and jiggle of my ass. *Awesome.* When I made it to the hallway, I turned to find Clint's heated gaze on my body.

"What are you looking at?"

"Your skin."

My eyes narrowed. "What about my skin?"

"It looks so soft and smooth, like tanned porcelain."

I crossed my arms, knowing Clint was never straight-forward enough for this to be a compliment. "Oh yeah?"

"I want to see it turn red and bruised under my hands."

"Who hurt you?"

Clint smirked. "We'll leave tomorrow night. I can brief you on the way to Portland. I'd like you to meet me at the Renaissance." He paused before asking, "Know it?"

I groaned. Of course I did. "That's the hotel where I tried to kill you."

"Precisely."

"Didn't peg you for the sentimental type."

A small smile flittered across his face. "Be there by seven. Pack for two nights. We'll come home Sunday." He turned to leave.

A thought sprung up. "What were you doing there the first time anyway?"

"At the hotel?" Clint stopped and peered over his massive shoulders. "Slumming."

"I knew it." Not that Clint's confession made a difference to the outcome of that particular assignment, but I wanted to figure out what he was. He defied the normal parameters of a human servant. He should've died that night and he should've stayed dead after Ethan stabbed him. "Go there often?"

Clint turned to face me with a pleased smile. "Every couple months, I get to have a few days off to enjoy myself."

"Don't you mean to enjoy the blondes?" Something about the night we first met never sat right; I needed to learn more about Lucien's right-hand man.

"Same thing," he said.

I snorted.

"Jealous?"

"You bang more than an outhouse door in a storm. No, I'm not jealous. I'm disgusted."

"By what? Me *banging?*"

"By the collective intelligence of women being too low to see through whatever act you use."

"There's no act. They see me for what I am, and I don't pretend to be anything else."

"Then I'm not disgusted. I'm appalled by their sheer lack of gray matter."

Clint shrugged and checked his phone. "Do you have a formal gown to wear?"

I made a face. "Of course not."

"What size are you?"

"Size awesome."

He gave me a blank stare. He didn't get it.

"Eight." You couldn't be my height with boobs and a butt and fit something smaller without having a serious eating disorder or model-worthy genetics.

Clint shrugged and started punching numbers into his phone as he walked away. More evidence that men didn't care about the number on the tag of a woman's pants, they just wanted to get in them.

3

Every time I held grocery bags in one hand and tried to unlock my building door with the other, the key stuck. No amount of supernatural ability helped me, either. Last time I used force, the key snapped in the lock, and I received a two-page letter from the Glenwood Agency, my building's management company, detailing the proper use of keys and how to correctly unlock the door. They threatened I would be charged if I failed to follow their *simple* instructions and broke my key again. All three of my feras had lost it at the condescending tone and demanded I rip someone's face off. I don't think they cared who I picked.

I hated Glenwood.

With a lengthy exhalation, bordering on a groan, I admitted defeat and placed the bags at my feet before unlocking the door. The key turned smoothly, as if it hadn't been stuck two seconds ago. I threw a foot into the building and my hip into the door before leaning down to pick up my groceries. Trained dancers cringed across the globe.

When I finally lumbered into the warmth of my building, I skidded to a stop.

The telltale scent of vanilla and honey flooded my nostrils, sending a shiver of foreboding down my spine at the same time it made my mouth water. Witches.

Nothing but trouble.

How did I miss the scent before? I shifted the weight of my grocery bags to bring feeling back into one of my pinkies. Oh right. *I haven't used the front door all week.* Been flying out the window, instead.

Sniffing down the hall like a bloodhound tracking a fugitive, I followed the smell to my new neighbours' front door.

Goddammit!

Not only did I live beside a coven of Witches, but I'd written them a letter, too, and insulted their singing. Not good.

I trudged back to my apartment with my groceries.

With another, smaller, fight with my key, I unlocked my apartment's door and swung it open. *What the heck?* I stared at the third biggest surprise of the day. Maybe second. Lucien's power trip and Vampire summit order fell into a different category.

Covering my floor were thousands upon thousands of mini-paper cups. I knelt down and scented the air, taking in short successive breaths. Tap water. I pinched the rim of one cup and lifted. It pulled at the surrounding cups. They were all stapled together.

Huh.

This would have taken someone days to complete.

Or magic.

There, beneath the smell of new paper and corroded pipe water, lay vanilla and honey. They figured out who sent the letter. And they had exacted revenge. I smacked my forehead with my palm and then raked my fingers down my face.

"Fuck." How the heck was I going to get the cups out? Even if I could move them all at once, I'd have to tip them to the side to get them through the door and the water would spill all over the wood flooring and rugs.

I was going to have to detach each cup, one by one. With rolled-up sleeves and my long black hair twisted into a ponytail, I cracked my knuckles and stepped into the fray. My groceries sat in the hallway to supervise.

Personally, I'd prefer a proper fight—hair pulling, name calling, bitch slapping and all.

BY THE TIME I MADE IT TO MY LIVING ROOM, drenched in stagnant paper cup water and on my last straw of patience, I saw two messages on my antiquated answering machine. I'd refused to replace the archaic thing despite the incessant waves of new technology. It reminded me of the one my mom had before she died.

I pressed the button and sat back in my chair. Wiping

sweat from my brow, I cringed as a husky voice I knew too well, and still dreamed of, floated in the air and licked my skin.

"Andy, it is me," Wick said, showing his age with his lack of contractions. "Do not delete this before listening... Please," he said in a rushed exhale of breath. "It is important."

The *big bad wolf* said please? If exhaustion hadn't prevented me from getting out of the chair and reaching for the machine, I still would've deleted the message.

"I cannot go to Portland."

I froze, listening intently. Of course Wick's pack was involved with the Portland Vampire Summit. I should've known better. Stupid of me. Lucien would want to demonstrate his power at a Vampire gathering by showing off his wolves.

"Steve is going in my place."

At least he didn't send John or Ryan, the Werewolves who openly despised me—John, because I'd hurt his mate in an attempt to escape, and Ryan, because I'd hurt his feelings in another attempt to escape.

Steve, indifferent at best, at least knew how to be inconspicuous, having been ordered to follow me in the past.

After a pause, Wick continued. "I am sorry, Andy. I cannot say it enough, and you are probably going to ignore this apology along with the rest, but I am. Truly sorry. Forgive me. Please call."

A second please? *Aww, he's being so sweet.* Still not happening.

Wick had no choice when he'd held me down for Lucien to blood bond me. My brain knew it, as did my heart, but logic and reasoning did little to assuage the hurt and sense of betrayal. He should've fought more, said more, done more, and his ineffectiveness at keeping me safe provided a rude lesson in loyalties. With a simple order, Lucien could force Wick to do very bad things to me.

My wolf might think Wick was a good mate, but I knew otherwise. He'd always answer to Lucien.

Despite all that, I wanted to forgive Wick. I *really* did. But in my nightmares, I saw his face on Dylan's body. Though Wick had little in common with the cruel Alpha from my past, I couldn't shake the images from the other night. If anyone looked up damaged in the dictionary, my picture would be there with a reference to baggage.

The machine beeped and started the second message.

"Andrea." The deep purr of Tristan's voice surrounded me. My heart rate increased. "Call me."

I laughed. My life was so fucked up. The last time I'd seen Tristan, the leader of the local Wereleopard prowl, he'd been bent over me, naked, trying desperately to heal me after he'd thrown me into a wall. I'd passed out and Wick ended up taking me to his place.

My mountain lion urged me to pick up the phone, or to shift and run to Tristan like some sex-kitten in heat. Maybe I was. First time for everything.

Tristan tempted something primal within me. The way he smelled... It would be so easy to be a mountain lion, to slip into the form like a worn housecoat and lose myself to the freedom of feline mentality. Forget the past. Forget Wick and Lucien and the SRD. Just be. My cougar represented everything safe.

At least to me.

Hikers and forest prey probably disagreed.

Sighing, I stared at the cordless phone on the table in front of me. Who should I call?

With feet feeling more like cement blocks, I stumbled to my room to pack.

4

As soon as I stepped onto the train, I knew why Shifters and Weres shunned the contraptions like E. coli avoided antibacterial agents on a petri dish. It smelled. Badly. A putrid mix of old man, sweaty socks, and cigarettes. My nose hairs didn't shrivel; they curled into the fetal position before they withered and died, leaving my nasal passage a dry, barren wasteland no longer capable of being harmed by the olfactory assault.

They could post as many "New and Improved" posters as they wanted, it couldn't hide that these pre-Purge death traps were better off in a museum than functioning as transportation. In the first years of the Purge, thousands died in train-related "accidents." A militant extremist group, opposed to the existence of supernaturals, started bombing and derailing all forms of public transportation, the protestors so angry they didn't care who they killed, or what they destroyed. With few security measures, trains posed no hindrance to their attacks and the activists hit them hard.

"Why aren't we flying?" I asked the guys, trying to unfurl my nose. This train had more than twenty passenger cars, and we got one of the fancy ones with private cabins. If this was what the expensive seats smelled like, how bad were the public ones?

I turned in time to see Steve step in behind me and blanch. One of the enforcer wolves in Wick's pack, Steve stood at medium height and build, with brown hair and light brown skin. Gem-cutting emerald eyes squinted, and his nose flared. The rancid train smell would be ten times worse to a Were, and he looked as if he'd discovered the meat in his dinner last night wasn't chicken.

"Because I hate flying." Clint answered my question and threw his bags into the overhead compartment of our private room before sitting down by the window.

Truth. I narrowed my eyes at Lucien's human servant. "There's more to it."

Maybe he couldn't survive a plane crash? I'd seen him die more than once—I'd ripped out his throat, and a Master Vampire skewered him with a sword, yet he managed to bounce back hale and hearty from both events. Even a human servant bonded to a Master Vampire had limits, and Clint surpassed those—like an Olympic runner competing against toddlers. Not for the first time, I wondered what box Clint ticked off on his government tax forms under "Entity Type." Human, maybe. Normal, no.

Since the Purge, every supernatural in existence came

out of the proverbial closet—Werewolves, Vampires, Fae, Demons, Angels, Skinwalkers. With an endless supply of possibilities, it might take forever to figure out Clint. I doubted he was a god. Or an angel.

Clint shrugged his giant shoulders and stretched his legs, effectively taking the seat across from him off my option list.

When I'd met him at the hotel earlier today, I'd brought coffee from Suzy's Gourmet Café. I knew it sucked. He took one sip of the drink they'd loosely referred to as a cappuccino and spat it out in a spray of milky brown liquid. His murderous look had hit me hard.

Game On.

"Excuse me." Steve slipped by and sat next to Clint's feet.

That left only one choice—sitting beside Clint. Dropping my head back, I stared at the ceiling. This was going to be a long trip; Clint, a human servant who appeared to be un-killable, Steve, the Werewolf with jewelled eyes and unknown motives, and me, badass SRD assassin. And none of us excelled in small talk.

"Come here, Shifter." Clint patted the seat beside him. "Get comfortable."

"You know that's not going to happen." The train lurched into gear, and I staggered. Either I remained standing, giving the two men a show most likely resembling a belly dance from a tornado on crack, or I sat down.

Difficult decision.

As soon as my ass hit the dilapidated cushion, Clint's hand drifted to my knee. I swatted it away, and hissed at him. The train rumbled to a start, and my body bucked forward before slamming back into my seat. It reminded me of the first time I rode a horse. Or at least tried to. Not my most successful moment—straddling a large passive herbivore when I could shift into a hundred and twenty-pound predator. The horse wasn't deceived by sight, nor my forest scent, and turned into a bucking bronco. The farmhands looked stupefied at Daisy's behaviour and gave me suspicious looks as I hobbled off the farm rubbing my aching backside.

I'd wanted to be normal. It had been during my supernatural denial stage of life—right before Dylan, and the worst years of my life that followed.

Sighing, I gazed out the window.

After breaking Dylan's control over me and destroying his pack in the process, I morphed into a rabid, hollow version of my mountain lion and ran off into the forest. It took thirty-three years to find my humanity—to walk in human form again and function, barely. I pursued the one job where my poor people skills were considered an asset, and that could possibly give me the answers I sought. What was I? What happened to my biological parents?

And then I met Wick. After botching an assassination attempt on Clint, I was captured by Lucien's Werewolf Alpha. My heart clenched at the thought of Wick's chocolate eyes focused on me, wanting me.

"Move," I ordered and sprang out of my seat, I gave

Clint little chance to pull his feet off the chair before I sat across from him. "If we have to ride this death trap, I want a better view."

Clint's smile widened. "Of me?"

I groaned and then abruptly stopped. Was that growling? My head whipped around to look at Steve. The hairs on his arms stood up and his yellow-shifted eyes locked on Clint. The human servant chuckled, ignored the Were, and looked out the window.

What are you doing? I asked, using my ability to mind speak to the Werewolf.

You're Wick's mate. He shouldn't talk to you like that.

I sputtered. Not knowing what part of his statement to address first, I stumbled over a couple words before I started over. *First, I'm not Wick's mate. Second, Clint's a flirt, and I'm not interested. Third, what is your purpose here? To aid Lucien's mission or to protect me on Wick's behalf?*

Steve took a deep breath before turning to me with an expression very akin to a parent talking to their misbehaving four-year-old. *Okay. One: even if you deny him, you're Wick's mate and will be treated as such until he removes his claim, which he hasn't.*

My heart beat hard in my chest, the pressure on my bones undeniable and painful.

Two: Clint isn't harmless. He wanted you as a toy and he still does. If I can smell his lust, so can you. Don't be stupid and don't underestimate him.

I shrugged. Clint's sexual hunger resembled the foul-smelling gym bag in the car. After a while, I got used to it and only noticed Clint's arousal when it spiked.

When did that happen?

And third. Steve mentally flicked up a third finger, counting down my questions. *What do you think?*

Wick sent him here for me. The dominant Alpha would hate the idea of his mate, or the female he claimed as his mate, being dragged out of country with Lucien's perverted human servant. I envisioned Wick pacing, making tracks through the plush throw rug in his living room.

How is he? I asked, and then I cringed. I'd promised not to talk or ask about Wick.

Devastated, he replied.

The word stabbed my heart, over and over again as I replayed Steve's voice in my head and heard the truth in his words. *Devastated.*

The train came to a screeching halt, pitching my body forward into Clint's lap. He looked down at me between his legs with my face an inch from his goods. The twinkle in his eye spoke more than any words he could say.

"Ugh," I grunted. "Get over yourself." I pushed off his legs to straighten up.

Clint's head dipped back as he laughed out loud; his gorgeous shoulders shook.

The sounds of people screaming stopped whatever response I planned to give.

"What's going on?" I brushed off my pants, feeling dirty.

"I'll check," Steve shot over his shoulder before he slipped out the door.

A rustle of clothing followed by the ring of swords unsheathing vibrated through the air a split second before the smell of anticipation and metal hit my nose. Sound travelled faster than smell.

"Getting excited?" I asked Clint as I cast a look over my shoulder. He had both his blades out. They reflected light in the small room, but I focused on his predatory gaze.

"You don't live as long as I do without taking moments to enjoy the small things in life."

"And how long is that?" Clint remained silent.

I turned back, needing to focus on the current threat, not the oddity of Clint. Time for that later.

Steve flung open the door to the cabin and slipped inside. The smell of crayons and fog wafted across the room—excitement and confusion.

"Trouble," he said.

"What kind of trouble?" I asked.

"There's fifteen to twenty humans going ape shit crazy in the train car three down from us. They're heading this way."

Clint chuckled and sheathed his swords.

I raised my eyebrows.

Clint cracked his knuckles. "Norms are nothing."

The sounds of angry yelling flowed down the corridor and into our compartment. A craggy old woman's voice hollered, "Mind your manners, young man!" Something padded like a purse thumped against somebody. I smiled and stretched my arm muscles.

"Doesn't sound like they're hurting anyone. Not exactly trouble in my books," I said.

Steve shook his head. "They're well accessorized and look determined."

"What do you mean *determined*?" Clint's tone mocked Steve's at the same time I asked, "What do you mean *well accessorized*?"

The yelling and cursing got louder—they would enter our section of the train soon. Steve checked the hallway before saying, "Their eyes glow like they're possessed, and they have knives. A few have guns."

Clint swore and unsheathed his swords again.

"Dude!" I exclaimed. "Next time lead with that!"

Steve shrugged at my accusatory glare and turned to the open door of our private cabin, revealing an empty hallway. I didn't want to think how he knew what possessed looked like. Or how I knew what he meant.

The door at the end of our train car slammed open.

5

There comes a point in a Shifter's life when the itchy sensation of dried blood and various parts of internal organs splattered against skin no longer fazes them. I was well beyond that point. What disturbed me was how good Clint looked slicing his blades through possessed humans—the attraction, ridiculous, the allure like the people who wanted to pet tigers at the zoo. Clint turned to me, somehow transforming his roguish smile into a suggestive one, as if he sensed my fascination.

Not happening.

I could admire the biggest beast in the forest, but it didn't mean I would dry hump it.

Steve shifted from Werewolf form, his nude body streaked with blood like mine, making us look like morgue escapees. He cast the human servant a wary look.

It's always unnerving to see him fight, Steve said in my head.

Agreed, I shot back.

We came together and stared down at the pile of dead bodies.

Clint joined us, stopping to wipe his blades on the clothing of the nearest norm. "A bit of a letdown," he said.

Steve grunted in agreement. I said nothing, but knew what they both meant. I felt silly for overreacting and shifting into my mountain lion. The humans posed no real threat to any of us despite their numbers and their military-grade accessories. They couldn't fight or shoot straight. The ceiling took more of a beating than we did. But I didn't share Clint's disappointment; instead, heaviness descended upon my chest and limbs.

"Maybe we could've saved them," I grumbled. "This is a PR nightmare."

Steve shook his head. "They definitely targeted us." Then, in my head, he spoke, *There's nothing we could've done, Andy. It was them or us.*

I know, I replied. And I did. throw down or get thrown down. Survival of the fittest. It still didn't *feel* good. I took down the bad guys, not helpless norms, possessed or not.

"We have sufficient witnesses." Clint pulled out his phone and punched in a number. I heard Lucien's voice answer on the other end, and Clint walked away from us as he relayed the events on the train.

Kneeling down next to one of the bodies, I flipped her over. A woman in her mid-thirties with brown hair. I peeled back one of her eyelids—hazel eyes, no longer glowing bright. Normally Demon possession turned eyes red, at least in my limited experience. I'd never encountered this before.

"Ever seen eyes glow like that?" I asked Steve, who crouched beside me.

"Nope." He pulled back the woman's lips to reveal uneven, but clean teeth.

I pointed to her nice clothes. "None of these people appear down on their luck. Normally, the homeless are the most vulnerable to demonic attacks."

Steve nodded and moved to the next body. I did the same. After searching all seventeen, we came to the conclusion nothing significant existed about any of them —a range of ages, races, and tooth alignment. All norms. No supes.

"Do you know what the summit is about?" I straightened up and watched as Steve tried to brush the drying blood off his chiseled abs with his bare hand.

"Demons," Clint's voice cut in, having walked back to join us. He tucked his phone into his jacket pocket. "And the Vampire Council's relationship with the demonic realm."

Pursing my lips, I glanced over my shoulder to find Clint staring at my ass. "A bit too coincidental, don't you think?"

Clint yawned. "Maybe. Maybe not. There's nothing significant to vote on at this summit. It's informative, and I'm not presenting. This—" he indicated the bodies strewn about with a twitch of his finger "—may not be what it seems."

"They looked and acted possessed to me."

"Yet their eyes glowed their natural eye colour instead of red, and they died like normal, unpossessed humans," Clint said, expressing valid points. After they died, the bodies of possessed norms often kept moving as the Demon inside vainly tried to keep control. These ones crumbled like weak, mortal norms.

"Then what do you think this..." I jerked my finger around, mocking Clint's earlier actions, "is about?"

Clint lifted his mountainous shoulders.

"What type of relationship does the Vampire Council have with the demonic realm? I was under the impression there was none," I said.

"There isn't." Clint leaned in. "But the Vampires want one."

"An alliance?"

Clint nodded.

"That's ridiculous." I stalked back into our private room and pulled down my bag, fully aware the men followed and received a full, jiggling view of my very bare booty. "Vampires are powerful enough as it is."

"Ah, but there's always more power to be had."

I ignored Clint's last comment and how much he sounded like Lucien. Disturbing how accurate he described vamp mentality with one sentence. I pulled out clean, non-bloody clothes, wanting to be fully dressed when the SRD authorities arrived to question us. For some reason, norms had a hard time questioning naked Shifters about murder, and I wanted to speed up the process.

Too bad I couldn't do anything about the blood caked to my skin.

With flashing red and blue lights threatening to give me a seizure, an officer headed in our direction. Middle aged and balding, he held himself with authority and planted himself squarely in front of us with a wide stance. He placed his hands above his holster, close to his gun and squinted at us over his pointy nose. "I'm Officer Stevens from the VPD."

"What's the Vancouver Police Department doing here?" Steve asked. "We crossed the border...didn't we?"

Officer Stevens nodded. "Partly. The other half of the train is still on the Canadian side, and since the train originated from Vancouver, we're taking an active interest. That and—" He abruptly cut off whatever he planned to say next and took out his notepad. "Now, one of the first responders told me one of you is an SRD agent?"

His hard gaze studied my face, but I didn't answer right away—too distracted by the sight of his uneven teeth. They looked like they were all at a party and not on speaking terms.

"That you?" He pointed his pen at me.

This cop meant business. I liked it. Squashing the urge to salute, I took a slight step forward. "I'm Agent McNeilly."

He nodded again and clicked his pen. "Tell me what happened."

"About twenty minutes into the train ride, we abruptly stopped. We heard screaming and yelling farther down the train. Steve went to check and discovered a number of humans with knives and guns. They appeared possessed, with bright glowing eyes instead of red. When they reached our train car, and saw us, they became severely agitated and aggressive. They started shooting and we defended ourselves."

"Three against seventeen? You were extremely *fortunate*," Officer Stevens said. Before he could question us further, his radio blared. After listening to the garbled message, he clicked it on and rattled off a bunch of numbers. When the voice responded on the other side, Officer Stevens's eyebrows pinched together, and he turned, giving us his back. He spoke cop jargon into the radio again. Another muffled reply. With heightened hearing, I heard the entire conversation, but I had no idea what a "five-thirty" was.

The officer swore under his breath. He turned back toward us and pasted a thin smile on his face. "Seems the SRD will be taking over this investigation. Claiming jurisdiction due to exclusive supernatural elements." He spat off to the side. "They can have it. You three—" he pointed to each of us in case we didn't understand "—are to remain here until they've had a chance to question you. I'll wait by my squad car to transfer chain of command when they get here." He handed me a white card. "If you recall anything pertinent to this event, norm-wise, please let me know."

"What about the media?" I wiggled my index finger at the news vans parked outside the crime scene tape and the reporters circling like vultures.

"I'll make sure they're aware an SRD agent is present and remind them of the confidentiality clause in the Canadian and U.S. governments' laws stating they can't release footage, names, or information revealing the identity of an agent."

"Well…"

"No one has yet to risk the consequences. At least, not in my career. So don't worry, your identity will be safe." He glanced at Clint and Steve. "Can't promise the same for you two."

The men exchanged a look and shrugged.

Officer Stevens took in their reactions, grunted, and stalked away, leaving us to wait for the SRD.

THE BLAND WHITE-BOY APPEARANCE AND NORM scent might've made it difficult to recognize the man in front of me, but I pegged him instantly. His bright hazel eyes, expensive cologne, and the condescending expression mixed with hatred, made it easy.

Agent Tucker.

I groaned. The last time I'd seen him, I'd leaped

across an interrogation desk to crush his neck with my hands. His fault. He'd asked about my feras, and he should've learned in Supernatural Beings 101 that was an off-limit question. Standing outside the train, Tucker's pissy face made it clear he hadn't learned his lesson.

"Andrea McNeilly." His voice scraped against my skin, despite its smooth undertones.

I made a point of staring at his fancy Rolex watch, a gift from dear old Daddy, before speaking. "That's Agent McNeilly, to you."

Tucker scrunched his lips and did a one-shoulder shrug, as if my correction was inconsequential. "Let's try to be civil. If you answer my questions truthfully, we can make this fast."

"I don't believe you'll be an impartial party. I'd like to request another investigator."

"Request denied."

"Then I'd like my request noted on the report."

"Just answer my questions, McNeilly."

About to ask how he'd distinguish the truth from lies without his shiny lie detector machine, I shut my mouth when he nodded over his shoulder. A large black man in a business suit stepped forward.

"This is Agent Nagato."

A Shifter. Agent Nagato's scent hinted at something feline. Bobcat, maybe? His fera probably hid somewhere out of sight. I, unlike Agent Tucker, knew better than to ask where it was. Regardless, the Shifter would act as a walking, talking lie detector. The body gave off a distinct oily scent when a person told a lie, and with our heightened senses, all Shifters and Weres could smell it.

Tucker took Steve aside to one of the train cars first and spoke, low and hushed. Even if I weren't able to follow along, Steve gave me a mind speech play by play—straightforward questions regarding the incident. Tucker's main focus centred on whether we knew or had any connections with the humans.

Amateur. He might not know I could mind speak with Steve, but he had to know separate interrogations were pointless. It took him well over an hour to arrive at the crime scene, and while we waited for him to grace us with his presence, we'd had plenty of time to get our stories straight. No one had separated us. Even with his lie-detecting Shifter, there were ways of evading the truth without directly lying. Not that we had anything to hide.

Unless he could read us. Maybe he looked for deviations in our mannerisms, unique ticks to tell him more than we intended. He might be purposely using inflammatory questions and insulting comments to get us to snap or say something we didn't intend.

The daddy's boy pranced back with Steve. No. He didn't possess those abilities. I'd bet my government paycheque he got his job due to connections, not skill. Besides, the three of us had enough control not to rise to any bait he set.

He took Clint next. The interview with him went the same, except Clint claimed to be a *normal* human. Tucker sounded unconvinced and asked where he knew him from. Clint did a surprisingly good job sounding ignorant without lying.

When Agent Tucker stepped out of the train after Clint, his eyes riveted to mine. His expression of excitement and anticipation didn't inspire me to jump up and down, saying, "Oh goody, my turn!" He smelled hungry, and that rang as all kinds of wrong.

Agent Nagato walked out and stood beside him. His nose scrunched up and he frowned. When he followed his boss's stare, his gaze met mine briefly before cutting away.

The courtesy of a private interrogation didn't extend to me. Tucker stopped and folded his arms, right before demanding, "Agent, recount all the events that took place on the train in a clear, factual manner."

I did.

Tucker tapped his foot and kept glancing up. He'd heard this story twice before. When I let my voice trail off after describing how we came to be in the current situation, the same hungry scent swirled around me.

"What were you doing on the train?" Tucker's nauseating voice interrupted my thoughts.

"None of your business."

"Truth," Agent Nagato's voice carried a deep rumbling, like the train we stood beside.

Tucker turned to the other Shifter. "Nagato, you don't need to respond to those types of statements."

Nagato remained silent, but the look he cast at the back of Tucker's head indicated he liked Tucker about as much as I did.

Tucker's gaze circled back to me. "As an SRD agent, it's imperative we know the nature of this trip. Business or pleasure?"

I bit my tongue. Fuck, which category would this debacle fall under? "Neither."

"Truth."

"That makes no sense," he murmured. "Are you currently on an SRD assignment?"

"You have access to my files, don't you? Why not look it up?"

"Answer me."

"No."

"I said, answer the question!" He shifted weight as if he was about to stomp one of his feet. Must've thought better of it, because he took a deep breath and returned to his regular stance.

"I did. No, I'm not on an SRD assignment. And if I had been, you'd have blown my cover." *Take that, asshole.* I identified myself to the emergency responders as an SRD agent, but I doubted he knew that. And if he did... Was that why he came? Did he personally attend this crime scene because he harboured resentment toward me and wanted to make my life miserable? Now that, I could believe.

"Truth."

Agent Tucker pursed his lips. His eyebrows bunched together. If it weren't for the raucous noise the train engines made when idling, I'd swear I heard the wheels in his head turning. "Are you on this train for a vacation?"

I snorted. "No."

Nagato nodded when Tucker glanced at him. "Are you here under someone else's orders?"

My back straightened. "Are we going to play twenty questions all night? If so, I would like my SRD union representative." I'd no idea if I had one of those, or even if I was in a union, but it sounded like the right thing to say.

Tucker's eyes narrowed. "Just answer the question and we're done."

"We're done now." I folded my arms.

Tucker leaned in. "Who's got control of you, *Agent* McNeilly?" He glanced at Clint, his gaze shifting over his body, probably still trying to place him.

It wouldn't take him long to figure out who I travelled with. Then he'd know a relationship between me and Lucien's court existed. *Fuck.* Face recognition software was a bitch.

Tucker turned back to me. "Sounds like a Conflict Of Interest. A COI is grounds for removal."

"Termination," I corrected. One implied the end of a job, while the other referred to the end of life. Personally, I saw a reason to distinguish between the two.

Tucker's eyes gleamed. I half expected him to squeal in delight; instead, he crossed his arms. "Sure."

"Are you threatening me? Again?"

Tucker straightened and adjusted his tie. "You misunderstand me. I'm looking out for your best interests."

Yeah, right.

"You're lucky, you know, that I'm not hauling you

and your travel companions in. This isn't the VPD. Hell, this isn't even Vancouver. We're an international organization for supernaturals."

"Haul me in? The local law enforcement and all the witnesses agreed the norms were possessed. Even the VPD is handing the scene over. This is clearly supe on supe self-defence."

He waggled his finger in my face. "But norms were killed."

My fingers itched to waggle right back, but I balled them into a fist and kept them close to my side. "The SRD and North American Law Enforcement Agreement clearly states any possessed norms forfeit their rights and protection under the Norm Charter of Rights because they no longer have control of their faculties and possess supernatural characteristics and abilities, such as increased strength and speed. For all intents and purposes, possessed norms fall under the supernatural classification. You know this. Supe on supe is SRD jurisdiction. Let us go."

"Be careful, Andy," he said and walked away. The feras in my head snarled, wanting me to attack his exposed back. Sometimes, it was hard to say no.

Nagato said a polite goodbye before following Tucker. His stiff back and jilted gait indicated he didn't like giving his back to a Shifter and a Werewolf one bit. I didn't blame him.

When the agents were out of supernatural hearing distance, Clint leaned over. "What's between you and loverboy?"

I choked on the label. "He hates me."

"You seem to inspire that reaction in a lot of people," Clint said.

Ignoring him, I glanced around. *Coffee.* Coffee would be good right now. There must be a vendor somewhere around here.

"Any particular reason he hates you?" Clint asked.

"Oh…" I waved a nonchalant hand in the air. "I tried to kill him."

Clint and Steve laughed.

"Did you guys see a coffee shop? I might go postal if I don't inject caffeine into my system."

Steve, bless his heart, looked around. "There's coffee on the train."

"Ugh. Did you *smell* that stuff? No way am I drinking that."

"Yet you go to Suzy's Gourmet Café?" Clint narrowed his eyes at me.

"For you. I got my morning coffee somewhere else." I couldn't hide the shudder that came with the memory of the first time I had a coffee from the place. I'd used it as a surveillance location. Many hours of scouting meant many coffees, which in turn, meant many sore stomachs.

The human servant grunted and turned away. Was he *smiling*?

"Why?" Steve asked.

"Um…It's disgusting?" I could think of a few more words to describe the brown liquid they served at the café.

Steve shook his head. "Why did you try to kill Agent Tucker?"

"He asked about my feras."

Steve sucked in a breath. No further explanation necessary. Everyone knew how sensitive Shifters were about their fera familiars. The death of the fera meant the death of the Shifter, and vice versa. During the Shifter Shankings, every redneck with a gun went out shooting any animal in close proximity to humans. The result included the extermination of many household pets, along with an estimated ninety percent of the Shifter population, including my birth parents. Or so I assumed. I'd hoped the SRD had the information in a file somewhere, but I'd yet to find anything.

Clint turned back. "You're supposed to be an assassin. Have you completed *any* successful hits?"

My mouth tingled as my teeth elongated. "I'll show you a good hit."

"Down, kitten," Clint said. "Why isn't he dead?"

"We were interrupted."

6

Whenever I read about Vampire summits, the stories filled the page with intrigue, danger, and lots of mind-blowing sex. The reality was far more boring. Maybe I should stop reading the pre-Purge paranormal romances I'd found in thrift stores. They might be hilarious, but they were also sadly misleading. Not that I wanted to bone a blood-sucker, but this was booooring.

When is the blood rage and feeding frenzy? I asked Steve.

Only you would want to see that. He sounded annoyed.

I hear it's pretty epic. I examined my nails before staring at the back of Clint's head. He sat at an enormous table in a boardroom while his assistants, meaning me and Steve, stood in the background listening to *hours* of boring Vampire conversation and debate.

Vampires liked to present themselves as refined to the

point of pretentious—sitting at elegant tables, using multisyllabic words and subtle hand gestures, wearing expensive clothes and having attractive staff mill around to attend to their every need—but I knew better.

They were animals, like me.

And who would you suggest they have the feeding frenzy on? Steve asked.

He had a point. *Everyone but us?*

Steve snorted, drawing the attention of everyone in the room. He made a bad show of coughing. Clint received a few dark looks and sneers of contempt. I didn't need to smell their derision to know they thought he should have better control of his slaves.

My phone vibrated to let me know I had a message. Pulling it out discreetly, I tapped the screen and found a text from an unknown number.

You, me, tonight.

Who is this?

I meant to text quickly, but it took five attempts to type with my thumbs. Ever since the time I accidentally told Wick I'd stopped for cocaine instead of caffeine and when Mel, my best friend, asked me to get penis instead of pedis, I lost my trust in technology and proofread all my messages.

Tristan.

Aware of my current location and whose company I kept, I bit back the laugh bubbling up my throat.

> Can't. Out of town. How'd you get this number?

I have skills.

Clint cleared his throat and shot a dark look over his shoulder. I put the phone away.

THE ELEVATOR DOORS SHUT SOFTLY AGAINST the stench of Vampires.

"If I have to hear any more complaining from either of you two, I'm going to leash Steve and make him watch while I spank you like the bad little girl you've been." Clint didn't sound as angry as his words implied. He looked like he enjoyed the idea.

Sniffing the air, I recoiled. He didn't just *enjoy* it, he was turned on. *Gross.*

Steve growled, not liking the dog reference. Werewolves could be so testy about species confusion. I didn't know why. I read somewhere wolves and domesticated dogs should be considered the same species since they produced viable offspring. Steve probably wouldn't appreciate the information right now.

"Whatever, Clint. Can we just go to our rooms for

the night?" I leaned against the elevator wall and sagged a little. "Are we done?"

Tonight's meeting lasted four hours as the Vampires debated the pros and cons of forming an alliance with the Demons. It took them half the time to figure out both groups included blood-obsessed sadomasochists who shared similar interests, and the rest of the night to agree Demons couldn't be trusted and might use the alliance to get a foothold into this reality and betray the Vampires.

Duh. I could've told them that in less than a minute and had time left to throw in a couple unsavoury and extremely unladylike words. My feet ached, and I blamed Clint and Lucien entirely for my pain and discomfort. At least we'd missed Friday's meetings and festivities due to the train delay.

"No," Clint said with a tone that brooked no arguments. "We go to the ball being held in an hour."

"Why?" I grumbled. "Its sole purpose is to provide an environment for vamps to rub up against one another."

"Precisely why we go. We need to see who *rubs up* against each other, who's avoiding who, and who's unable to control their minions..." Clint gave me a pointed look after the last statement. *What's his deal?*

"So I have to wear the contraption?"

"Yes." Clint smiled. "You have to wear the dress."

The elevator door opened, and I sulked down the hallway to my room without saying another word to the two men.

"Do you need help?" Clint asked, calling after me.

I did, but I'd never admit that to him. He wasn't asking to be helpful. I turned to give him a tight smile. "I'll manage."

Clint smirked like he knew I lied and already envisioned the trouble I'd have getting into the dress. I flashed him the bird and stepped into my room.

There, draped on a padded pink hanger on the outside of the closet, hung layers upon layers of structured gown. I stared at the dress with trepidation and decided to down a couple mini-bar bottles of booze before attempting the impossible.

It took thirty minutes to figure out how to shove my body into the dress and another ten to admit I needed someone to zip it up.

I need help, and if I ever hear anything about this, I'll rip your throat out.

Who am I to refuse such a gracious call for assistance? Steve's voice laughed back at me. *Especially when you ask so sweetly.*

A growl escaped my lips. He was in the other room and couldn't hear it, but the deep rumble through my chest alleviated some of the tension hiking up my neck. When he knocked on the door, I swung it open and yanked him into my room by his shirt. Steve smirked and twirled his index finger in the air, indicating for me to spin around. "Suck it in, baby."

I held my hair out of the way and would've exhaled in relief when Steve pulled the zipper up if the corset allowed that sort of freedom.

"Thanks," I wheezed and turned around.

Steve raised his phone and snapped a picture.

I held my hand out against the bright flash, too late. "Uh... What the fuck are you doing?"

"Taking a picture."

Blinking away the white spots, I grumbled. "I know that." I crossed my arms.

Steve glanced down, then his tanned face turned fire-hydrant red and his eyes cut away. He suddenly became enraptured with the screen of his smart phone. I followed his original look down. My folded arms accentuated my already propped and exposed chest. The girls looked ready to pop. *Wowza!* I dropped my arms to let them hang by my sides. "Why did you take a picture?"

"Wick asked me to."

Before I could reply with something catty, my phone beeped. I had to dig my cell out of my cleavage, causing Steve's eyebrows to rise into his hairline.

"Well, where else could I put it?" I asked, then realizing his possible answers, quickly added, "Don't answer that."

"Too easy."

I checked my phone and read a one-word text from Wick:

Hot.

A silly little smile spread across my face, and I turned so Steven wouldn't see it. Despite everything, Wick knew how to push my buttons—all the right ones. And he was correct, I did look hot.

The ink-black dress Clint provided fit my tall frame with a deep plunging neckline that defied the term "sweetheart." Soft black lace accentuated my bronzed skin tone and hung over some fancy material—chiffon? Satin? Taffeta? No idea. But the gown flattered my figure in a way I didn't know possible. The contraption looked like a black widow spat out a wedding dress, but in a good way. I would never be the pink, puffy, princess-dress type. Clint pegged me well enough to pick out the right gown and that disturbed me.

Steve cleared his throat. "We should go before Clint's gruts get all twisted."

"Gruts?"

"Man-panties."

I laughed and followed him out to the hallway to find Clint propped against the wall with his arms folded, waiting. He looked like a gentleman with his classic good looks, black suit, and tie. He gave me an efficient once-over, his eyes widened slightly and his mouth relaxed.

"What?" I snapped.

Clint shrugged. "You clean up nice." Pushing off the wall with his shoulders, he straightened his suit. "Although I'm hurt you asked the mutt for help instead of me."

Steve lifted his chin in a short jerk.

"Relax," Clint said. "We all have an act to follow tonight. Don't forget it for a second."

I crossed my arms.

Clint's gaze dropped to my chest.

Oops! Cleavage.

I quickly uncrossed my arms to let them dangle at my side. "So you're a method actor?"

"Sure." He straightened his tie. Spinning on his heel, he sauntered down the hallway. "Follow me, slaves."

Steve offered his arm, and we walked linked behind Clint.

Once we entered the ballroom, we let Clint walk farther ahead and made a pit stop at the bar. Making a show of being a good servant, I ordered Clint's favourite drink—Glenfiddich, neat, along with scooping non-alcoholic punch for myself. When we caught up, Clint snatched his drink from my hand without looking or acknowledging my presence. He was convincing as a power-tripping, egotistical human servant. Method actor, my ass. This was every day for him.

"Dog," Clint addressed Steve over his shoulder. "You will patrol the perimeter and keep me posted on anything unusual." When Steve hesitated, Clint turned to him. "You're dismissed."

Steve made a small bow and withdrew, blending in with the myriad of black suits in the room. *He's such a dick,* he sent to me.

I know, I replied before turning my attention to the man in question.

Clint tilted his head at me. "Why are you looking at me like that?"

"You should treat others the way you want to be treated." I sipped my drink and waited for his response.

Clint's brow furrowed. "That's not going to happen."

"Why not?"

Clint ducked his head close to mine. "I'm not going to walk around blowing everyone."

I didn't choke or spray my punch all over because I'd expected some sort of innuendo or inappropriate comment, just not that one.

The corners of Clint's lips twitched. He took a slow sip of his Glenfiddich, watching me over the rim.

"You're disgusting," I said.

"Yet, honest."

I looked at my half-empty punch glass and regretted my decision for the non-alcoholic version. "I'm not nearly drunk enough to have this conversation."

Clint reached out for my glass, but I pulled away. "Like I'd let you get me a drink. You'd probably throw roofies into it."

Clint shook his head. "Relax. You're a Shifter. I'd try horse tranquilizers first."

I spun on my heel and headed to the bar. Despite coming to this event fully aware I'd have to play a servant role and Clint had asshole-like tendencies, it still made it difficult to stomach. I hated acting like someone's bitch. It stirred up a lot of suppressed memories. I wanted to embed my fist into Clint's face, and that would ruin our entire charade. Not even an hour into the ball, and I needed something stronger to drink.

It would calm the three feras screaming in my head, as well.

When the bartender handed my drink over, I thanked him and walked away from the bar, only to have a heavy blanket of almond spice envelop me. My mouth watered, and I rapidly swallowed in quick succession to prevent drooling all over my gown.

Growing up, I had a Dutch best friend in high school —Maartje. She told everyone to call her Marsha because she hated people butchering the pronunciation of her name. I called her Marty. Her family, a group of giants defying the vertical limitations of normal humans, taught me to have a great appreciation for all things almond. Almost every Dutch dessert contained the ingredient in some form—banketstaaf, amandel koekjes, and a whole slew of other desserts I couldn't pronounce without spitting.

Marty grew up and moved out. She didn't bake, and no longer having access to her mother's pastries meant our friendship quickly fizzled out.

That and she slept with my boyfriend at the time, Caden. He was a dick. I think the loss of free kerststol and chocolate sprinkles to put on my toast hurt more than her betrayal.

But one of my favourite smells, to this day, was almond. Scenting it thick in the air at a Vampire summit though, sent a wave of fear splicing through my body. Only one supernatural smelled that strongly of almond.

Demon.

I spun around and took another few gulps of spit to prevent the nearby waiter from offering me a bib. The heady scent surrounded me, drawing me closer, begging me to approach. A bright smile beamed through a haze of scented fog as I stumbled toward the source.

No! my cat screeched. She clawed at my head, yowling. My teeth elongated, and I stopped walking, shook my head, and waited for my vision to clear.

"You're no fun," a voice that could only be described as verbal sex slithered around my skin. Appraising me from a not-so-safe distance towered a Demon dressed in human clothing, a man close to seven feet tall with muscles straining against his tight V-neck shirt and dark form-fitting jeans. Dark eyes framed with dark brows, jet-black hair, and olive skin, watched as I assessed him. How'd I not notice him before? He stuck out like an elephant at a mouse convention.

"Why aren't your eyes red?" I blurted out.

A slow, sensual smile revealed sparkling white even teeth. "I'm not possessed."

My eyes narrowed.

He chuckled. The sound vibrating deep in his chest caused an unnatural heat to spread through my body. Why did I keep reacting to him like this? I needed to get laid, but geez! I hated Demons... Didn't I?

My wolf growled, vibrating my skull. *Yes! Yes, I hate Demons. I despise them.*

"Silly Shifter," the Demon interrupted my internal battle. "I wear a human form to hide my true nature." His voice trailed off in a low purr.

He waited for me to respond, but nothing came out. Nothing came to mind. Still paralyzed from his voice, I stood there doing my best statue impersonation. My falcon screeched inside, defying the Demon's power and breaking his hold on my body.

I glanced down, and my breathing hitched. My toes stood inches from the salt and blood line of the Demon summoning circle. If my feras hadn't clawed, growled, and shrieked me back to reality, I would've walked straight through the line, breaking the control over this powerful entity from hell and serving myself on a platter. My skin prickled and I shivered.

I fucking hate Demons.

"I'm glad someone's got you on a leash," I said and took a step back, putting a safe distance between my toes and the salt line.

The Demon's head fell back, laughing. The sound stirred my loins again, but I didn't want any stirring in that area from the presence of pure evil. My heart beat hard in my chest, so hard I heard nothing else. The Demon kept trying to lay some sort of sex mojo on me. *Fuck that!* I refused to be Clint's bitch, and I sure as hell wouldn't be this guy's. Singing a song about independent women and bringing my feras close, I pushed against his power. Now that I knew what I fought against, I could turn my unnatural and unwanted arousal into anger. And I had barrels full of rage at my disposal.

"What is your name, human?" the Demon asked.

"Like I'm stupid enough to give you that." Names held power with Demons, and it worked both ways.

"Would you prefer I call you human?"

"Call me whatever you like. I don't plan to meet you again."

The corners of the Demon's full mouth twitched. "I'll call you *Carus*, then."

My head snapped up before I could rein in my reaction. *How did he know?*

Something more disturbing crooned in the back of my mind. Like the evil angel sitting on my shoulder, the voice from the darkest part of my soul sounded like a deranged hobbit. *What could he tell me?*

The urge to give in to the voice and ask turned palpable—a bitter taste on my tongue. There would be a cost for his information. Demons always charged for their services, and I wasn't willing to pay any price he set.

The Demon noticed everything. He'd cocked his head to listen, probably hearing my sharp intake of breath and fast-beating heart. His nose flared and his mouth opened in a large toothy grin. He inhaled a long drag of air, as if savouring the scent of my changing emotions—the surprise, confusion, the desperation for information, and the abhorrence when I realized I *wanted* something from him.

"Goodbye, Demon." I turned and hurried the hell away from him, taking some of the fastest steps I'd walked in my life. Turning my back on someone, something, that could tell me what I'd spent the last fifteen years trying to discover...

Demons all had their own special powers, and this one was a Seducer. No doubt in my mind. Better than some of the other types, maybe, but boasting a human form meant he was very powerful and dangerous—one of the highest calibre of Demons in existence. I knew my limits. He was well beyond anything I could take.

Not prey, my cat hissed. I agreed.

7

When I escaped the thrall of the Demon, I found Clint standing nearby, mouth on the rim of his drink, laughing at me with his eyes. "I hoped he'd get you to dance naked," he said.

Nice backup. "What's a Demon doing here?"

Clint swirled his drink. "They brought him in for consultation."

"Seriously?"

He nodded.

"Do you require my services for anything else?" I spoke through gritted teeth, not exactly doing the obedient underling act justice, but not exactly caring, either.

Clint's face crinkled, but he chose not to make a lewd innuendo for once. "You may mingle."

With a slight bow, I stalked off to patrol the perimeter opposite Steve and observed the Demon from a safe distance. Who summoned him? Odd he didn't mind being displayed like a rare animal at the zoo. I'd be screeching at someone, but he calmly paced his circled cage and watched the crowd with more vigilance than Clint. Everyone gave the summoning circle a wide birth and no one approached. Apparently, Clint was the only one willing to let his servant get close and personal enough to see what happened. Maybe he planned it all, betting on my strength to showcase the power of Lucien's horde.

Lots of Vampires rubbed up against one another, but I didn't know Joe from Schmoe. Clint slowly perused the room. Every time he blinked, I envisioned him taking mental notes, or saving images for his spank bank. I didn't ask him which. Not one interaction escaped his notice. His attention shifted around the room all night, appearing to take everything in—very perceptive.

But he didn't see the Vampire lurking in the shadows observing him.

You have an admirer, I said to Clint.

To give Clint credit, he didn't whirl around like a fourteen-year-old girl after being told her crush just stepped in the room. He didn't even turn in my direction; instead, he pulled out his cell phone.

Seconds later, mine beeped and I had to dig it out of my cleavage. Super classy.

Clint texted:

Who?

Using mind speech, I answered while getting myself

another drink at the bar. *Don't know. Looks like a young Rob Lowe. Definitely a Vampire and definitely watching you. He keeps moving so he's at your back.*

Clint's lips twitched. My phone vibrated.

Ian.

Friend or foe? I asked.

Both. Approach and ask him to
join us.

Relieved to finally do something other than walk a circuit of the room, I sashayed over to the Vampire. So intent on staring at the back of Clint's head, he didn't notice my approach until I stood a few yards away. He turned to me with an annoyed expression and opened his mouth to say something, probably a scathing dismissal, but I beat him to the punch.

"Clint humbly requests your company," I said, completing the final steps to put me within striking distance. Not sure what a fight in this dress would look like, but I had a knack for improvising.

Ian's face lost all expression. His eyes vamped out for a few seconds, and I wondered if I'd have to shift and claw his pretty face. Instead, he bent his head in a slight bow and reached forward to take my hand with Vampire speed. My muscles stiffened as I tried not to flinch. Wrapping my arm around his, he turned us toward Clint. "It would be my pleasure."

Nothing rubbed me the wrong way more than

walking alongside a Vampire. My normally animalistic grace looked clunky and inelegant next to the gliding blood junkie. Not something I experienced often and definitely not something I liked. I did the whole gangly awkward thing when I was fifteen. No need to go back there.

Ian pulled up a few feet from where Clint waited with an unreadable expression. "Clint."

"Ian."

When I moved to withdraw from Ian, he clamped his hand down on mine, freezing me in place. "This one's a rare treat."

"Lucien's."

Ian's fangs flashed as he spoke. "I smelled him on her."

Eww. I smelled like dead meat and blood? I had no idea Lucien marked my scent along with the fang scars on my neck. *Fuck that!* My beast rumbled deep in my core and anger bubbled up from the source. I stiffened my leg muscles and took a deep breath.

"Have you heard any news?" Clint changed the subject.

Ian paused and glanced to his right. "Nothing new. Most are in favour."

"Those opposed?"

"The Pharaoh," Ian said with a soft voice, barely forming the words.

Clint nodded and then raised his glass in a silent salute before taking another long sip.

"Why don't we drink together?" Ian's fingers stroked my hand. I tensed.

Clint reached out and placed his empty glass on a tray of a waiter walking by. "We don't share the same taste in vintages."

Ian chuckled. "Why don't you get another whiskey while I sample *her*?"

Clint shook his head. "Lucien's," he said with a steely voice.

"So you said." Ian let my arm go and gave me a long appraising look before turning on his heel and slipping away.

8

Ignoring the red blinking light on my answering machine, I threw my bags on the bed and let a big sigh of relief escape. I'd never been happier to be home. Or at least, not in the last week. What did that say about my life?

The rest of the Vampire summit dragged like a party for the dead and dreary, and after the tête-à-tête with Ian, Clint insisted we linger another half hour before allowing us to return to our rooms. He refused to answer any of my questions about his exchange with the Vampire.

Now home and wanting nothing more than to crawl into bed and forget the Vampire drama and love-life complications, I made myself a late-morning coffee instead and turned on the television.

A bobblehead newswoman with perfect Lego-block hair stared seriously into the camera. "And new information has surfaced regarding the train incident that happened three days ago across our southern international border where seventeen norms were slaughtered by three individuals. Due to privacy agreements, we can't divulge the name of the SRD agent involved, but the Werewolf has since been identified as Steven Daskalov, the underwear model."

What? Steve modelled underwear? *No way.* I'd have to bring this up later...and maybe look up some old photos on the Internet.

The newswoman kept talking. "The name of the third person, and the only apparent norm in the trio, has yet to be ascertained. What we can tell you is laboratory tests on the blood have confirmed the seventeen norms were under some sort of compulsion. The type of compulsion or possession remains unclear, but it appears the Train Killing Trio will be cleared of all—" I turned the television off, threw the remote on the couch, and sat on the ledge in front of the bay window. I stared out the glass at absolutely nothing until I couldn't stand the flashing red light of my answering machine any longer—a bright beacon cutting into my paradise.

With a groan, I dragged myself out of my cushion of pillows and pushed the button.

"McNeilly, it's Agent Booth. You need to come into the headquarters. Now." Booth's raspy voice sounded exactly how I remembered it—like she drank the dregs of a beer can the day after a party and didn't realize there were cigarette butts in it.

Crap. Did she plan to rip me a new one for the train

incident? At least Booth contacted me. If Tucker had phoned, I'd probably go postal. After playing Clint's minion for two days, I'd used up all my douchebag tolerance.

I glanced at the clock. Five minutes to ten. Thanks to taking a red-eye flight back late Sunday night, plenty of time remained in the workday. Not wanting to talk to the agent until I had to, I pulled my laptop out to whip off a quick e-mail.

> *Dear Agent Booth,*
> *I received your voice message. I will be in shortly.*
> *Sincerely, Agent McNeilly*

I quickly read over my message and my heart stopped. What the fuck just happened? Instead of what I wrote, the following words stared back at me:

> *Suck it Agent Booth,*
> *My ass received your voice message. My ass will screw you over shortly.*
> *Sincerely, Agent McNeilly*

I deleted and retyped the message, only to have the same thing happen again. I typed each letter slowly, watching the screen. My computer autocorrected "Dear" to "Suck it," "I" to "My ass," "be" to "screw you," and "in" to "over." Experimentally typing, I discovered more errors. "The" changed to "stupid," "a" to "lame," and "is" to "dumbass."

Scratching my head, I searched the computer settings. Under autocorrect, someone had manually entered the alternate words. Either a perverted old man lived inside my computer, or I was the victim of a hacker. Besides annoying the crap out of me, the autocorrect did no damage. It didn't retrieve any important information. My heart stopped. *Did it?*

I narrowed my eyes and stared at the screen. Only one group I knew preferred pranks to real fighting. Those bloody Witches! I understood my letter may have offended them, but no more than their singing.

They crossed a line with this little parlour trick and the invasion of my home, and needed to be put in their place. My muscles tightened as I prepared to launch out of my seat.

Gah! I didn't have time to deal with them now. Nor could I afford another supe on supe crime scene if it escalated. Tucker would wet his panties at the possibility to write me up. No, I had to find out what Booth wanted first. Wasting ten minutes of my precious time, I fiddled with the settings until they were back to normal. Then, I retyped my e-mail to Booth and clicked the send button.

When I walked into the lobby of SRD headquarters, I got a sense of déjà vu, spotting the same two security guards who greeted me last time. Guard

One sat at the sign-in counter behind a computer, while Guard Two stood sentry with his legs shoulder-width apart and his arms crossed in front of his chest. They carried themselves with importance, but their bland looks and blander personalities meant my nicknames worked. I could do better, but I didn't care.

Guard One, with sandy hair and green eyes, looked up abruptly and stopped typing. "Can I help you?" he asked as I approached the desk.

My nose flared as I took in more of his scent, recognizing it, owning it. A growl rumbled in my chest. "You're my new neighbour."

Guard Two turned to me. A quick sniff confirmed he was also one of my Witch neighbours. His eyes narrowed, and he started to silently mouth an incantation. The energy in the air intensified, humming with power.

I held my hand out to stop him—like it would do much if he threw a spell at me. "I'm not here for you two."

Guard Two pushed back his plain blond hair, and his lips formed a thin straight line. I remember thinking these two were the most boring Witches I'd ever come across. Now that I knew of their nightlife activities, I might have to revise that statement to something else.

I preferred them boring.

"Why are you here?" Guard One hissed.

My mountain lion paced in my head. She didn't like being on the receiving end of a hiss. She preferred dishing them out.

"You don't remember me?" I waited, but the blankness in their eyes told me they had short-term memory issues. "I'm Agent McNeilly."

As soon as I spoke my name, Guard One's face transformed—he looked like he wanted to shoot himself. Guard Two looked like he wanted to shoot me. I propped one hand on a cocked hip. "Agent Booth is expecting me."

Guard One hesitated, as if he needed a moment to collect his thoughts before re-entering diligent SRD employee mode. He tapped away at his computer and after reading something on his screen, turned his attention back to me. "Sign here. I'll buzz you through."

I picked up the pen and signed, aware that both Witches watched me, as if I represented an undiscovered specimen. Did they want to dissect me?

"Nice trick with the autocorrect on my computer." I kept my voice low so they had to bend forward. If they pissed me off anymore, I'd smash their heads together. Let them try throwing a spell at me then.

Neither of them acknowledged my accusation, but Guard One leaked nervous fumes, and the second Witch's scent contained nothing but hostility. I'd have to work to instil a sense of fear in that one.

"Thank you." I placed the pen down and sauntered toward the sealed entrance. After Guard One buzzed me in, I turned in the doorway. "Don't think I'm letting your petty retribution go."

Guard Two crossed his arms and gave me the best pissy diva face I'd seen since last week's rerun of a model reality show.

I ignored it and headed to the elevators.

The only downfall of coming into the SRD headquarters to see Agent Booth, besides an uncertain fate, was the inevitable reunion with her receptionist, Angelica. I liked calling her Angie because it made her eye twitch.

Ethan, a rival Master Vampire, had enslaved Angie and her fellow Wereleopards. I sliced off his head to pay my debt to Lucien, but I had help. If it weren't for Allan and Clint, I'd be another notch in Ethan's belt. And not the fun kind.

When I'd scouted Ethan's lair, they captured me. Mark, a Werehyena employed by Ethan loved to play with knives and other people's skin, my skin. He made Angie watch while he took a scalpel knife and made multiple incisions all over my body.

As I lay naked on an operating table with the beginning injuries of a torture marathon, Ethan summoned Mark to a meeting. Got to love bureaucracy. Angie, ordered to stay in the room, but unable to help me, didn't stop me from shifting and flying away.

I owed her.

And I hated owing a pint-sized Barbie doll with unnatural curves. She indirectly put me in the whole Clint Assassination situation in the first place, being the one to contact my rogue handler. I wish that made us even, but Ethan controlled leopards, like Lucien with his wolves, and she'd had no choice, forced to do everything Ethan commanded. Probably the only reason she still had employment with the SRD.

That's if the SRD knew. Did Agent Booth keep Angie's transgressions to herself, holding it as leverage so the Wereleopard would do her bidding? It fit. Probably something I'd do, too.

Taking in a deep breath, I stepped off the sterile metal elevator with its characterless gray carpet. The sight greeting me had the air sticking to my lungs. My throat dried, my chest hollowed.

Tristan stood in front of Angie's desk, leaning over to speak to her. At my entrance, he turned to face me.

As good looking as I remembered, Tristan's angelic face inspired sinful thoughts. Six solid feet of muscle, with rich black hair contrasting sharply with bright sapphire eyes and fair skin.

At the sight of me, his dark eyebrows shot up and a slow smile grew on his face. When his intoxicating scent reached me, honeysuckle on a warm summer's day, along with the standard Wereleopard citrus and sunshine aroma, my knees grew weak. Maybe I should sit down.

"Andy," Tristan purred. "You didn't call."

Glancing at Angie, I took in her sucked-on-a-lemon face before she shuttered it with cold indifference. Tristan followed my gaze. I was not sure what passed between the two Wereleopards, but Angie stood up briskly and straightened her stretchy dress before sashaying down the hall. Despite walking at a brisk pace, she managed to swing her hips like a wrecking ball—boom, boom, boom.

"Andy." Tristan's voice snapped my attention away from the receptionist's butt.

"Tristan."

"I'd like to take you out tonight." His eyes sparkled. Able to smell my own desire and panic, Tristan had to be well aware of the impact he had on me.

"I got back into town this morning. I won't make a great date." I shuffled my feet on the office's short pile carpet.

"I disagree."

"I think you'd reconsider that statement if I fell asleep on you," I said.

Tristan's smile grew. "I like the idea of watching you sleep."

Flustered, I opened and closed my mouth like a fish tossed on a riverbank by a hungry bear, then words stumbled out. "I...I don't know what to say to that." Honesty was the best policy.

Tristan took another step closer, his movement muffled by the carpet. "You don't need to be nervous around me, Andy."

My heart fluttered, and although tempted to insist I wasn't nervous, I refrained. He'd scent the lie.

"Let me take you to dinner."

"Tomorrow night." The words shot from my mouth before the thought went to the processing section of my brain. The part that would've said *No, sorry, can't. Busy, you know. Things to do. Witches to beat up.*

The smile Tristan flashed melted my core into a puddle of goo. I'd have to check later to see if my panties were still on, his devilish grin better than any stiff drink.

"Andrea," Angie interrupted, having returned from her runway strut. "Agent Booth will see you now."

She sauntered back to her gray industrial desk displaying the same passive facial expression she wore on the way out. Her scent betrayed her, though—she was upset. What existed between her and Tristan? Lovers? Friends? Exes? Something ugly flared up inside me at the idea of her sleeping with Tristan.

Mine, my mountain lion hissed, and then encouraged me to rake my nails across her face. I took a shuddered breath and reined in the possessive fera before I turned the reception area into a girl-on-girl battle room, without the mud. Women didn't need to be enemies just because they liked the same guy.

Warm fingers caressing mine snapped my head to reality. Tristan brought my hand to his lips and placed a soft kiss on my knuckles. "I'll pick you up at seven."

My hand fell limp against my body when he released it. He brushed by me on the way out, his scent clinging to the air long after he left. I wanted to vacuum the air and bottle it.

"He'll only hurt you." Angie tapped away at the keyboard in front of her computer's flat screen, not bothering to look up. Probably editing her online dating profile.

I didn't know what to say to that either, so I glared at her head. Angie must've felt the death stare, because she sighed and looked up. "Do you need help finding her office?"

"No," I bit out.

Spinning on my heel, I made my way to Booth's

office. When I knocked on her door, she barked out, "Enter!"

I opened the door and let myself in. Agent Booth gestured to the chair in front of her desk and then proceeded to ignore me while she tinkered at her computer, most likely sending one irrelevant e-mail after another. I had an office job once. I got it.

With an unsupervised moment, I took the time to analyze Booth. Middle aged with graying black hair, gray eyes, and a large hooked nose. She wore trendy age-appropriate business attire, showing her personal style with purple-rimmed glasses and green eye make-up. Maybe she liked to dress as the naughty librarian with her gentlemen callers after hours.

The disturbing image of Booth in a lover's tryst flashed in my head. But something else put me on edge. My brows pinched together to join as one. Agent Booth had no scent. She hadn't the last time we'd met, either. I'd never encountered a scentless human, norm or supe, unless the individual dabbled in some heavy magic. Instinctively, I knew this wasn't the case with Booth, and it made my skin ripple. My mountain lion wanted to open her up and find out what lurked inside. Did the other supes notice? I gripped the padded armrests of the chair and told my feras to shut up.

My phone vibrated, but I ignored it, not wanting to take my eyes off Booth. When I sat in her office, I was on her time.

"It's okay," she said without looking up. "You can get that."

Booth kept typing away, not sparing any attention my way. Who was texting me? Not many people had my number. Curiosity got the best of me, and I fished it out of my purse to read the message from Wick.

I miss you.

My cheeks heated.

I need space.

Did Wick even mean his words, or had Lucien ordered him to pursue me? The Master Vampire needed a way to control me, and dammit, Wick was the perfect tool. I couldn't be with someone I couldn't trust.

I will give you space, but we're mates.
We will be together.

As if he stood right beside me, I heard his voice, rough and sensual against my skin. So sure and confident. I chucked my phone back in my purse and played with some of the objects on Booth's desk.

"I have a job for you." Booth spun her chair to stare me in the eye.

I set the weird lizardman paperweight I'd been looking at back on her desk. "Excuse me?"

"I have a job for you." She said each word slowly and succinctly as if they were single sentences and I was a dumbass. Her deep, dry voice made me thirsty.

Frowning, I ran a finger down the statue. I thought

she'd want to discuss the train incident. "Why not get O'Donnell to contact me? He's my handler."

A small smile appeared on Booth's face as she leaned back in her chair. "He's on vacation. And this is a...sensitive matter. The less people involved, the better."

Normally, I'd be flattered, but..."I don't like the sound of this."

Booth tapped her manicured fingers along her desk. "It's a simple retrieval."

"Then why the hush-hush?"

"Do you want it or not?" Booth folded her arms.

I mirrored her actions and sank back in the chair. "I don't usually do retrievals. I want more information before I agree."

"The target escaped from one of our labs."

I blanched. "You want me to retrieve a *specimen* for you?"

"Yes. And we'd prefer no one else find out. It would be a PR nightmare."

I refrained from mentioning how that seemed to be going around. No need to remind Booth of the train incident a few days ago if she didn't plan to bring it up. "Timeline?"

"Open, but the sooner the better."

"Rate?"

"Same as a standard hit."

I shook my head. "A retrieval's more difficult. Easier to kill than to collect. Double."

"Done."

Her quick acceptance meant I should've asked for triple.

"I'll have Angie give you the file." Agent Booth pushed her chair back and stood up. "Don't mess this up or I'll look into your whereabouts the last few days." From her tone, it sounded like she already knew.

Crap. What were the implications of that? I'd try to hang around and find out, but I knew a dismissal when I heard one.

9

Of all the shitty coffee shops in all the Lower Mainland, and I kept walking into this one. The last time I'd sat in Suzy's Gourmet Café, I used the dive as a shelter to wait for Angie to finish work so I could follow her home. Now, I waited for Herman. That this coffee shop offered the best surveillance location for not one, but two of my targets, spoke volumes about the shady downtown Vancouver neighbourhood. A realtor's nightmare, maybe, but a criminal's paradise, undeniable.

I studied my mark through the window. The file gave me little to go on. It had been *cleaned*, meaning they'd weeded out all the information they weren't comfortable with me having. Apparently, in this case, that included everything except what the guy looked like with a vague warning to avoid skin-on-skin contact. His name was Herman—no last name. He escaped a week ago, which made me wonder why Booth delayed requesting my services until now. Did she only just learn of it? Or had they tried using other agents for the retrieval already?

Outside, the man moved with reptilian-like grace, slithering between oblivious norms as they huddled under their umbrellas and forged along the sidewalk after work like drones. A small man, with slight shoulders and thin arms and legs, I had the biggest urge to dub him Pee Wee Herman, but that would result in more attachment than I could afford. Giving targets nicknames placed in the top ten things not to do on the job.

Too far to see his face clearly, all I could discern was his cautiousness—he kept looking back and forth before stepping into shops and alleyways, probably looking for a place to sleep for the night. If he'd been in the labs for a while, he'd have no resources or friends to draw on. The file didn't list any known associates, but that didn't mean he didn't have any.

I'd been lucky that Randy, the pawnshop clerk down the road, recognized Herman's photograph. Having worked in the service industry a few lifetimes ago, I knew it was more difficult to remember faces than the cop dramas on television let on. Unless something stood out, faces of the general public blurred. The same went for supes with scents.

Herman had an average appearance—mouse brown hair and lightly tanned skin like mine that hinted at ambiguous ethnicity. If it weren't for his awkward gangliness and slit eyes, he'd blend right in.

Randy, making sure to get an eyeful of my cleavage, was more than happy to tell me Herman pawned an old woman's watch, probably stolen, and where he'd seen him walking to—Suzy's Gourmet Café.

Legally speaking, if I contracted a disease or stomach ulcer after consuming coffee on the job, would I be entitled to worker's compensation?

Staking out the coffee shop, I'd hoped it was only a matter of time before Herman showed his ugly mug again. I liked being right.

Herman walked in front of the café and glanced in the window to where I sat. My gaze drifted off his shoulders and out to the street behind him. Years ago I learned never to watch a target's face. Eye contact risked people remembering me. I preferred not to get close enough for a mark to truly see me, because if they saw me again and again, the amount of red flags going up would send a bull into a fit.

No eye contact.

Act like I didn't see him. *I'm just another norm, caught up in my daily routine, doing my thing*. He was inconsequential.

Herman ducked his head and shuffled around the corner, which led down the side of the building. I waited a couple minutes before slipping out of the coffee shop to follow him into the alley.

Only to find it empty.

The long alley lacked any nooks to hide in and the side door to the Renaissance Hotel had to be opened from the inside. I'd learned that tidbit from my brief reconnaissance for the Clint Assignment.

Sniffing the air, I tried to locate any traces of

Herman's scent. No sign of the target anywhere. There should be a fresh smell, distinct from the usual alley odours, and then I'd own it. I'd track him down wolf-style.

That can't be right! I lifted my nose and drew in long drags of air, then short successive huffs, hoping to catch something, but nothing existed except the stale stench of urine, garbage and the regular homeless that frequented the alley. No new scents. My wolf growled.

Herman didn't have a scent.

Aside from noting I already deeply regretted taking this assignment, something else became very clear to me —Agent Booth lied about why she wanted this quiet— the target was like her. What, exactly? No clue. But I planned to find out.

IO

While staring at my reflection in the mirror, I realized two things: one, I should show off my cleavage more often—it was a shame to keep these girls hidden—and two, no matter how hard I tried, I couldn't hide the churning in my stomach, tingling in my chest, or the breathlessness I felt; my panic as evident as finding Waldo in a nudist colony.

The doorbell rang and my heart stopped.

You kill people for a living for fuck's sake. Get a hold of yourself.

For tonight's date, I wore a low-cut V-neck wrap dress with black bow-tie pumps. Despite the attire contrasting sharply with my normal day-to-day style and personality, I looked good. I said farewell to my reflection and stalked to the entrance of my condo. Taking a deep breath, I opened the door to Tristan

His full lips curled up in a sweet smile that spread across his face, revealing even white teeth. I found myself grinning back. The dance in his eyes said he didn't use this smile often—it belonged to me.

He wore dress pants, the expensive designer kind, a matching jacket, and a white shirt with a blue-stitched inlaid design. The colour a perfect complement to his sapphire eyes. I wanted to trace his shirt's pattern with my fingers, and had to snatch my hand back.

His citrus and sunshine scent swirled around me like a hot summer's day, and I wanted to bask in the warmth. An image of us rolling around in sheets smelling of him made my face heat, and a purr erupt from my chest. When I opened my eyes, I'd taken a step closer to Tristan, my face inches from his throat.

"Why do you smell so good?" I breathed.

A deep rumbling purr harmonized with my own in answer. Tristan dipped his head and nuzzled my neck, rubbing the bridge of his nose against the soft, sensitive skin.

Heat intensified quickly throughout my body. God, I wanted this man, and I didn't know him.

I gripped his shirt and pulled him closer, drawing in the smell of his skin. The pulsating in his chest morphed from a rumble to a chuckle. The sound vibrated through my body, melting my core into molten lava. I squeezed my thighs together to stop the throbbing between my legs.

Tristan gently gripped my hands and pried them loose, and I released his shirt. He squeezed before letting them go. "I plan to court you properly, Andy. If we stay here much longer, my good intentions will fly out the window."

With a nervous laugh, I stepped back. Tristan's gaze raked over my body and rested unabashedly on my chest before his gaze made its way to my face. He held his hand out. "You look lovely. Shall we?"

THE BEGINNING OF THE DATE STARTED LIKE most, at least I assumed it did—not a lot of experience in the dating department despite my almost eighty years of existence. Spending the last fifteen years as an assassin and over thirty years prior to that as a mountain lion meant few learning opportunities. Sure, I'd *interacted* with the opposite sex, but not on an emotional level.

I held my breath the entire way to the restaurant. Tristan seemed amused by my nerves and did his best to put me at ease, but he couldn't stop me from fidgeting. I hadn't technically been on a dinner date in decades. Not since Dylan. And that hadn't turned out well for me in the end.

When we got to the restaurant, I was pleased to find Tristan selected a place with quality food without the pretentious atmosphere and exorbitant prices. Maybe he suspected throwing money at a meal wasn't the way to impress me.

We ordered our food and after the wine came,

Tristan leaned forward, his brilliant blue irises boring into mine. "Do you have any hobbies?" he asked.

Out of everything he could've asked, I hadn't expected this one. Not sure why. "I've been an assassin for the last fifteen years. There's been no time for hobbies."

Tristan leaned back and savoured some of his wine. "You can fling that in my face all you want, Andy. It's not going to scare me off."

I pursed my lips. "Perceptive."

"And I imagine your tactics were very successful in the past." After a pause, he straightened up and placed his elbows on the table. "I don't scare easily."

I took a sip of wine to hide the silly grin easing onto my face. Glancing at Tristan over the rim, I could tell from his knowing smile, he wasn't fooled.

"So. Before you became an assassin. Before you accumulated whatever bad history you have...which I hope you'll confide later...did you have any hobbies? Did you paint?"

I snorted before I could stop myself. Not very lady-like. "I have about as much artistic talent as a cluster of colour-blind hedgehogs in a bag."

"I thought all hedgehogs were colour-blind."

"I read somewhere they have cone-like nuclei in their retinas, so theoretically, they should see some colours."

Tristan blinked. "Not your average reading material."

"No. Maybe I should've said moles instead?"

"Now those, I know, are flat out blind." Tristan relaxed back into his glass of wine.

I nodded. "And a more accurate description of my painting abilities."

"So we won't be doing any nude sketching of each other later?"

I took another sip of wine, ignoring the images of Tristan's naked body flashing through my mind. Not going there, not yet. "Why'd you ask about painting anyway?"

Tristan shrugged. "Seems to me women are always saying how much they want to paint."

He wasn't wrong. I'd recently watched two romcom movies that had the main character saying something similar. "I really did want to paint at one point in my life. But I'm not sure what I did with a paint brush and a sheet of paper could ever be described as painting."

Tristan chuckled. Silence fell over the table while he swirled his wine, and I stared down at mine.

"You obviously like to read," he said. "That's a hobby."

"Why does it matter?"

"Reading?" He frowned.

"No. Why do my hobbies matter to you?"

"Our animals want each other—that is abundantly clear—but I want to get to know you, Andy. Find out what you like, what you want, what you've been through."

Warmth radiated from my chest, and I fiddled with my fork, determined not to let him see how his words affected me. I loved how he said my name—all purr. "Why me?"

A long pause made me look back. With his head tilted to the side and his brow furrowed, Tristan looked at me like an unfinished puzzle. Setting his glass down gently beside his plate, he leaned forward and held my hands across the table. "You asked why I smelled so good earlier."

My throat constricted. I nodded.

Stroking my hands with his thumbs, he met my eyes straight on. "Do you not know why you find my scent irresistible? Why yours feels the same for me?"

The idea that my scent elicited the same response in Tristan sent a searing bolt of goodness straight to between my legs. Then I thought about what he said, what he implied. It was a weird sensation to experience a mix of polar emotions—dread, excitement, apprehension, and anticipation swirling around my head until I broke free and spoke.

"We can't be mates," I said. "You're a leopard." *And I'm a mountain lion, not to mention a wolf, a falcon, and something dark and twisted that I don't want to define.*

It was impossible to keep the tone of disappointment completely out of my voice. Why did I want him so much? My life would be simpler with only one love interest. Hell, it would be easier with none.

Tristan's eyes twinkled back at me. "You think Werewolves have a monopoly on the mate thing?"

A couple of weeks ago, when things started to heat up with Wick, I'd threatened he might have to share me if my mountain lion or falcon wanted to mate with another, not knowing if it was possible. I'd been making it up to put space between us. Once again, I found myself cursing my own ignorance. Had I grown up in a Shifter home, or not receded into the primal part of my being for three decades, I would've known this stuff. The Internet could only provide so much insight, and it often became buried under pages and pages of ignorance and stupidity. *Gah!*

Wick's response to my threat had been to research big cats. He found they weren't monogamous. Mountain lions specifically lived a solitary life and met other adults for the sole purpose of reproduction.

Wick.

The back of my throat ached. I grabbed my water and gulped down mouthfuls of cool liquid to wash away the thickness growing in my esophagus.

I glanced across the table at Tristan. What would he make of the research? Regardless, the information Wick found was based on big felines in nature, not supernatural Weres or Shifters, like me and Tristan. It certainly didn't cover how my Carus status affected my ability to mate. I hesitated before saying, "I've never heard of feline Weres being mated. How's that possible?"

I made a point of researching supernaturals. Not just to find out what the fuck I was, but also because knowledge was power. The better I knew my targets, the better I could take them down. That being said, I never discovered answers regarding my nature. It was very probable I missed out on other information as well.

Tristan laughed. It was a short bark that sounded borderline bitter. "We don't go around announcing it or throwing it in people's faces. The mating bond is sacred and not discussed outside the prowl or potential mates. It's our biggest vulnerability and the Shifter Shankings served as a glaring message to the rest of the supernatural community to keep our mouths shut. The Werewolves had already blabbed, but for the rest of us, the mating bond is kept secret. The decision to enter into one is not taken lightly."

I frowned. "You would pass on being mated?"

Before Tristan could reply, the waiter arrived with our meals. We had both ordered steaks, extra rare. Not exactly a surprise. Nor was the wide berth the servers and some of the other patrons gave our table, having deduced we weren't normal. What I could never figure out was how supes weren't outed before the Purge. What normal human would want to eat raw steak, unless they harboured a supernatural predator deep inside their psyche?

My mountain lion purred as the tender meat hit my tongue and awoke my taste buds. I reined in my reaction so I wouldn't freak out the table beside us. They were an older couple, norms, and from the quick glances they kept casting our way, it was safe to assume we made them nervous.

We ate in companionable silence, savouring the flavours in the meat. Or at least, I was. The mate thoughts kept trickling up, though. What would Tristan have said before the waiter arrived?

Stop it. Just relax and enjoy the moment. Great steak.

When the waiter cleared our plates, Tristan gave me a

sly look before telling the waiter we'd finish our wine and then he'd like the bill. No dessert.

"Not here," he whispered to me. "I have plans for our *dessert.*"

It was a good thing I was sitting, or I'd have melted to the floor from the look he gave me. I gripped the sides of my chair and smiled back, hoping he didn't realize how much the flashing of his pearly whites disarmed me. His grin grew.

He knew.

I I

Using my limited knowledge of dates, I'd say this one went well: awkward start, delicious dinner with good conversation, romantic walk on the seawall while the handsome love interest held hands with the socially inept lead female. Everything textbook perfect for a popular chick-flick movie.

Tristan gripped both of my hands in his strong ones. The waning crescent moon reflected off the water and illuminated the deep blue pools of his eyes. They mesmerized me as he pulled me close on the narrow section of the seawall. The ocean breeze brushed through my hair and whipped it around. Tristan leaned down. I closed my eyes.

A high-pitched wail shattered the exquisite silence. Our heads snapped away, and my muscles tensed.

A growl ripped from my throat, not quite wolf, not quite mountain lion.

Crazy-eyed norms swarmed us. Scrambling over the

edge from the ocean, they looked more like versatile climbing lizards than humans. Their eyes shone with the same possession as the norms on the train. My heart pounded against my breastbone as my cat and wolf pushed to take over.

"What are those?" Tristan released my hand. He slipped out of his jacket and rolled up the cuffs of his shirt to expose his forearms. He had nice arms—smooth skin rippling over veins and muscles. The first human who reached him got a fist in her face, sending her flying backward.

"Possessed humans." I kicked one pump off and grabbed the other from my foot. I chucked it at a large man still lumbering over the wall. It beaned him in the head and sent him falling back into the water.

"Nice," Tristan said, before judo-throwing a barrel-chested man with a bald spot into a nearby lamppost. He started to unbutton his shirt.

Before I had a chance to pick up my other shoe for a weapon, another woman grabbed my wrist and yanked on it, pulling me toward the edge of the wall. I broke her hold with a white-belt defence move and knocked her off with a flurry of hand strikes.

"There's too many," Tristan said after flinging another one over the wall. He abandoned the buttons and ripped off his shirt. "Shift."

Cursing, I used a series of moves to put a bit of distance between myself and the three humans launching themselves at me in an uncoordinated effort. Shifting quickly to my mountain lion form, I shook off the remnants of my little black dress and wasted no time pouncing at the humans converging on Tristan. Weres took more time to shift, and it was their most vulnerable state.

Ripping the throat out of one man, I quickly tackled another, clearing an area for Tristan. He'd already removed his clothes and curled into a tense ball as the change took him. Skin folded over skin, blood and other liquids oozed out, bones cracked, fur emerged. The older and more powerful Weres shifted quickly. Tristan shifted into a leopard faster than I'd seen any Were before, which told me he had to be over three hundred years old.

Rounding on the possessed humans, we made quick work of those remaining. Slashing, ripping, gutting. A natural hierarchy existed between animals, humans included. Big cats always came out on top.

My mountain lion enjoyed the sensation of physical superiority. Though jealous not to be let out, my wolf relished in delight as I overpowered weaker individuals. I liked not being dead.

Shifting back to human, I took a moment to study those we'd killed. I didn't feel sorry. Not even guilty—just sad. They were possessed with the same glowing eyes as the ones on the train. But it was either them or me, and that wasn't a dilemma in my books. Clear choice.

My falcon squawked and urged me to launch into the summer air. Looking up to find Tristan, my breath hitched, stolen from my lungs at the sight of his naked body. Even splattered with the blood of our attackers, it was magnificent. Well-defined muscles rippled with the slightest movement. He'd send Adonis into a pouting fit, winning whatever competition they entered. Following the V down to between his legs brought a smile to my lips and a flutter to my heart. He'd definitely beat the Greek gods in one department.

"Should I flex?" So caught up in admiring Tristan's naked form, I didn't realize he watched me until he spoke.

My attention snapped to his face and warmth flushed my cheeks. He responded by casting his gaze down my body. While taking a slow perusal, he stepped closer and closer. Couldn't exactly chastise him for doing exactly what I'd done, now could I? But if it was possible to do a full-body blush, I accomplished it then and there. "I don't usually let a guy get me naked on the first date."

Tristan laughed. "Now that, I believe." He bent to pick up my clothes. I tried really hard not to look at his butt. And failed. Nice. Very nice. Sculpted and hard, corded with muscle.

Breathe.

I wanted to sink my teeth into it.

Shaking my head, I croaked a "thanks" and took my clothes from Tristan. He shot me a crooked grin before finding his own stuff. I slipped into my ripped clothes. Where did the thought about biting his ass come from—me or the cat?

Did it matter?

After putting on his own clothes, he walked up behind me, placed his undamaged jacket around my shoulders, and pulled my body into his. My bare feet shuffled against the rough pavement. Strong arms enveloped me. He bent his head so the bridge of his nose ran along the soft skin between my neck and shoulder, like he did at the beginning of our date. Taking a deep breath in, he scented me. His shoulders dropped, and his arms relaxed as if the action gave him comfort. Maybe it did. I certainly felt better.

"This is going to sound wrong," he mumbled into my neck. The brush of his soft lips on my skin sent shivers down my body. "But I enjoyed fighting beside you."

I laughed and turned to face him. "I guess this means our date is over."

Tristan tilted his head. "Why would you say that? We still have dessert."

DESSERT HAD TO WAIT. FLASHING RED AND BLUE lights accompanied by wailing sirens flooded the night. The good ol' Vancouver Police Department put the SRD to shame with response time.

Covered with dirt, skin caked with blood, and wearing shredded clothes, we made quite a sight. But on a positive note, I'd found both my shoes.

"This could get ugly," I said.

"Do you want to run?" Tristan asked. "We could shift and be gone before they reach us."

"No. They'll find my DNA, and I'm in the system. Besides, someone had to see us to call it in."

We both glanced around the empty seawall and the surrounding ocean. The crescent moon and city lights from the North Shore and Lions Gate Bridge reflected off the water. I couldn't see or smell anyone in our proximity. My skin crawled as if snakes slithered across it. Someone or something watched us.

Police cruisers pulled up from both ends of the seawall while others screeched into the nearby parking lot. Officers flung their doors open, and used them as shields while they aimed their guns at us.

"Hands in the air!" One of the policemen in front of us bellowed.

We complied.

"Get slowly to the ground—" he continued.

"Wait!" Another cop yelled. This voice sounded familiar. "I know her. SRD agent. Stand down."

And just like that, the guns went away, and we watched Officer Stan Stevens stalk over to us, carefully skirting the crime scene. His face remained serene, but his soap and leather scent flowed in the breeze and carried his wariness to us in greeting.

"Agent Andrea McNeilly?" He planted his feet wide and kept his gun hand loose near his weapon. "We keep running into each other."

Not on purpose. "Hello, Officer Stevens."

He grunted and pulled out his notepad. "Tell me what happened."

I recounted the events while other police officers

sectioned off the area with yellow crime scene tape. I didn't leave anything out. The other cops milled around with crime scene tape and cordoned off the area. One placed a yellow marker by my bloody heel.

A van pulled up and investigators in white body suits hopped out. Some carried floodlights, others lugged lab collection kits.

"So more *possessed* humans?" Officer Stan clenched his jaw after he scribbled down our statements. He held his pen tightly, turning the tip of his forefinger white.

"It looks that way. Although they weren't possessed in a way I've seen before. Other than on the train."

"Any witnesses?"

"No. Just us."

"If this wasn't becoming commonplace all around town, I'd cuff you both and haul your asses in. You may have to come in for further questioning, but I have a feeling this will be turned over to your agency like the other cases."

Other cases?

Dead air hung between us as Stan studied my face.

"But?" God, I hoped there was a "but" in there.

An investigator approached us and with a nod from Officer Stevens, started swabbing the blood splattered across our bodies. Another man with whiskey on his breath took my hand and collected the skin, blood and hair from beneath my nails. I didn't fight or question any of the evidence collection. I wanted out of here. After Whiskey-breath finished with my hands, he tapped my chin. I opened and he quickly swabbed the inside of my cheek.

Officer Stevens watched with an expressionless mask and remained silent until the crime scene investigators left.

"But—" Officer Stevens continued as if no time lapse had occurred "—our crime lab can now identify a discrepancy in these possessed humans' norepinephrine levels. We'll know shortly if you're telling the truth. And if you're not, your agency can spend their budget hunting you down. You're not in the norm jurisdiction. I wish the SRD would respond faster so we didn't have to freeze our butts off waiting to transfer the chain of custody to them."

"So we can go?"

"Consider it a professional courtesy. Unless you want to wait around for your people to show up? We could, uh, we could find you a blanket or something." He waved his pen-holding hand at my body.

Huh? Oh, he meant my outfit, or lack of one. I tugged at my dress, trying to cover a bit more of my upper thigh without exposing my crotch. I gave up and pulled Tristan's jacket closer around me. "Did they say who was coming?"

"Agent Tucker, again." The tone Officer Stevens used earned him some serious brownie points with me. Apparently, he didn't think much of the daddy's boy, either.

"We'll head out," I said.

Tristan took me to a late-night coffee shop that served ice cream and offered no judgment for my shredded clothes and disarrayed appearance. We'd found a public restroom to clean up, but traces of dirt and blood still smeared our skin. No one seemed to care. Frankly, the amount of chest Tristan's ripped shirt exposed and the way the entire staff gawked at him, they'd probably let him do anything. I ordered mocha almond fudge in a waffle cone bowl and a cappuccino with cinnamon.

Tristan placed his spoon down in his empty bowl. "You asked me earlier if I'd pass on having a mate."

Too busy shovelling ice cream into my face to vocalize a response, I put my spoon down instead. I swallowed a mouthful of ice cream too quickly, and the onset of brain freeze set in. I winced and pinched the bridge of my nose.

Tristan laughed and reached out to hold my hand, waiting for it to pass. Light flashed in his eyes. "Finding a mate is a gift." He squeezed my hands. "And not something I've experienced until now. But it's not the same thing as the norm concept of soul mates."

My brow furrowed. Fine lines might permanently etch my face after this conversation. "I thought they were one and the same."

Tristan pulled back, letting my hand go. "That's what Werewolves would have their females believe."

I gaped.

"Once the mating process is complete, it's essentially the same. We will have no other, want no other, and go mad with grief if the other dies. But there is more than one potential mate in the world. More than one person can complement our predator and self. A mate is not half of one soul, but a match for it."

Tristan rendered me speechless. What he said went against everything I'd been told by Dylan and Wick. Thinking back though, Wick never claimed to be soul mates. He claimed to be my mate as if he was the one and only. Did he purposefully lie by omission, or did I assume? The wheels in my head turned so fast, some nuts and bolts spun right off and clanked around in my head.

Tristan sighed, as if sensing my inner turmoil. "Think about it. Considering the vast numbers of their population, how is it that every female Werewolf is fortunate enough to find her mate?"

"Some are forced unions." My voice came out blunt and hard.

Tristan's face screwed up in disgust before he looked up at me. His sapphire gaze blazed with an intensity that made me want to leap across the table and soothe him. After a pause, he said, "We'll explore what *that* was later."

Huh. Guess I still harboured some baggage from Dylan. Not a surprise. If I could smell the air bruised with my pain, so could he.

Tristan took a swig of his coffee and continued as if

the interlude didn't happen—as if the scent of burnt cinnamon didn't roll off him in waves, or he didn't clutch his mug hard enough to turn his fingers white. Any tighter and the cup would shatter. "If you took forced matings out of the equation, the number of existing true matings far exceeds the natural probability of one female Werewolf finding her one true soul mate in the entire world population of Werewolves."

It made sense. How else could Wick and Tristan both claim they were my mate? I savoured my last spoonful of ice cream—delicious—while I considered Tristan's statistical analysis. "What is it you do for work?"

Tristan's attention fixated on my mouth as it closed over the spoon again, just in case any ice cream lingered. He licked his lips. "Security."

"Didn't peg you as a security guard."

The sound of Tristan's laugh trickled down my spine and liquefied it. "I'm not. I specialize in security systems. I own a company, which provides personal detailing for a special price."

"And what would my price be?" *Oh my god, did I just say that?*

"For you?" Tristan leaned in. "I'm sure we could work out some special pricing. But don't distract me from my point, you little minx. I've run the statistics and the probability doesn't match reality. And it doesn't take into account the extended lifetime of Weres, nor that their true mate may not be turned for a number of years."

"You've had some time to think on this."

He rewarded my astuteness with a large grin. "I lead a prowl of Wereleopards. It's come up a few times."

"With Angie?" My mountain lion started pacing from one side of my skull to the other.

Tristan's head snapped up, his expression pinched. Then his nose flared, and the tension in his shoulders disappeared. "Jealous?"

I shrugged. "She seems attached."

Tristan's smile flattened into a grim line. "Her feelings are misguided. There is no history between us, not in the way you believe."

"Why would she bother if you weren't mates?"

"I don't pretend to understand the inner workings of any woman's mind, especially Angelica's. But suffice it to say, my position of power is an attraction to her. She's a powerful Wereleopard, and we're all drawn to power. Like I'm drawn to you."

Sharp sapphires held my gaze. My heart beat, seeming to pump twice the blood, hurting my chest. My mountain lion pushed against my control and urged me to leap across the table. "I need to pee."

Tristan shook his head. "I believe the bathroom is in the back."

I bolted to the washroom.

Clarity came at odd times in my life. This particular instance it happened while I held a power yoga squat over the toilet. Why did I run away from Tristan? Now apart, I wanted to run back and see his smiling face. I wanted to trace his laugh lines with my tongue.

I washed my hands, read the plaques by the

mirrors, and made my way back to my seat, drawing the attention of more than a few people including my own date.

"What has you so amused?" Tristan asked.

"Plaque in the bathroom."

His eyebrows rose.

"It said cats are just tiny women in cheap fur coats."

Instead of being offended as a less secure male feline Were would've been, Tristan's head dropped back as he broke out laughing. My cat pressed for me to act. I ignored her. When Tristan got control of himself, he said, "Think I might have to get one of those made for the prowl house. I'd like to show it to you sometime."

My breath caught.

I'd like to see the prowl house and a whole lot more.

"But tonight..." He leaned in. "I think I need to get you home."

My eyebrows rose.

"Slow and steady wins the race."

The drive back to my place was quiet. It gave me time to reflect and analyze the man I sat next to. He drove a black Lexus LF-CC. I asked because I had no idea what to call it. I'd never given cars much importance, but the sleek one Tristan drove acted as a vehicular panty remover. The inside, finished in white-and-brown leather with brushed metal and wood accents, matched Tristan's calm, smooth style, but what really did it for me was the hybrid decal.

Everything about Tristan spoke of good taste and money, yet he didn't throw it in my face. He was the exact opposite of the type I usually went for. But look where that got me—Dylan.

What about Wick?

Guilt lanced through my veins. Exponentially better than Dylan, but in the end, Wick had still hurt me and because his connection with Lucien, he could hurt me again. Trying to get the bad taste out of my mouth, I took out a piece of gum, then offered one to Tristan.

"Yes, please. Could you take it out for me?" he asked, glancing quickly in my direction before returning his gaze forward to focus on the road.

"Here you go." I held out the stick of gum.

The corner of Tristan's lip curled up in a half smile. He opened his mouth and flicked another glance my way.

I reached out to slip the gum in his mouth. Before I could withdraw, Tristan leaned forward and placed his warm mouth over my fingers, clamping down before slowly reclining back into his seat. He sucked the gum stick out of my hand and dragged his teeth along my skin.

"Thanks," he said.

"You're welcome," I stammered, still staring.

Tristan laughed and pulled into my building's driveway. Too soon, in my opinion. He leapt out and walked around to open my door. My heart fluttered. Would he kiss me goodnight? I took his hand and let him walk me to the front entrance. We both paused to spit our gum in the garbage.

Before I could thank him again for the best date I'd ever had, Tristan spun me to face him. Holding my hands, he looked me intently in the eyes.

"Freedom of choice, Andy. You only enter into a mating if you want to."

He placed a finger on my lips to stop whatever I was going to say. Not that I could remember what that was. His skin tasted salty and sweet. I wanted to dart my tongue out and lick him.

As if distracted by the sight of my mouth, he paused and stared at my lips before continuing. "Let's be clear on something. I don't want you to, and it's not easy for me to say this, but you can walk away. From me, from Wick..." He paused to give me a pointed look. "Or both. Your animals have told you who's a good choice, a good mate. You can take or leave that information."

"Oh."

Tristan smiled slowly and leaned in with an infectious grin. He slid his hands up to cradle my face, before drawing me in. "For the record. I think you should choose me."

He pressed his soft, warm lips to mine. His scent, mixed with our desire, swirled around me. He pulled me closer and deepened the kiss, angling my mouth for better access. His tongue sent electric pulses down my body. My nipples hardened, heat coiled low in my belly, my knees weakened. I gripped the back of his shirt and clung on. His arms circled my body, supporting me against the toned planes of his muscles. Crushed against his hard chest, my lungs fought for air. Who needed oxygen anyway? I lost myself in his kiss, in him, surrounded by the pulsing sound of our hearts, beating in unison.

And then he pulled away.

Limp in his arms, it took me a moment to regain my footing and think clearly.

"Your choice," Tristan whispered into my ear before fully withdrawing. He ran a finger along my lips and gave them one last look, as if imprinting them to his memory, before he walked away.

12

When staring at Randy, the pawnshop owner, across the display case full of necklace pendants that doubled as cocaine snorters and pill cases, I wondered, not for the first time, how ironic life turned out to be.

Bonnie and Adam McNeilly, the adoring couple who raised me instead of my birth parents, were devout Christians, and believed in seeing the good in everyone. After years of failed fertility treatments, they pursued the adoption option and ended up with me. Born during the first years of the Purge, my papers said nothing of my biological parents being supes. At the time, no one thought anything about the increase of orphans coinciding with the Shifter Shankings.

Not until over a decade later, when seemingly normal teenagers started stumbling into the woods, plagued by visions and heightened emotions well beyond teenage angst, to meet wild animals they'd eventually bond with and shift into.

Then there were some pointed questions asked at the adoption agencies.

My parents never got any answers. They never asked for them. They told me they loved me no matter what and saw the beauty and goodness in me, even if I didn't. If only they knew what really lurked deep down inside.

I imagined it looked something like Randy's face.

Deeply scarred from some past abusive recreational activity, whether drowning cats without tying the bags closed, BDSM without a safe word, or using his own face to sharpen the blades of a lawnmower, Randy's features had more crevices than the Marianas Trench. Pockmarks decorated the valleys and hills of his skin, and his lips twisted permanently into a sinister sneer. He was one of my best informants and all it cost was a low-cut shirt and turning a blind eye to his blatant eye-groping of my body.

"Saw him again." Randy's voice grated against my eardrums, deep and gravelly. He leaned in to get a closer look at the girls. He never made direct eye contact. I gave up correcting him long ago. I knew he had no other way to relate to women, so I looked past his lack of social skills. The inside of Randy probably outcompeted the outside for scarring and damage.

"When?" I grabbed a dented lighter from the countertop display and flipped it open and closed.

"This morning. When I opened shop he was waiting for me."

"What did he pawn?"

"This." Randy held out a shiny object. When I reached for it, he pulled his hand back, making me lean forward before he let me snatch the object out of his hand.

Cold to the touch, the figurine's rough edges brushed my skin. I moved it around in the light. A weird lizardman. Much like the one on Agent Booth's desk. But this one was different—smaller and cruder, the lines not expertly smoothed out. I sniffed it. A rose and citronella smell clung to the figurine, making me think of an older woman's perfume or soap.

Hmm. Booth and Herman, both scentless and both in possession of weird figurines? Part of me wanted to barge into Booth's office and demand she tell me about Herman. The more rational part realized that action might sign my death warrant. Agent Booth went to extremes to guard her identity. If I let on I knew she and Herman were the same kind of supe—one that landed Herman into the lab as a specimen—she wouldn't hesitate to take me out. If I were Booth, I wouldn't either. I needed to find out what this figurine represented on my own.

"I wonder where he got it," I mused.

"Huh?" Randy asked.

I repeated my question.

Randy shrugged. "Same place he probably got the watch. Ripped off an old lady."

"Thanks for the tip."

"Uh-huh." Randy licked his chapped lips.

Stepping out of the pawn shop, I wondered how I

was going to find an old lady missing her watch and an ugly lizardman figurine. Time to hit up the SRD search engines and pay the good ol' VPD a visit.

IT TOOK MUCH LONGER THAN NORMAL TO GET home in rush hour. Relieved not to be greeted by another Witch prank, I sank into my couch and closed my eyes.

My cell phone vibrated. I looked down at the call display. Wick. The bridge of my nose started sweating. How did I feel about him? Should I tell him about Tristan? My finger hovered over the Accept button. My stomach sank. Chickening out, I hit Reject instead.

My cell beeped two minutes later with a text from Wick.

You went on a date with Tristan???

I stared at the screen and wondered what to do. How'd he find out? Another message dinged before I had a chance to type anything.

I'm coming over.

I fumbled with my tiny cell phone, trying to type as quickly as possible.

Bad time.

He didn't reply.

I groaned and slogged to the kitchen to flick on the electric kettle.

I hadn't seen Wick since he dropped me off after the blood bonding. He'd driven me home in silence. Well, near silence. He kept mumbling how sorry he was until I told him where to shove his apologies...or something like that. I might've used stronger words.

Wick had wanted to come in. "I want to hold you," he'd said. But for once, I didn't want him anywhere near me. He'd done enough *holding* already. I sent him off with a few curses and insults. He'd looked so sad, hanging his head in shame as he slunk back to his shiny black SUV with his metaphorical tail between his legs. God, part of me had wanted to call him back and let him wipe the bad memories from my mind, and my soul. The other part of me had known, I wouldn't, couldn't, tolerate anyone's touch at the time, let alone *his*. Too fresh, too raw. Had things changed?

The water started to boil when the tires of Wick's SUV squealed outside as he rounded the corner by my building. Pulling two mugs out with shaky hands, I chucked a tea bag in each one. I'd prefer coffee, but guessing at Wick's current emotional state, soothing chamomile might be better.

Might.

A homeopathic remedy against the whirlwind force of Wick? Wishful thinking. Maybe he'd just go away and

I could avoid this confrontation. He had no right to be upset with me.

The buzzer went off. I visualized Wick standing there, glaring at the intercom while pressing the button for my unit down and not releasing it. I buzzed him in and braced for the storm.

Wick blew past me when I opened the door. "This is what you meant by space?"

He spun around in the living room. The full force of his rage made me stagger back a step. Ten times worse than I'd imagined. His rosemary scent, normally full and sweet enough to make me drool, ran foul, laced with the stench of burnt cinnamon and the jealous odour of old cat piss. He wore his heart on his sleeve. Betrayal, evident in his eyes.

Even pissed off, Wick looked good enough to eat. With blond hair cut short, chiseled features, and broad shoulders, he looked like a present-day Norse god. His eyes held my attention; not blue like the Norse, but a rich, chocolate brown. Right now, bright yellow ringed his irises as Wick's wolf fought for control. "You are not to see Tristan again."

His pain and jealousy sent my stomach to the floor. Then I remembered what Wick had done. "You have no right barging in here demanding things of me. Not after what you did." *That's right, keep the anger close. Don't jump his bones.*

"I had no choice. You know that." He clutched the bottom of his shirt, clenching his fists. "We are mates. Why would you date someone else?"

Many replies sprang to mind. Some to placate his anger and ease his fears. And some to push him farther into unbridled madness. But I couldn't lie to Wick, nor intentionally hurt him, no matter how upset I was, no matter how much I hated Lucien's control over him. He deserved the truth.

"I have a connection with Tristan, too." My voice came out quiet, barely above a whisper. If he'd been a norm, I'd have to repeat myself louder, but Wick heard everything. He flinched, as if the words slapped him in the face. His eyebrows pinched together, and his lips compressed into a straight line.

Now both of us hurt. Great. Somehow, that didn't make anything better.

Wick looked down at the floor. His jaw clenched and unclenched, his hands fisted and opened, fisted and opened. Then his scent changed. From sour air and burnt cinnamon, the scent evolved to the steel and iron aroma of determination.

And the musky coconut of desire. My knees buckled.

Before I could say anything, Wick enfolded me. A hand fisted my hair at the back of my head. His hot mouth closed on mine, demanding. His tongue penetrated my mouth and brushed mine. He backed me into a wall and pushed his rock-hard body against me. He'd always played on the soft, safe side with me, sensing the bruised nature of my past, but today, right now, his actions demanded a response, a confirmation of my feelings. My heart punched against my breastbone, my body flushed with heat. My brain emptied of all intelligence, leaving me light-headed.

I tried to speak, but Wick stole my breath away, sucking it from my mouth. He hoisted my leg up and ground against me. And the shameless tramp that I was I kissed him right back with as much passion and frustration.

As quick as it happened, it ended. Wick untangled himself, leaving me weak, speechless, and extremely aroused.

"I will have your heart, Andy."

When I managed to lift my gaze to meet his, triumph glittered back at me. The corners of Wick's lips tugged up into a smile.

"You owe me a date," he said.

Before I could reply, he stalked out the door.

13

A text at three-thirty in the morning could often be a hilarious drunk-dial from a friend, but in my line of business it never meant anything good. It had me wishing the crazy, off-key Witches were the reason I fumbled around in the dark trying to find the light switch and my phone on the bedside table at the same time. I didn't function well half asleep.

The text came from Allan.

Lucien's.

Before I could process the command and think of a fitting response, like *bite me*, but wittier, another text came in from Allan.

Now.

Groaning, I staggered to the bedroom window and

flung it open. The cold night air hit me. Shucking off my cozy, warm pajamas, I stretched my arms out wide, willed the change and leapt into the air. The only benefit of being at the beck and call of a Vampire was the night flying. Savouring the smooth flow of air beneath my wings, I angled to Lucien's mansion.

How kind. They left a window open. Sweeping into the main banquet hall, I shifted so my human feet skimmed the ground. Slick move. Too bad it was wasted on only two people in the room—Clint and Allan.

"Kitten." Allan held out a white fuzzy robe, befitting a five-star hotel. He was the largest Japanese man I'd ever seen, and not sumo wrestler big, not professional body builder big, just massive stature and well-toned muscles big, like Dwayne "The Rock" Johnson, but *bigger*. And drool-worthy handsome. But he knew it. If it weren't for his decaying scent, allegiance to Lucien, and his hard-on for scaring the crap out of women, he might've been a romantic option.

Lucien definitely had a preference when it came to choosing his backup thugs.

Allan, reading my mental dialogue like a book, laughed, then shook his head. "Maybe one day, kitten, you'll see things our way."

Ignoring that, I stepped into the robe and gave Clint a pointed look. "Very thoughtful, Allan. Thank you."

Clint sneered and looked away.

Allan folded the soft robe closed around me and leaned in to whisper in my ear—a pointless move considering he said it loud enough for Clint to hear. "Wouldn't be right to face a Master Vampire without clothes."

I snorted. Been there. Done that.

"Nothing I haven't seen." Lucien strolled into the room. Wick trailed in after him.

The sight of Wick sucked whatever smart-ass comment I was going to make out of my mouth in a giant whoosh of air. "Whatthefuckhappenedtoyou?"

Wick walked straight to me as if to give me a reassuring hug, and then his gaze flicked to Lucien. He rocked back on his heels and stopped a few feet short. Gashes on his face meshed together as I watched, and dried blood encrusted his shirt and pants. A lot of blood.

"It's not all mine," he said.

"But I saw you a couple hours ago!"

"Humans attacked Wick's pack tonight. *Humans*." Lucien cut in, saying the H-word like it soiled his mouth. "Sound familiar?"

Nodding, I tore my gaze away from Wick's soulful eyes, deep pools of melted dark chocolate. "Yes. We were attacked on the train by humans and I..." My voice trailed off when I realized what information I was about to reveal.

"And you?" Lucien probed.

Clearing my throat, I continued. "Got attacked by more the other night."

"When?" Wick demanded.

"Where?" Clint frowned.

"With whom?" Allan asked with a sly smile. He

already knew. The bastard plucked the information out of my head.

"Last night, on the seawall...with Tristan." I said the last part quietly. Not that it made a difference given the supes in the room.

Wick growled and looked away.

"Tristan? The Wereleopard prowl leader?" Lucien asked.

I nodded.

"Interesting development." The room fell silent as the wheels visibly turned in Lucien's head, probably calculating how to use the relationship to his advantage.

While he thought on that, I turned to Wick. "Is everyone okay?"

Wick nodded his head without looking at me. Again, burnt cinnamon and old cat urine rolled off him. Jealousy—an ugly emotion, an even uglier smell. He clenched his hands into tight fists by his side.

Allan's phone rang. We all turned to him, but he ignored it. Apparently, he preferred keeping his attention on all the pissed off supes in the room.

"Answer it," Lucien said.

Allan nodded and slipped the phone from his inside jacket pocket. Two seconds later, he grunted.

"Care to share?" Lucien asked.

"The Wereleopards were attacked, too," Allan said. My breath snagged in my lungs.

Allan turned to me. "Your lover's okay. The possessed humans almost dragged one of the women into the water, but otherwise they're all fine."

Memories of my kiss with Tristan slid under my skin and my breath caught. Wick's head snapped up. His nose flared and a deep angry red spread across his face. Yellow eyes glared at me. If I wasn't careful, his wolf would jump me.

Lucien made a thoughtful sound and stroked his chin. He turned to me. "Andrea."

My eyes narrowed. "Lucien."

"You will find out who is behind the attacks."

"Why me?" That came out more petulant than I would've liked.

Lucien glared as if to say, how dare you question me. He waited to let the message set in. "Because you're mine to toy with."

"You stole that line from a movie."

He crossed his arms. "Did not."

"Did too."

"It does sound familiar," Wick added.

Lucien shot him a dark look and then waved in the air like he had an invisible wand and it erased the last few minutes from our memories. "Not relevant. You will do this."

Sighing, I thought about being ornery, saying something like "make me," but we both knew he could. I didn't want to push my luck. "I'm on assignment right now. I don't have the time."

"Make time," Lucien shot back. "Your connection with the SRD is exactly why I'm assigning you this task."

I frowned. "I've been attacked twice, and the SRD is

sucking ass with this investigation. Not sure I'm the best option."

"You kill people for a living, and the humans are only attacking supes when there's more than one," Lucien said with a flat voice, as if it should have been obvious.

"Uh, hello?" I waved my hand. "Supe here."

"But..." Allan cut in. "You're a loner."

"Hey!" My hands flew to my hips.

Allan did a manly version of rolling his eyes. "You don't run in a prowl or a pack."

Ready to launch into a tirade about the benefits of flying solo, I stopped and thought about what he said. "The humans are only attacking supes when they're in numbers," I whispered, connecting the dots.

Wick nodded. "I'm telling my pack to disperse."

"Wouldn't it make more sense to attack supes when they're by themselves? Easier targets and all?" I asked the question out loud, not expecting an answer. I was close to something. But what? I went over the facts and what they had in common.

"Water!" I blurted out.

The men looked at me with blank faces.

"All the attacks happened near water. The train runs along the coastline, I was walking on the seawall, Wick's place is in Kits and Tristan's is near Burrard Inlet." I ticked the events off with my fingers.

"And they were trying to drag supes into the water." Clint dusted off his suit jacket as if joining the conversation soiled him in some way.

"I would like this situation resolved quickly and

quietly." Lucien's gaze flicked to the window and the lightening horizon. "And I would also like my bedtime snack."

Clint strode out of the room without needing further prompting. I thought on Lucien's motivations. The vamps hadn't been attacked yet. Was he sending me out on a wild goose chase as a pre-emptive strike or did he want to save face among his Vampire friends? If it looked like he couldn't control his area, the masters without territory would be quick to swarm if they perceived weakness. Most Vampires coveted Vancouver for its lack of annual sunshine.

Clint walked back into the room, escorting a blonde woman in an outfit best described as black string.

"And that's my cue to leave," I said, drawing unwanted attention from the men.

The blonde gave me a vacant stare, or maybe it was her confused face. Hard to tell.

"I'll walk you out..." Wick trailed off. His brow furrowed.

"To my car?" I finished, raising my brow.

Wick cast his gaze down, probably figuring out his next plan of attack.

Clint laughed. Allan and Lucien were too busy staring at the meal in anticipation.

"Join me?" Lucien asked Allan, who nodded. They both smoothly glided to the woman. She looked delighted at the attention.

"Pick this one out yourself?" I asked Clint, jerking my head toward the blonde.

He smiled. "How'd you know?"

"You're predictable." I shot the words at him as I strode past to the window.

"Andy," Wick called out.

"Yeah?" I shucked the robe. My back was to the room, but Clint's heated gaze burned into my backside and the sound of Wick's sharp intake of breath bounced off the stark walls.

"I'll call you."

Laughing, I willed the shift and flew into the night.

"Did that woman turn into a bird?" I heard the blonde ask right before she gasped. In pain? In delight?

Thankfully, I made it out of range before I found out.

14

Whenever I talked to real cops, usually at the side of the road with crazy windblown hair and a guilty expression, they'd tell me ninety percent of their job involved paperwork. Looking around the downtown Vancouver Police Department precinct, I could immediately tell they told the truth, and nothing but the truth.

A beefy police officer led a man with stooped shoulders and a sullen expression through the main room in handcuffs. The prisoner shot the officer a panicked look. "You're not going to call my mom, are you?"

The policeman exchanged an exasperated look with another officer before continuing onward, taking his charge through double swinging doors. I'd never been in this precinct before, so I wasn't familiar with the layout. My guess? Destination: holding cells.

The woman ahead of me in line with the too-short, too-tight dress and knee-high pleather boots leaned over the counter and traced her finger along another police officer's forearm. He snatched his hand back and cleared his throat.

"Sweetheart, I've got some moves that would help you loosen up," she said.

"Are you soliciting a police officer?" The man with the pinched face looked up. I squinted to read his name tag—Officer Gallows. He had a lean face, with deep-set features, lending him an eastern European look. Dark bags under his eyes spoke of a long shift.

The sex worker shrugged. "I'd help you relax, is all I'm saying. Free of charge. It's not against the law to try to help a handsome officer, is it?"

Gallows rolled his eyes. "What can I help you with, ma'am?"

"I'm here to bail a friend out."

"Done this before?"

She nodded.

"Then you know the drill." The officer started presenting form after form for the woman to fill out and sign over the smooth off-white counter. When she finished, he called another officer over to take her to get her friend, or at least that's what I assumed.

Before I had a chance to step forward and make my request, an irate man bumped in front of me and yelled, "I pay your salary!" while pointing an accusatory finger at the officer.

Gallows let his breath out slowly before standing up. "Jim!" he bellowed. "Get this guy out of here."

The crazy man kept yelling, but it became more and

more incoherent as he rambled on. Another policeman, presumably "Jim," came over and grabbed him by the upper arm. "Come on, Billy. Time to go. You don't want to spend another night in here."

"But the cucumbers!" Billy slurred. "All the cucumbers." He sagged a little in Jim's grip, making it easier for the officer to haul him away.

I raised my brows at the desk clerk. He shook his head. "Guy's not playing with a full deck, if you know what I mean. Got caught stealing cucumbers, of all things."

Laughing, I stepped forward. He shouldn't have told me that.

"What can I help you with, ma'am?" Officer Gallows asked. Somehow his face unpinched a little.

Not liking the label, I smiled instead of telling him off and leaned forward, letting my animal magnetism speak for me. I had a way with men. Sometimes I used it to my advantage, like now. Sure, I could use my superior intellect, but I'd found through my fifteen years as an SRD agent, my animal magnetism worked better and faster. No other Shifter I'd met possessed this trait. I might have to hit O'Donnell up about this later. I let the magic roll off me in waves and wrap around the officer. When Gallows's eyes glazed over a bit, I knew he fell susceptible to my charms.

"My name's Agent McNeilly. I'm with the SRD, and I'm investigating a rogue supe we believe is targeting old women for theft in order to sustain himself. I'd like to speak to someone regarding recent crimes in the area."

Being government agencies, I'd once naïvely thought the SRD and local police would share databases and information, especially considering the Purge occurred eighty years ago. Not so. Hatred, fear, and ignorance ran deep in the government organizations. Both hoarded data, guarding it like dragons defending their treasure. I'd have to get a Supreme Court-issued subpoena in order to officially view the VPD's files. I shot the idea down for many reasons—I'd have to talk to a judge about matters Booth preferred to keep quiet, the whole process took eons, approval was highly unlikely, and even if I came out successful, every cop in the building would be shooting the back of my head with death stares.

"We don't usually grant that kind of access."

I leaned against his desk, and purred. "Are you sure?"

The officer's tired eyes widened. "Maybe we could make an exception?"

"That would be great," I said.

"Jim?" Gallows's voice strained. Realizing only the two of us could hear, he straightened up and called out in a louder voice. "Jim!"

"What?" Jim grumbled, walking up behind me. "Why do you always give me the crazy ones?"

I turned and gave the officer a dark look.

Realizing I'd heard him, he straightened and plastered a wide, albeit fake, smile on his face. "Present company excluded, of course."

Gallows exhaled the breath he'd been holding. "Could you please assist SRD Agent McNeilly here with access to our crime database?"

Jim's eyebrows rose.

"Just do it."

Jim hesitated and then looked at me. I poured on the wide-eyed, big-boobed charm, even if they weren't *that* big.

"Right this way." Jim held his arm out. After I graciously took it, he led me to a large room filled with desks. Cops milled around everywhere.

As soon as we were through the main doors, and out of Gallows's hearing range, Jim spun me around and squinted at me. "Now cut the crap and the cute girl act. We don't share resources with the SRD. What are you really here for?"

Fuck. Well, that didn't work. Apparently my wide-eyed, big-boobed charm didn't work as well as I thought it did. Jim had seen right through it. He had one hell of a poker face. If only my position with the SRD and my competence earned me professional courtesy with the VPD. Normally, my assignments required little research. My biggest challenge usually involved finding a way to get in and get out without getting dead. Why'd Booth choose me of all people? Surely, the SRD had better agents for this job.

I scanned the room for a way out and my attention snagged on a familiar face.

"Officer Stan Stevens," I blurted out.

"What?" Jim said.

"I'd like to speak to Officer Stevens."

The cop stood speechless for a half minute, while he worked out his jaw, clenching and unclenching. Probably deciding whether to throw me out on my ass or to let me speak to his comrade.

"Stan!" he bellowed over his shoulder. "There's an SRD agent here to see you."

Everyone in the room, all twenty-odd cops halted what they were doing before turning their heads in my direction.

"Send her over, then," Stan yelled back. Once he spoke, everyone went back to what they were doing.

Jim grumbled and led me to Stan's desk.

"Agent McNeilly," he greeted me with a friendly smile and offered his hand, then indicated for me to take a seat at his desk.

Something happened when he sat back down. He flicked the "cop mode" switch. Stan's eyes squinted at me across the old dilapidated wood desk that had taken one too many beatings from outraged criminals.

"Your eyes are red." Stan leaned across his desk.

"I'm not sleeping well."

"Sure you haven't been drinking?"

"Geez!"

Stan shrugged.

"Well your eyes are glazed." I folded my arms. Stan's face screwed up in a puzzled expression. "Sure you're not eating donuts?"

Instead of laughing at my insanely hilarious joke, Stan gave me a flat stare that told me how much he appreciated my humour, which is to say he didn't. At all.

"What are you here for, Agent?" he asked.

"I'm trying to track down a target."

He folded his arms and sat back in his chair. "What *kind* of target?"

"The kind you don't want running around your streets, increasing your caseload."

"Why not give me the name and let the VPD handle it? Or is it supe on supe?"

Since I didn't know if the victim was a supe or a norm, it meant she would be considered norm until proven otherwise. This case technically fell under the VPD's authority. Only supe on supe crime went straight to the SRD. I did a mental eye roll. "Please don't take this the wrong way, but I'm more equipped to handle the situation."

"How so?"

"I work for the SRD." I gave him a pointed look, but Stan gave me a blank stare.

"So?"

Exhaling slowly, I stared at the ceiling. "So...generally it takes a supe to catch a supe."

Officer Stevens gave me the once-over, skepticism clear on his face. "What type of supe are you?"

"The badass kind."

The cop waited for me to elaborate.

"Didn't anyone ever tell you it's rude to ask a supe that question?"

Stan shrugged and quickly added himself to the list of people I had little patience for.

"I need to see a list of all elderly women who were victims of robbery in the last week."

Officer Stevens blinked.

"Now," I said.

He crossed his arms.

"Please?"

Stan grunted and leaned forward. "How will this information help you?"

"My target is getting a source of income somewhere. This might lead me to that source." I'd found nothing in the SRD records, but that meant little. The need for sharing resources between agencies glared like an ugly neon sign. If the necessity was so apparent to me, why hadn't someone done something about it?

Stan tapped his finger on the desk and stared blankly at his computer screen.

"Look. Are you going to help me or not?"

"What's in it for me?"

"Reciprocation?"

"Why would I need your help?" Stan scoffed.

I leaned forward and let my eyes shift yellow as my cat pressed forward. "I am very helpful in certain situations and I would let you take credit for the takedown."

Letting my face relax and de-animalize, I waited for his response.

With a thoughtful expression on his face, Stan nodded. He pulled out his keyboard and started tapping away at the buttons. "I need a promotion," he said as he clicked through some screens. "I'm tired of this off the street bullshit." A quick glance my way. "No offence."

"None taken," I murmured.

"One hundred and thirty two," he said.

"Excuse me?"

"One hundred and thirty two cases reporting elderly women being the victims of robbery over the last seven days in the Lower Mainland."

"Are you kidding me?" I cursed. "What's the world coming to?"

Stan shrugged. Years of working on the job desensitized him to the ugliness of society.

"He pawned a watch and figurine. Can you narrow it down by items stolen?"

Nodding, Stan's fingers flew over his keyboard. "Fifty three."

"Still too many."

"Well, do you have any more information?"

"No." I drummed my fingers on the ends of the chair's armrests. "Could I get a printout, please? I have to start somewhere."

Looking at the sheet, I grumbled a "thank you" to Stan before stalking out of the precinct. Somewhere turned out to be almost everywhere in the Lower Mainland.

15

After watching five back-to-back I-slept-with-your-best-friend episodes of daytime television, the epitome of not-so-great programming, I came to the conclusion women existed in the world far skankier than me. Yes, I technically dated two men. But they knew about each other. That made it okay, right?

And I wasn't sleeping with them.

Yet, the devil on my shoulder whispered. Since running into the almond-spiced Demon at the Vampire summit, this voice had gained strength and assertiveness, as if the sheer force of seduction had awakened an evil part of my brain. But that didn't make sense. I knew evil lurked inside of me, but it wasn't in my head. It holed up in my gut.

Wick told me to dress comfortably. I tried to search on the internet what that meant date-wise, but every site said I should wear something that made me feel comfortable and sexy on my first date. Yoga pants? Running gear? Not sure if that's what Wick meant.

I caved and texted Wick.

> What do you mean by comfortable?

Like comfortable.

> If I knew what you meant the first time you said that, I wouldn't be asking.

There was a long pause before he replied.

No heels or skirts. Wear something you can move in.

> We're not going hiking are we?

Some people thought huffing and puffing up the side of the mountain provided excellent stimulus and good dating options. Not a fan. At least, not in human form. My mountain lion and wolf would *love* it. But not human me. If I planned to get hot and sweaty with a date, I could think of better activities—like sparring.

I have something else in mind.

I settled on black cargo pants, military boots, and one of my favourite Chuck Norris T-shirts—the white one that read, "Chuck Norris Forecast: Cloudy with a 90% chance of pain." Flicking my hair up into a quick ponytail and pinning back the short layers that framed my face, I was ready for some physical dating activity or kicking ass. Should I stretch? I glanced at the clock—fifteen minutes to spare.

A quarter of an hour to overanalyze my actions. Was this date a good idea? Probably not. But like an addict, I couldn't shake this need to be near him.

Halfway through my leg stretches, I heard Wick's truck pull up outside the building. I could only get so limber anyway. After buzzing Wick in, I fished my wallet out of my purse. I pulled out a couple twenties along with my credit card and license, and slipped them into one of my pant pockets. One of my biggest pet peeves included trying to do something active, like hop a fence, and getting smacked in the face with my purse or worse, getting it caught on barbed wire. Made subterfuge a bit difficult to achieve.

Wick knocked, and I opened the door for him. His presence filled the space. Ripped jeans and a faded shirt never looked better. Tall and imposing, he should have an intimidating effect, but all I got from him was warmth. His rosemary scent wrapped around me, embracing my skin and leaving me light-headed. I retreated to allow him more space to enter.

Wick took a step forward and then another, pressing his body against mine. He slipped his hand up to the back of my neck and leaned down for a kiss, his lips firm, yet soft. My toes tingled, but when I started to really get into it, he pulled back with a smile.

"Damn you," I breathed.

Wick chuckled. "You ready?"

"As ready as I'll ever be." Using the flat of my hand

on his solid rock chest, I pushed him out of my apartment. Locking the door behind me, I glanced at the Werewolf over my shoulder. "I hate surprises, you know."

"I think you love to hate surprises."

"I don't have to wear a blindfold do I?" I asked as we walked out of the building.

His mouth twisted. "Not today, no."

When the meaning of his words sank in, my body heated instantaneously as if struck by lightning. "You're not playing fair."

He leaned over and whispered into my hair, "Never intended to."

Always the gentleman, Wick held the door open for me. I found his traditional values charming and often in conflict with his heated gaze and dirty innuendos. The man didn't swear often and rarely used contractions, but he warmed my heart and body and made me want to dance the horizontal mamba.

We drove twenty minutes out of town through twisting forest roads.

"Hunting?" I guessed, for the third time.

"No." Wick smiled, but kept his gaze on the dirt road. "Let me guess, you were the kid that snuck into her parents' room and found all the Christmas gifts because you couldn't wait until the big day."

"No." My voice didn't sound convincing to me at all, and the smell of my little white lie filled the cabin of Wick's truck. He nailed it. When I was little, I knew all my parents' hiding places and snuck around to find out what I was getting for Christmas. And my birthday. No need to tell him the extent of my neurosis. My father ended up locking the presents in the shed.

A smile spread across his face and I dug my hands into the leather upholstery. I wanted to wipe his grin off...with my mouth.

I knew the moment Wick detected my arousal. His smile widened into a satisfied grin, and he relaxed into his seat. Staring at the contours of his face and his expression's nuances wasn't helping me douse the flames. I shifted in my seat and looked out the window. *Oh look! More trees.* My mountain lion begged for release and sent me images of us winding around old tree trunks and sinking our claws into tender soil and bark. My wolf howled and wanted to run.

Going through a series of rugged switch backs, heading up a wooded mountain, I guessed as many possibilities as I could for what Wick had planned. The activity distracted my wandering brain, and kept it from slipping into the gutter.

With each guess getting more and more outlandish, Wick laughed and kept shaking his head, enjoying my discomfort of the unknown.

"Hang gliding?"

Wick shook his head again. Taking his eyes off the road longer than I liked, he gave me an appreciative look. "You already fly."

"True." Sitting back in my seat, I drummed my fingers on the doorframe to the Rocky anthem, the one where he's running and punching at the same time, while I thought of possible outdoor activities that required forested mountain tops. The potholes littering the gravel road jostled us as the truck continued its slow ascent up the mountain.

When we pulled up to our location, I started laughing. This possibility never occurred to me. "Paintball?"

"You like to fight, but I cannot persuade you to spar with me again. I thought this the next best thing."

"Last time we sparred, we ended up naked," I said, my voice flat.

Wick's smile grew. "I know."

I snorted and popped open my door. We jumped out of the truck and Wick escorted me to the gear-up location. The man actually winked at me as he handed me paint-splattered coveralls. Holding them up, I figured out two things—under the myriad splashes of crusty paint the mechanic-style coveralls were originally blue, and the mechanic who wore these was the extra, extra large type.

When I glared at Wick, he raised his brow in challenge and stepped into his own outfit. It fit him perfectly. What were the odds of a six-foot-seven mechanic donating his used gear to a paintball business? My eyes narrowed.

"You're kidding me." I grumbled, stepping into the outfit. It fit exactly like I expected—awful. Scanning the remaining outfits, I admitted defeat. All that remained were the extra smalls and the extra soiled. Smelling the teenage body odour from where I stood, I'd brave the tripping hazard over cloaking myself in a stench that industrial-strength cleaner couldn't fix.

I looked like a beginner snowboarder trying too hard

to be cool by wearing clothes several sizes too big to be functional. How some of the professional guys and girls pulled off gravity-defying feats with pants that couldn't stay on their bums, was beyond me. Mine would be around my ankles and my face would act as a snow plow down the entire mountain.

"Briefing in five minutes!" A young man bellowed at all the paintball hopefuls. "Meet under the covered picnic area." He waved and pointed at the only picnic tables in sight in case we didn't understand what he referred to. Looking around at some of the people we would be playing with and against, it was probably for the best.

Wick swatted my butt as he sauntered by me to the meeting area. "If you can't hack it, you may as well admit defeat now."

"Never!" I ran the zipper up hard to emphasize my point. It caught a bit of flesh. I winced from the brief flash of pain, but bit back a howl. I'd be damned if I let Wick know I hurt myself with clothing. He'd never let me live it down.

Plunking down beside Wick on the nearest picnic table bench, I rolled up the legs and sleeves of my coveralls to allow more functionality.

The man who yelled at us earlier swaggered into the area and started stalking back and forth along the covered cement that I could only assume was meant to be his stage. Although he still suffered from post-adolescent acne, I estimated him at least mid-twenties. Something about the way he smelled and carried himself. He wore camouflage combat fatigues.

"My name is Darryl, and I'm your moderator for today. This voice..." He pointed a stiff finger at his mouth. "...is law. If you hear me yelling, you stop shooting. Right away. No exceptions. Violators of this rule will be removed immediately."

Oh yeah. This guy took himself very seriously. How many rejection letters did he receive from the local police departments in response to his applications? Did he list first-person shooter games as his relevant experience?

"Paintball is a very safe sport," he started. "Correction: paintball is a very safe sport *if* you wear your mask." He paused, as if taking the time to remember his place in the lecture. "There are occasional injuries in paintball, but serious ones are almost always caused by people taking off their mask." He paused again and waited for the young teenaged boys in the front to stop talking. He fixed them with a cold stare. "DON'T TAKE OFF YOUR MASK."

Drill Sergeant Darryl propped his leg up on the edge of a bench and rocked forward by swaying his hips. "Why do I harp on safety all the time? Because too many paintball players have think it won't happen to them." He used a girly, high-pitched voice to mock said players, to which I took offence. I'd bet my entire stash of chocolate-covered almonds the players who most often demonstrated that attitude were young men, not ditsy girls.

"I've been around paintball for quite some time now so I know how much you people like being told, time after time, how to be safe. But since players continuously break basic safety rules, it bears repeating, again, and again, and again.

"With the exception of the designated safety areas where there are nets to prevent accidents from occurring... DON'T TAKE OFF YOUR MASK."

Darryl went on another tirade about the importance of using only the paintballs they provided, but I'd already tuned him out. Instead, I cast my senses out to the forest and enjoyed the sounds and smells. The sweet tang of pine, cedar, and fir trees filled my nose—a soothing balm to my frazzled nerves. When people stressed out, they liked to go to their happy place, which usually involved soothing music, massage therapy, and floral fragrances. My place was the forest.

Hunt, my mountain lion prodded. My bones ached, willing me to change, and boy did I want to. I shushed her instead and listened to the wind whistling through the leaves, joining in a sweet harmony with the bird calls. Music to my ears.

After the monster inside me rose up to destroy the shackles from Dylan's forced union, and half his pack with it, I'd fled into the woods and survived as a mountain lion for thirty-three years. It took that long for me to find my humanity. Find it. Piece by piece, I'd put myself back together, but I wasn't finished. I didn't need a session with a psychiatrist to tell me that.

I shook my head and tuned back in to reality. Darryl pointed at players and sides, and I discovered Wick and I were on different teams.

"What?" I stumbled over the word. I'd drifted so far

into my thoughts, and missed the selection process. Had Wick requested opposite teams?

Wick swatted my butt again before marching off to join his group. He winked at me over his shoulder right as the horn blasted.

Damn him! He did this on purpose. I stuck my tongue out at him and turned to run in the opposite direction to establish a position. When the horn blasted for the second time, it was game on.

I intended to win.

AFTER THE FIRST ROUND, I REGRETTED WICK positioning us against each other. Our teammates rubbed arms, legs, and bums from paintball welts, while Wick and I remained unscathed. It was fun wreaking havoc on norms in the form of brightly-coloured paint, but it would've been nicer to do it side by side. There was no way they'd allow us to play together now. It would be too stacked one way.

I wanted to get Wick. We managed to evade each other the entire first round, but this time, I was gunning for him. Sneaking around the side of the designated safe area, I positioned myself downwind from where all the screams of outrage, shock, and pain came from. I'd always heard getting hit with a paintball compared to being snapped on bare skin by a thick rubber band—it stung. If that was the case, these norms were the biggest lot of babies I'd ever met.

Letting my falcon drift close to the surface, my eyesight sharpened. A dark figure moved in the brambles near the deer path ahead of me. About to step closer, something tugged at my senses.

Come to me, a voice echoed in my head. I froze. An overwhelming urge to walk into the forest on my right consumed my body. I hadn't felt anything like this since...

Since I was fourteen, and walked into the forest to meet three feras.

Sweat beaded on my brow and the bridge of my nose. I wiped it away, while fighting the compulsion to move.

Come to me, Carus.

Leaning forward, I tried to locate the animal. A branch snapped and my attention darted to where the sound originated from. The forest hummed with the sound of summer insects. My heart beat loud and heavy in my chest.

Underbrush rustled. *There!*

A flash of orange.

Pop! A sharp sting, much like a rubber band on bare skin, radiated across my right butt cheek. I yipped and jumped three feet in the air.

Whirling around, I found Wick with an ear-to-ear grin and his paintball gun resting over one of his shoulders. If he had a leg propped up on a recently deceased moose, he'd look like a hunter from a photo.

"Tagged you," his whiskey voice crooned. "Knew you'd go downwind."

Reaching back, I rubbed my bum—and instantly regretted it. Pulling my hand away, it was covered with goopy, yellow paint. Lifting my fingers to my nose, I discovered the paint smelled faintly of fish.

Gross.

"How's your butt?" Wick asked.

Looking over my shoulder at it and the giant yellow paint smear across the back of my coveralls, I shrugged. "It stings."

"I think we need a time out."

My eyebrows rose.

"And you can explain to me where you were," Wick continued. "Because your head definitely wasn't in the game."

Wick sounded like my dad after a high school basketball game gone wrong. I'd been dumped by my first boyfriend right before warm up and my drive for playing the sport instantly evaporated. My dad waited until we got home before he accused me of sandbagging. I'd run out of the room crying. Later, when he discovered from Mom the reason for my meltdown, he'd knocked softly at my door, came in and gave me a giant Dad hug. The kind I used to get when I was a kid and hurt myself on the playground. He didn't bother with a "there's plenty of fish in the sea" speech, for which I will be forever grateful. He'd said, "That young man's an idiot. I didn't like him anyway."

It was the last time I hugged him. And one of my

most cherished memories. He died in a car accident two days later.

Shaking my head, I shifted my focus back to the present and the smug-looking Werewolf in front of me.

"Obviously," I said. "You'd never get a shot on me if I was paying attention."

"Let's head to the safe zone." He turned and started marching through the forest ahead of me.

"Sure. Just one thing." I said, sighting Wick through my scope.

"What's that?" Wick half turned toward me.

"This," I said, right before I shot him.

16

With the rain spitting in true West Coast fashion, Wick and I took cover under the netted tents, the ones Darryl referred to as the Safe Zone. The other players cast relieved glances our way when they saw us sitting this round out.

I needed a time out before I could talk about what happened in the forest. A fuzzy feeling fogged my brain. What could I say? I had no idea what happened.

One thing for sure, in addition to finding the person behind the supe attacks and capturing Herman either for the SRD or Booth's private agenda, I needed to speak to Donny, my handler. And soon. The old Shifter knew my situation and might be able to tell me what was going on. If my To-Do list got any longer, I would have to hire a personal assistant and that was plain ridiculous.

Did PAs go on coffee runs? I could use a cappuccino right now, with cinnamon.

To distract Wick from pestering me further on the forest incident, I asked him if he had any siblings.

"Three younger brothers," he answered.

"Your poor mother."

Wick smiled, but it looked slightly droopy.

A thought hit me. "I'm so sorry. Are they still alive?"

The question might seem harsh to a norm, but given the extended lifetime of Werewolves, it wasn't. Weres were all born as norms. They became supernatural by contracting the lycanthropic virus, usually not by choice. Unless they died of unnatural causes, all Weres, like Vampires, outlived their norm families.

Wick shook his head. "No. They're long gone. I keep tabs on their families though. From a distance."

"You didn't make contact after the Purge?"

Another sad smile. "I maintained more distance after the Purge."

"Are they anti-supe?" My heart sped up. That would be too cruel a fate for Wick.

"No. But it's safer for them if no one associates them with the Alpha of the Lower Mainland. I would never forgive myself if they were harmed because of me. I caused enough pain for my family."

I looked away, sad for Wick. What he said made sense. It was the right thing to do, but Wick would probably trade his power to have his family back. His tone and the brooding look in his eyes spoke volumes.

"What did you like most about having siblings?" I asked, trying to lighten the mood.

Wick paused and then laughed. "Well, I was the oldest."

I waited.

"I teased and picked on my brothers. Ruthlessly. But I would beat up anyone else who tried to hurt them."

I laughed along with him. The image of Wick as the protective older brother wasn't a big leap for his personality or the position he held in his pack.

"What about you?" He asked the question I hoped to avoid, but, of course, I'd set myself up, opening this can of worms.

"I was adopted."

Wick frowned. "But did you have any siblings?"

I shook my head. "No. My parents found the adoption process so painful and drawn out, they didn't have it in them to go through it again. Great parents, but I lived a lonely childhood."

Wick nodded. "Did you ever look for your birth parents?"

"Yes, but I never found them." I looked up at the mesh ceiling. "I was born in the first year of the Purge."

Wick nodded. He knew my age, but he'd given no indication he'd made the connection. Until now. His face softened, and he reached out to take my hand. "The Shifter Shankings."

"I don't know if my birth parents put me up for adoption to protect me, or because they were killed. My documentation said nothing about supes. It was too early in the Purge for that. I hoped the SRD stashed private files somewhere, but I've yet to find them."

"So your parents could still be alive." I nodded.

"And you could have siblings."

A pause. "I hadn't thought of that."

"If you could choose, would you want a sister, a brother, both?"

I hesitated. "I'm not sure. As a kid, I always hoped for a brother. Now, I think I'd be happy with anything really, anyone."

Wick squeezed my hand.

17

When faced with uncertainty, or in my case absolute confounding bewilderment, when confronted with my man situation, I found it best to hide in a dusty library that no one under the age of one hundred frequented. Something about being surrounded by old books, each with their own past and smell, comforted me.

Although our date ended on a sombre tone, Wick managed to lift my spirits when he dropped me off. Cradling my face in his hands, he stared into my eyes with a strange look, not reverence or devotion, but something close. Then he kissed me. The tenderness he conveyed in that one kiss, the compassion, understanding, acceptance, and desire, all in one, melted my heart, sending my mind into a tailspin. The date with Wick had been a bad idea, my mind divided, my heart more conflicted.

None of the books on the shelves in this library could

tell me what to do about a confused heart. I walked up and down the aisles, running my fingers along the thick bindings of the books, leaving a trail in the dust.

My hand recoiled when one of the books zapped it.

Shaking my hand, I glared down at the culprit. With gritted teeth, I pulled the book off the shelf, trying to ignore the tingle running down my arm. My mom always told me "curiosity killed the cat," but that life lesson never really stuck. If something stung me, I wanted to know why.

When palming the dust off the cover didn't work completely, I took a breath and blew. Hard. The *Encyclopedia of Mythical Creatures* stared back at me.

The shock lessened to a distinct numbing sensation. Or maybe I'd become acclimatized. Desensitized. Before I could open the book to see what all the fuss was about, my phone beeped with a text from Mel.

Lunch?

When and where?

Sushi Town on Main. 2pm. Today.

I looked at my watch—a cheap plastic sports issue from the local department store that cost under twenty bucks. I refused to pay more for a watch I'd lose in a shift. I only loved one watch and I never wore it in fear something would happen. My mom gave it to me for graduating high school. She'd told me my dad always planned to get me one, but he'd passed before he could.

Looking at the time, I had an hour before Mel wanted to meet.

You're on.

Sweeeeeet!

She often defied her age of one hundred and ten years old—thirty years my senior. She acted and texted like a boy-crazy teenager.

Shaking my head, the book stinging my hand drew my attention once again. Leather bound and thick, it reeked of so many supes it was hard to distinguish one scent from another. I opened it to the first page. The small print blurred together, and I had to move the book in and out before my supe vision kicked in and focused.

But I didn't get to read much before the poignant mix of mischief and trouble filled the room. The heady scent of coyote made me smile. I slapped the book closed and shoved it under my arm.

Donny O'Donnell stood at the end of the aisle. My new handler was old—wrinkles creased his face, showing he smiled more than frowned. His coyote familiar, Ma'ii, slipped into the room after him before the door swung closed.

When I first met Donny, he'd hooked me up with various wires to a lie detector contraption for Agent Tucker to interrogate me at the SRD headquarters. They thought I'd gone rogue. Technically I had, but it was against my knowledge. My handler, Landen was to blame for that debacle.

The machine was completely pointless. O'Donnell could scent a lie from the truth, but Agent Tucker hadn't trusted him. His previous addiction to technology made me wonder why he now trusted Agent Nagato. Maybe he only used Nagato for on-call work where he couldn't drag the machine along with him.

When Agent Tucker had asked about my fera, I leaped across the interrogation table and strangled him. Donny hadn't moved to stop me or help Tucker. I'd liked the old man ever since.

Agent Booth had been the one to stop me from squeezing the life out of Tucker. Sometimes, when I was having a particularly bad day, I thought about the look of panic on Tucker's face or how his eyes bulged when I'd tightened my grip. The memory made me feel better.

I knelt to scratch the fera's head on the bridge of his nose. Ma'ii tended to bite me in sensitive areas, like the soft skin at the back of my ankle, when I annoyed him or Donny. Navajo for coyote, I'd once commented on the redundancy of Ma'ii's name when we first met. He hadn't been amused. For an animal that represented trickery and pranks, he didn't have much of a sense of humour.

My mountain lion hissed at the attention. She should be getting the good loving, not the coyote. My wolf didn't like it much, either, and mentally paced back and forth. My falcon couldn't give a shit. She liked anything that pissed off the cat.

When I stopped scratching Ma'ii, he bumped my leg

with his nose. *More,* his voice crystal clear in my head. I'd learned one of my special skills as Carus was the ability to mind speak with any animal familiar. And recently, I extended that to anyone supernatural. Which left a big question unanswered—what was Clint? Was I able to speak to his mind because he was a human servant, or was he more?

Ma'ii jabbed me again, and then tried to nudge my hand into action by lifting it with his snout. *More!*

Go scratch yourself, I huffed back at him.

The coyote's ears drooped, and he sulked down the library aisle to Donny, who obliged and started scratching him where I left off.

"Reading?" Donny asked.

"Wasn't planning on it." I waved the book in the air. "But this one caught my attention."

Donny squinted at the title. Feeling sorry for him and his aging eyesight, I closed the distance between us and handed the book over. He jumped when it contacted his skin. Must have shocked him too. When he read the title, he started laughing as if it made all the sense in the world. "Fitting."

I raised my eyebrows, but Donny shook his head.

"I have questions." I took a seat at the table closest to us.

"I figured." Donny pulled out a chair and joined me. "Agent Booth said you were looking for me."

"Yeah." I leaned forward, about to launch into a retinue of questions, when I remembered my manners. "Oh! How was your vacation?"

A small smile appeared on his face. "Is that where I was?"

"Agent Booth lied to me?" Really, this didn't come as a surprise. I already knew there was something hinky about the assignment she set me on. That she was able to lie without tipping her hand, either by scent or any other classic tells was worth mentally noting.

Something flashed across Donny's face, too fast for me to analyze. "She's a woman with many secrets."

"But she's a woman?"

The confusion on Donny's face made me laugh. "Oh come on! Surely you've noticed she lacks a scent. I want to know what she is."

"Some things are better left undiscovered."

"So you know what she is."

"No one can ever really be sure of anything."

I reached across the wooden table and jabbed him in the chest with my finger. "Nice evasion tactic. Don't think you're slipping one by me. I'm going to let you get away with it for now, only because I have bigger questions I want answered." I paused as sharp teeth sank into my skin. "And tell your fera to release my calf muscle. I barely poked you."

Donny laughed. "Tell him yourself."

With a grimace, I settled back into my plastic chair and looked down at Ma sitting at my feet with my right calf in his mouth. He'd taken offence to my finger attack on his Shifter, but not enough to break skin.

I'm sorry I touched your Shifter. He's fine. Please release my leg.

Ma looked up at me with soulful eyes. *Watch yourself, Carus. I will fight you.*

I had no doubt Ma would put everything into a fight for his or Donny's life. I didn't fear the possibility because I would never dream of attacking either of them and if I did for some justifiable cause, they were both old. Really old. When it came to fighting, the adage about getting better with age only worked to a certain point. Donny and Ma were well past that.

"So what did you want to see me about?" Donny leaned back in his chair, much like I envisioned a therapist would, minus the pencil and notebook.

"I want to know more about what I am."

Donny nodded and waited.

"And I was hoping you could fill me in, since you seem to know so much."

"I am not an expert."

"You know more than me."

"What is it you know?"

"I know only what you've told me. Feradea, the beast goddess, singles out a chosen one every five hundred years or there about. The chosen one is called the Carus and can shift into more than one shape and talk to not only other Shifters' feras and Weres, but all supernatural beings."

Donny sat up. "I didn't tell you that last part. About communicating to all supernaturals."

"Yeah. Thanks for leaving that out. Why the big secrecy?"

"I didn't know." He squinted at me. "How'd you find out?"

"Doesn't matter. What I want to know is, why me? Why didn't I bond to one fera like all the other Shifters? Why did mine get internalized, instead of staying physical to walk beside me like yours?" What about the big bad monster that lurks inside? I didn't ask the last question. Having only met Donny a handful of times, I couldn't bring myself to reveal something so private, so hidden, despite my gut telling me I could trust him.

"Well I can't answer why you. You'll have to ask Feradea. We covered the lack of a prophecy the last time we spoke, so you can stop giving me dark looks like you're going to be forced to go on some epic journey to save the world."

I faked wiping sweat off my brow. "Thank goodness for that. My respect for you just went up."

"How'd you get your forms?"

I squirmed in my seat and looked down. It was a sensitive topic for any Shifter. Each experience was unique and private. The metaphysical meeting of souls held a sacred place in every Shifter's heart.

"Let me tell you what I think happened. After you hit puberty, you had a compelling need to walk into the forest, like all Shifters. Except when you finally did stumble into the bush, you were greeted by more than one animal."

Fidgeting in my seat, I met Donny's eyes but didn't answer. I didn't need to. Donny missed nothing. My sheer discomfort would confirm his guess.

"How many forms do you have?"

"Three."

Donny waited. He was good at that. Letting the silence fill in and ask the questions for him. It spoke of years of patience.

"Mountain lion, peregrine falcon, and wolf." Watching Donny's face, I could tell from the twitch in his mouth and slight furrow in his brow he hadn't expected my answer. I folded my arms, feeling defensive. "What does it matter?"

"Animals symbolize extraordinary power for people around the world. Totems or spirit guides act as messengers and protectors. Surely you know this."

"I do. But feras are not the same as animal totems or guides."

You are so young, Ma's voice snickered in my head.

"I disagree," stated Donny. "A fera is a companion, a guide, and an integral part of your soul."

"So my soul got smashed up into four pieces?"

He shook his head. "Not exactly. The fera becomes a part of you. Merges with you. Reinforces the essence that is your soul to make it stronger—fills in the gaps to make it more whole." He gave me a stern look.

I pursed my lips.

"Think of your soul as a bucket of rocks. Your feras are the sand that fills the space between."

"I feel like there's an insult in there somewhere."

"There's not." Donny glanced skyward as if asking Feradea for patience, or help. "Why are you being so difficult?"

Relaxing into my chair, I forced my arms to unfold. "What do my animals tell you, then? What do they mean?"

Donny's face morphed into the smart old man look, as if the wrinkles on his face held all the knowledge of the world. "The wolf is smart, a teacher to guide your steps. The mountain lion is a leader that never hesitates to pounce and teaches you assertiveness and understanding of the natural flow of our environment. The peregrine surprises me. It's the illuminator to show the past, present and future—it's observant, seeing the bigger picture."

"Why does it surprise you?"

His eyes twinkled. "Pegged you as a raven. The trick-ster that inspires change."

"Isn't the coyote the trickster?"

Donny gave a sly grin. "It's true the totems for coyote and the raven are very similar in different indigenous cultures. Both are considered pranksters. The raven is often darker and more mysterious, the keeper of secrets. The lessons the raven doles out are more sinister and spiteful. The coyote understands the balance of wisdom and foolishness, teaching us to laugh at our mistakes."

"Fitting." I glanced down at Ma. "But the coyote doesn't laugh at himself."

A small smile. "Figures he already knows everything."

I snorted. "It's too bad I didn't bond with a coyote or a raven then. Sounds like a good match."

"It's not too late for that."

"What do you mean?"

"Just as you've taken in three feras, you can take in more."

I blinked. It was the most intelligent response that came to me. After a pause, I managed to speak.

"What?"

"You're not limited to three feras. Going back to my bucket analogy, your current feras have only filled the bucket part-way. There are still some holes between rocks. Still room for more sand. Other Shifters only require one fera to satisfy the void. You require more. Your first three feras are the foundation in which you must build on." Donny gave Ma an adoring look. "It's quite a gift."

"Doesn't sound like much of a gift," I huffed.

Donny's face glazed over with a faraway look.

"It's the greatest gift a Shifter can have."

I crossed my arms, not buying it. "Sounds more like a burden."

"Ahh," Donny sighed and nodded. "*Lumentum.*"

"What the hell is that?"

"Latin."

"You know Latin is a dead language, right? Am I going to have to search this shit on the Internet or are you going to clue me in?" I regretted my harsh tone as the words left my mouth. My ignorance wasn't Donny's fault. "Sorry, Donny. I—"

"No need for an apology, Carus. I sense your frustration. *Lumentum* translates to *Burden of the Beast.*"

"Are you calling me a beast?" I pressed my hands into the side of the heavy oak table.

Donny's eyes met mine. "Are you saying there's not one deep inside you?"

I froze as ice slithered through my veins and gripped my heart. "How'd you know about that?"

"I think you need to read this." Donny handed me a book. I took it from him without reading the title because I recognized it and the zapping sensation—the *Encyclopedia of Mythical Creatures*. "Seriously?"

With a small smile, Donny nodded. He pushed his chair back to get up. "The Carus must walk his or her own path."

When I started to complain, something sharp jabbed my ankle. I looked down and glared at Ma.

Leave the old man alone, Ma glowered back at me. *He needs to rest.*

And you need your beauty sleep.

Ma bared his teeth and growled, but somehow it didn't come across as threatening.

18

Mel was late. Not a surprise, but with each passing minute, guilt crushed me where I sat. My phone only possessed so many games to distract my mind from rehashing feelings of inadequacy, or from reminding me of how many things I had yet to do.

In a four-seater booth at the back of the sushi restaurant, I pressed the text option on my phone and typed out a message for Mel cancelling our plans. She probably hadn't left yet, anyway.

"Soooooo sorry I'm late." The blonde bombshell blew into the restaurant like a mini hurricane. Heads turned in her direction. Despite craning their necks at awkward angles, most of the male patrons remained fixated on Mel as she made her way to the table I'd held for the last half an hour.

Wearing light jeans with thick threading, probably designer, and a light pink T-shirt with a snug fit and the word "Juicy" across her chest, Mel looked every bit the Hollywood actress trying to blend in. Except she wasn't. She was a Werewolf.

Her hourglass figure, big hair, and piercing blue eyes got a lot of wanted and unwanted attention.

Unfortunately for her, a member from Dylan's pack was not impervious to her charms either. David forced a union on her, binding Mel to him until his grisly death.

To an outside observer, Mel and I had little in common—from our physical appearance, to our wardrobes and mannerisms. But during the eleven years of surviving in Dylan's ruthless, soul-breaking, and sadistic pack, we'd bonded. On the inside, we had the same damage, same baggage, and same knowledge of how bad shit could really get.

Mel recuperated better than me. Light and bubbly. Every now and then, however, I caught a glimpse in her eye—a flash of sadness or a quick look of panic—as if some action or sound reminded her of the past.

"So..." She slid into the seat opposite me after giving me a friendly hug and peck on the cheek. "How's everything going?"

I picked up a menu and tossed it to her across the table. "Better order a lot. I don't even know where to start."

Usually when I talked to someone and summarized all my problems, it helped clarify and prioritize things. This time, not so much. It had nothing to do with Mel. I told her everything about my two cases—Herman and the unidentified supe responsible for the attacks. Going through the details, I realized how little I had to go on. And how much I was screwed.

Mel listened to it all. When I first met her, I thought I'd hate her. I wanted to. She was the closest living thing to a real life, walking, talking Barbie. Who wouldn't hate that? I'd assumed her brain would be as empty as a plastic doll's and she'd be a shallow bitch.

Turned out, she was neither and I had to have an honest moment with myself to reflect on how I judged people on appearances.

Mel didn't interrupt me the whole time I talked, and her eyes didn't glaze over once. A true friend.

"I have nothing to go on for the supe attacker," I finished.

"Supe Slayer."

"Pardon me?"

"That's what the newspapers are calling him...or her." She waved her hand in the air. "It."

"Really? They figured out that there's one person behind the attacks? That's amazingly perceptive for the media."

Mel nodded. "I read about it in the paper today."

"You read?" My eyes widened.

Mel laughed and flicked rice at me. "Bitch."

"Takes one to know one."

An old joke, and not even a good one, but we giggled like little girls anyway.

"Sorry, you were saying?" I took a sip of my green tea. "What did the newspaper say?"

"Besides a lot of anti-supe 'they had it coming to them' drivel? Not much. But one thing they mentioned stood out to me."

When she stopped to plop another sushi roll in her mouth, I grunted and poked her with my chopsticks. "Spit it out already!"

Mel opened her mouth and let the full sushi roll fall out and flop onto her plate. Her eyes widened and her lips trembled.

Given her history, I might've felt bad if she smelled sickly sweet, like fear, but she didn't. I folded my arms. "You know I have no patience."

Mel winked and popped the sushi back in her mouth. Chewed it quickly and swallowed. "In all the cases, the supes were dragged to the water. There have been some reports of supes washing up on riverbeds."

Placing my chopsticks on my now-empty plate, I drummed my fingers on the table. "We knew there was a connection to water. The river information is good. Might be able to use the locations to find a common source. Geographic forensics, here I come."

"And somehow in the midst of tracking carcasses, you're going to go knocking on the doors of little old ladies? As if they haven't been traumatized enough by a lizardman mugging them, the big bad Carus is going to interrogate them."

I flicked wasabi onto her plate with my chopsticks.

She recoiled and shook her head at me.

"I resent that," I said, in case she couldn't tell by my wasabi assault. "The old ladies won't have a clue I'm a supe. I have more tact than that."

Mel took a deep sip of her tea before speaking. "Are you looking for one or two elderly women?"

"Just one. Missing the two items Herman's pawned."

"Well, who's to say he didn't get those two items from two different women?" Mel's brow rose.

My stomach dropped as realization hit me like a slab of cold ham on the face. I gave the cop the parameters for women with both items stolen, not one or the other. I could go to every single one of these women and face the very real possibility none of them were Herman's victim.

"Who's to say he stole them at all?" Mel interrupted my slew of mental cursing.

Sighing, I stared at the ceiling. It was possible.

"Where else would he get them?"

"Known associate?"

"Big words, little girl."

"New cop drama on TV."

I rolled my eyes. "He doesn't have any." That I knew of. His file was cleaned.

"What about the agent lady?"

"Booth?"

Mel nodded. "You said you suspected she has a vested interest. Any old ladies in her life? Maybe there's a connection?"

Good logic, but... "Why would she need me then?"

Mel shrugged. "Maybe she doesn't know the old lady in her life is helping Herman out. It makes more sense though."

"How so?"

"Well, it would be an awfully big coincidence for him to mug a little old lady who just happened to have the same weird lizardman statue as Agent Booth. More likely he got it from someone they both know."

Huh. "Never in my life have I been gladder you're not as dumb as you look."

Mel burst out laughing, spraying a little rice over her plate. She slapped a hand over her mouth but continued to giggle.

We grinned at each other while the waitress topped our teapot. When she looked at our table covered with rice and wasabi, her lips curled down.

"I'll have to pay Officer Stan another visit." He was my best bet. I doubted Booth would leave her personal information unmonitored in the SRD databases. One search at work and I'd have to face the wrath of my supervisor. I glanced at my watch. "And soon."

"Enough of this!" Mel exclaimed, drawing the attention of the other patrons in the restaurant. She glanced around and lowered her voice. "Tell me about your date with Wick."

"How'd you know about that?"

Mel snorted. Somehow the sound came off more ladylike than when I did it. "He's my Alpha. We're all attuned to his emotions. He was nervous yesterday and then really happy. I knew it had to do with you..."

I waited.

"...and Steve told me."

I laughed and plopped another dynamite roll in my mouth. "What's he feeling now? Wick, I mean. Not Steve."

Mel tilted her head. "I'm sorry. I couldn't understand you with all that rice in your mouth."

I swallowed, smiled, and repeated my question. Trust Mel to throw in an etiquette lesson after spraying food on the table herself.

Mel didn't answer right away. Her head bowed, she picked up her green tea and inhaled the steam.

"Mel?"

"He's nervous again."

I slumped in my seat. "Why?"

She took another deep sip of tea before placing her cup back on the table. "Maybe because he's wondering if he's enough."

"Enough for what?"

Her look practically speared me through the forehead. "Enough to win your heart over that mangy cat."

"Ugh!" I threw my hands up. Taking a moment to collect my thoughts, I ate three more California rolls, chewing them viciously. Making sure I swallowed before starting my tirade, I pointed my chopsticks at Mel in an accusatory manner. They shook a little. "First. You shouldn't fling insults. You haven't met him. It's not fair to judge him. Second..." I inhaled a long breath of air, filled with the aroma of sushi and tea. "I don't know what to do! My cat wants Tristan and my wolf wants Wick."

"I don't get it. Wick and you go so well together. You barely know Tristan."

"I've spent more time with your Alpha, sure, but he could be ordered to hurt me at any time. All it takes is one command from Lucien. I'm struggling with that especially after Dylan."

Mel watched my face intently as I spoke. Something changed in her eyes. They started out angry, flashing yellow, but now something else showed—something softer and more sympathetic.

"I'm sorry. You're right. It's just that...well, Wick is a good Alpha. A great one. After Dylan's pack, I thought I was condemned to a lone wolf life. And that didn't sit well with me or my wolf. It's unnatural. You know a shewolf needs a pack and the protection it offers. Wick represents safety and home for me. He's fiercely protective of all of us, and I guess—"

"You want to protect him, too," I finished for her. I got it. I really did.

"I know you won't intentionally hurt him, and you deserve to be happy more than anyone."

I returned her smile with a weak one of my own.

"What do *you* want?" Mel asked.

"I honestly don't know."

19

L ast time I saw Officer Stan Stevens, I got the distinct impression he liked me about as much as walking barefoot through a yard full of doggy doo-doo, but when his gaze flicked up to meet mine from across his desk, it wasn't hatred filling his expression or clogging my nose, it was hope.

Before I could utter my request, Stan leapt out of his chair and grabbed his jacket. "Time for you to scratch my back," he barked.

I had the choice of either standing there, staring at said back with a gaping mouth, or following him to find out what the heck he meant.

One quick car ride later, during which Stan drove like a possessed maniac and shaved years off my life, we arrived at an abandoned warehouse in the industrial zone off Hastings Street and Commercial Drive.

A couple of blocks from the water, crime scene tape cordoned off a large building with broken windows and graffiti. Patrol cars sat scattered around the entrances and cops milled about. Some looked green in the face. Some walked around, shifting their eyes back and forth as if the boogey man planned to jump out at them any minute.

"What's this?" I asked. Stan had refused to enlighten me during the four-minute race car drive.

"Murder scene," he said, opening the door and jumping out.

The air rushed into the cab of the cruiser, and with it, the smell of blood. Bracing myself for more, I got out and shut the door behind me. The dense summer air filled with the scent of death, rushed to fill my nostrils.

"Ugh." I wiped at my nose as if I suffered from bad allergies. "How many dead?"

Stan's head snapped around. "How'd you know there was more than one?"

"Too much death in open air for only one body."

Stan nodded. "Let's go."

I followed him to the building. We paused briefly after ducking under the tape for him to sign us in and mumble "consultant" to the other cop, but otherwise, it was a straight march into a large unadorned room.

The full force of the smell hit me. The room blurred. I staggered and reached out to clutch the first thing my hand could find and dig my nails into—Stan's arm. His solid bicep acted as an anchor while my brain fought to clear the sensory overload.

Stan, bless his heart, stood like a statue and said nothing. Several seconds flew by while my eyes processed what my nose had already told me.

Dead bodies lay sprawled and piled on top of one another in the centre of the room. Squinting at the mass of bone and blood, I looked for more information. Various stages of decomposition. Even with drafts slicing through the room, the odour stung my nose. No need for me to shift to a wolf to tell they were all norms.

It was hard to determine where one body ended and the next started. The blood spatter and shredded clothes left them practically naked in appearance. Along with the stench of their decaying bodies came wafts of their last emotions, so strong they imprinted the room with it. Sickly sweet fear and the hot metal reek of pain.

"What do you see?" Stan's voice cracked in the middle of his question. He cleared his throat and tugged at his uniform's collar.

I pulled down on my shirt, firmly putting it in place before zipping up my yoga hoodie. As a glorified SRD assassin, I'd seen death before, been the cause of it, but never on this scale...never like this. I lifted my chin in an attempt to look confident. *Focus*. "Around twenty norm bodies in various stages of decomposition." Sniffing the air, I absorbed more detail. "The freshest about two days old, the oldest I would say at least three months."

"Sexual assault?"

"No."

"Torture?"

I sniffed again. "They were in pain during their final moments, and scared shitless, but the pain isn't excessive, not what you'd expect for torture with this many victims.

My guess is no. Their deaths weren't swift, but they weren't tortured."

Stan nodded. "The coroner will confirm, but those results will take a while. They're all norms?"

Stan's disappointed voice had me turning toward him. "Yes, all norms. Were you hoping they'd all be supes so it wouldn't be such a waste? Or so you could hand it off to the SRD and go home?"

Stan shook his head, unruffled. "I'm no supe hater. I hoped we'd found the Supe Slayer location. The maps led us here."

Frowning, I looked around the room again. "Maybe it is."

Stan's brow furrowed.

"The Supe Slayer uses humans for his attacks," I explained. "These could be the norms he controlled. At least now we know what he does with them after they're no longer useful."

The smell of acrid, burnt cinnamon and sickly sweet fear clogged my nose. I choked on the thickness of it. Anger and fear. Stan's genuine emotions instantly raised my respect for him. He hadn't hardened into an unfeeling stone.

"How do you know that?" Stan demanded.

I turned to face him full on. "Did you honestly think someone could go around attacking supes and our community wouldn't take an interest in it? Let's just say someone looked into it."

Putting the pieces together, Stan scoffed at me. "The SRD assigned *you* to find the Supe Slayer?" He looked more confused than affronted. "Agent Tucker informed us he was running point."

The agent's name provoked a growl. Stan took a half step back.

"Don't expect a lot from him," I said.

"Don't worry. On principle, I expect nothing from the SRD. No offence."

I waved his comment off. As an assassin, I'd had little contact or involvement with headquarters. Everything had come through my handler. The SRD had a reputation of swift justice, namely taking out supes-gone-bad, but things had changed. The more I learned about the SRD, the more I realized something was off.

An SRD agent should've been at this scene, but I'd seen none. Where were they?

"No offence taken," I said to Stan. "But to be clear, I wasn't referring to the SRD when I said someone else had taken an interest. Other powerful groups want to find the culprit."

Stan thought on it for a moment. He opened his mouth and started to form the word "who," but when I shook my head, indicating I would say no more on the matter, he shut his mouth, nodded and turned back to the murder scene in the room. "What do old ladies have to do with this?"

I blinked. *Oh!* He meant my search request. "That's another case."

"Will you share your Supe Slayer information with me?" He didn't look over. Instead, he asked with his gaze forward and alert. He probably didn't want to give away how much he cared about my answer, or how much he wanted me to say yes, but his set jaw and steely iron scent gave him away.

"I'll share, if you do. My...associate...wants this person caught." What should I call Lucien? Definitely not using "Master." That rubbed the wrong way. I hesitated before adding, "I can't promise you'll get to take the person or persons down though."

Stan nodded. "Just keep me in the loop. I don't care who you're working for."

"Deal."

We examined the pile of humans. The crime scene investigators finished with their pictures and measurements, and started pulling the bodies down.

They took one after another from the pile, snapped more pictures and let the medical examiner view each one before packaging them up for removal. Stan was right. This process took time and it would be days, if not weeks before the lab results came back.

"Pick up anything else?"

"The smell of death is too strong for me to detect any trace or subtle scents. I might sneak back after the bodies are removed to see if it's better then. And yes, I'll let you know."

"I'll give you a ride back to the station."

"Perfect."

Climbing back into the car, Stan faced me before turning the key. "You came to see me about something before I dragged you here. What was it?"

I rolled the window down, intent on getting some

clean air to clear my nasal passages. A slow smile spread across my face. "I need to dig into my boss's personal life."

Stan's information proved extremely helpful. Agent Booth's mother lived in town. At the ripe age of eighty, she fit my profile perfectly. If she ever decided to answer her phone, I planned to meet her. Maybe she would have the answers I needed. Maybe she'd be another dead end.

A light breeze moved through the cherry trees, bringing soft floral scents to me as I walked up the stairs to my building. Then a familiar scent stopped me in my tracks. Spinning around, I gawked as Tristan sauntered up the steps behind me. Fitted jeans and a sports jacket accentuated his athletic build. His sapphire eyes, mesmerizing, locked me in place. *This must be how a cobra feels when a mongoose runs around it.*

"Andy," Tristan purred. His hand slipped around my neck, and he pulled me slightly forward for a kiss. His lips soft and gentle on my own, stirred my body into wanting things from him, things that weren't exactly soft or gentle. His purr deepened, vibrating against my chest, making my nipples hard.

"Tristan," I breathed. Gently pushing him back with shaking hands, I smiled. "You always overwhelm me."

His bright even teeth flashed at me. "I'm all about reciprocation."

Desire sprung up instantaneously, sending shivers of anticipation across my skin. Tristan's nose flared and his smile grew.

"Damn," I breathed. "You're good."

"Can I come in?"

"Can you behave?"

His dimples answered for him, but I pulled the door open and waved him inside. "Well, come in anyway."

Tristan laughed and reached above me to hold the door. "Ladies first."

Ducking under his arm, I walked into the building. Tristan followed. When I glanced over my shoulder, I found his gaze glued to my ass.

"What are you doing here?" I asked, unlocking the door to my apartment.

"I figured I'd impose myself on you. If I called first, I have a feeling you'd try to avoid me."

"Why would I do that?" I shucked my shoes off and motioned Tristan to come in by waving my arm through the air in a giant half circle. *Smooth.*

He didn't answer right away. Instead, he stepped into my apartment and took a deep breath. The small smile and closed eyes told me he liked the smell of my place. Pulling off his shoes, he walked around and observed every object, piece of furniture, and wall hanging as if he was in a museum. "Not many personal items," he noted. "None, in fact."

"Professional habit." Not trying to throw it in his

face this time, it was the truth. I only had one personal item in my place. A colour copy of a photo with my parents sat on my bedside table. The original sat in a box along with a handful of other keepsakes. The storage facility was in a remote location, and I made a point to never visit.

"Nothing at all?"

"A picture of my parents."

He spun around, interest flashing in his expression. "Where?"

"Bedroom." I nodded at the door off the living room.

Tristan tsked at me. "Trying to get me in there already? Without offering me coffee first?"

"I'll make us some now." Rummaging around in the kitchen, I set up the coffeemaker and pressed the start button. Aware Tristan took a seat on the sofa in the living room, I called out to him. "So why did you think I would avoid you?"

"You had a date with Wick, and you're probably confused."

"How'd you know?" I asked as I walked out of the kitchen and into a wall of emotion. Cat urine and burnt sugar, jealousy and longing, conflicted with Tristan's clinical tone.

I sat down beside him without breaking stride or staggering. I deserved an Emmy Award for that.

"About the date or your mental state?" Tristan asked.

"Both. Neither. I don't know. Explain."

Tristan took a deep breath and exhaled. "Angie felt the need to inform me. I think she followed you."

"She's not my type."

Tristan laughed and shook his head. He reached over and wound a strand of my hair around his finger. "She thinks you're not my type either."

I snatched my hair away. "And what do you think?"

"I think you're exactly my type."

"Smooth."

Tristan shuffled closer on my couch.

"But seriously. Your type is tall, ethnically ambiguous women with prickly personalities and unusual supernatural abilities?"

He laughed, again. Then his expression turned thoughtful. "Before you, I'm ashamed to say I went for petite women with big curves..."

"Big boobs, you mean," I interrupted. My girls weren't small, but they'd never be described as big.

Tristan dipped his head to acknowledge my point. "And not particularly intelligent. I didn't believe I deserved better. Still don't."

At least he was being honest, but still, his type bothered me. My shoulders bunched up. "In other words Angie?"

Tristan hesitated before nodding. "She's actually very bright. But regardless, I've never slept with her, nor do I ever plan to—something she's well aware of."

It's not that I didn't believe him. He spoke the truth, his statement came out blunt and to the point, no skirting, no hedging or avoidance, no oily scent of a lie. I still didn't like it. Tristan might not be interested in Angie, but could Angie say the same? Doubtful.

"Now, I'm of the mind that not too big and not too small, is *just* right." His gaze drifted down my body.

My heartbeat fluttered and the heat pooled between my legs. I switched topics. "Are you angry?"

"About what?" he asked, leaning in to nuzzle my neck and inhale my scent.

"About my date with Wick."

Tristan withdrew, his expression serious. "No. Not angry. Jealous. I want to clamp my teeth around his face and rip it off. But I understand. You need to make a decision about both of us, and that can't be easy."

"No. It's not."

Tristan's angelic face held nothing but sin. "Give me a couple of hours to do whatever I want, and I'll help you decide."

I pushed his face away. A couple of hours? Geez. How could comments and innuendos like these make my heart race and my body heat up when Tristan made them, yet when Clint threw almost identical lines at me, I turned to ice and wanted to bash his head into a wall?

Good mate, my cat purred.

Yes, yes, I know, I told her. *Settle down.* I guess it didn't matter what Tristan said to me, a cheesy pickup line or absolute smut, it just mattered that it was him saying it. The presence of a potential mate bond held its own pull and allure.

The little devil on my shoulder piped up. *What will it be like when you're bonded?*

A wave of heat crashed through my body, and my fingers ached with need to reach out and grab Tristan, to rip off his clothes and pull him to me. I jumped off the couch and glanced around the room. "Coffee should be ready now. It stopped gurgling."

Ignoring the twitch of Tristan's lips, I dashed to the kitchen.

Tristan cleared his voice. "So what have you been up to?"

As I made coffee for the two of us, I updated Tristan on my two tasks and where I was currently in the investigations, which didn't take long. Biting back the bitter taste of discouragement, I handed a cup to him. He'd asked for half cream, half coffee.

"Thank you." He took a sip and purred. The sound warmed my body. I'd never get tired of it. My cat clawed at my brain.

Good mate, she whined.

I shushed her and asked Tristan to repeat what he'd said, completely missing it while I settled my raging lust-bunny hormones.

As if he knew the internal struggle I went through, Tristan smiled. "If all your leads have dried up, why not request the assistance of a Demon?"

If ice could flow through my veins, it would be warmer than the rest of my body. The idea of summoning a Demon froze every vein in my body. Dylan had liked summoning Demons. One in particular, Bola. I still had nightmares about him. The smell of sickly sweet sweat rolled off my skin.

Tristan's nose wrinkled, and his eyes narrowed. "I take it you're against the idea."

The statement, although perceptive, surprised me. I expected him to demand the story, the history behind my reaction. His leopard, if it was anything like my mountain lion, would be clawing the inside of his head. While his face showed no strain from any internal struggle, his scent gave him away. Anger, heaps of it.

"Only a little." I lied.

Tristan watched me closely. "They're not all bad."

"Have you met a good one?"

His lips quirked, and I suddenly wanted to crush my mouth against them. A totally ridiculous reaction after experiencing the debilitating fear of my Demon flashback. What was wrong with me?

"No," Tristan said. "But Ethan used to pay Witches to summon them. The key is the agreement. Worded right, both parties walk away satisfied."

I grunted. "Satisfying the Demon is what concerns me."

"Will you tell me what happened?" He ran a finger down my cheek.

I wrung my hands together and looked down at them.

"Andy?"

"Yes?"

"I learned long ago that a woman's will is like a strong tree. Bending with the wind, but breaking under force." He ran his fingers down the length of my hair surrounding my face. "You are too precious to me to batter answers out of. I doubt I'd be successful anyway." Cupping my face, he kissed me, the pressure on my lips brief, but lingering. "Will you tell me about it? If not now, maybe someday in the future, when you're ready?"

"It was a long time ago. Not worth mentioning," I mumbled into his lips. Leaning forward, I tried to get him to kiss me again.

He pulled back farther, so his lips still brushed mine as he spoke. "Anything that elicits such a response from you, inspires that magnitude of fear, is worth knowing about."

He ran his hands down my back and gripped my hips. I wanted him to pull me against his rock hard body and grind against me. I certainly didn't want to talk about Demons anymore, but his comment niggled something in my brain—the still functioning part. "And why's that?" I nipped at his bottom lip. Would he use the information against me?

"So I can ensure you never feel that emotion again. Not with me. And because I want to know everything about you. The good and the bad."

I pulled away and grabbed my coffee mug. The good *and* the bad. Tristan mirrored my actions in slow motion as he studied me. I inhaled the rich smell of my drink and tried to find the calm I normally found in the action. Intently, his gaze sought mine over the rim of the mug as his brows furrowed. He might be thirsty, but I drank to put a physical object between us—as if the coffee alone could hold off Tristan's powers of seduction. I gave the coffee bean a lot of credit, but I think I overestimated it in this case.

Clearing my throat, and my head, I decided to give

Tristan a glimpse of my past. "My last pack's Alpha liked to summon a Demon when his equally sadistic Witch friends came over to play."

"Dylan," Tristan hissed. He gripped his coffee mug so hard I worried he'd shatter it.

My heart beat faster at Dylan's name spoken out loud. I hadn't told Tristan much about Dylan, but he'd filled in the blanks, the silence of things better left unsaid.

He's dead. I reminded myself. I tore his throat out forty-eight years ago. *He's dead.* He couldn't hurt me anymore. *Dead.*

Tristan stiffened. The smell of fear rushed off my body in waves. Suddenly, he plucked my mug from my hands and set it on the coffee table before wrapping his strong arms around me. Resting his head in the crook of my neck, he drew in my scent and whispered to me, "He's gone, Andy. He can't hurt you anymore."

Smoothing my hair, he talked softly into my ear, his lips brushing the soft tissue. "I'll never let you hurt again."

20

Tristan lied. Not intentionally. But when he gently excused himself after ensuring I wouldn't try to stab myself with a fork, his absence cut deeply. How could I become attached to him so quickly?

Good mate, my cat purred.

Honestly, I'm getting sick of you, I told her. *I get it. Find something new and more helpful to say.*

The mountain lion huffed and receded to the back of my mind, while my wolf grunted and my falcon cackled.

That goes for you, too, I said to the wolf. She pawed at my brain, but then went quiet, leaving me to return my thoughts to Tristan.

The last thing I wanted to do today was knock on my neighbours' door all hot and bothered after Tristan's visit. It would send the wrong message. But I had to get this over with before I lost my courage, and as the Wereleopard moved farther and farther from the building, my body cooled and my brain started reeling from all the things I had to do.

Not many sounds or scents drifted from the other side of the door. It must've been well lined with rubber by a contractor who took pride in his or her work. I tapped on the door, and braced myself for Witch mayhem. What was the worst they could throw at me without notice? The intel from the other side came through garbled. A fierce bouquet of lemon and pepper first squeaked through the cracks and tickled my nose, then smoke in foggy weather. Ahhh... Surprise and confusion.

The door swung open, revealing Guard One and Two from the SRD front desk. Two other men stood behind them, peering over their shoulders. One, short with typical Irish looks, and the other, tall with messy brown hair and a sour expression. The sight of four male Witches sent my prepared speech and introduction tumbling out of my head.

"Where are the women?" I blurted the first thing that came to mind.

Guard One frowned. "There are none."

"So four male Witches living together? An all-male coven?"

Guard Two leaned against the doorframe. "Female Witches are high maintenance."

"What do you want?" Guard One asked. His tone demanding, but he ruined the effect by wringing his hands and shifting his eyes.

"I'd like to make amends and discuss business." There. Very professional.

The two nameless, unknown Witches cast confused glances at each other, then at me.

"I'm Andy. Your neighbour." I held my hand out, but no one took it. The creases between their brows smoothed out before reforming, and I dropped my hand to my side. "The one you've been playing practical jokes on?"

Nothing.

"Whatever." I turned my attention back to Guard One and Guard Two, the Witches capable of speech. "Are you going to invite me in, or are we going to let the rest of the building know our business?"

Guard Two's eyes narrowed at me. "Are you going to attack us?"

"Of course not."

With Guard Two giving the okay, the others drew back and ushered me into the ultimate man cave. Sitting down between two bowls of chips, I looked around their living room and realized I'd interrupted a video game marathon.

"Nice place, you have," I said, glad they couldn't smell a lie. I stood up to accept a glass of water from one of the Witches. As if I'd actually drink it. Who knew what they'd put in it. "Interesting choice of décor."

"You didn't come here to fling fake compliments at us, so why don't you cut the crap and get to the point?" Guard Two grabbed a beer out of the mini-fridge beside him and shut it with his foot.

"Maybe we should start with introductions," I said. My glass of water looked more unappealing as I watched him drink the cold ale.

The nameless Witch with the dark hair and blue eyes started to speak, but Guard One shot him a threatening look. The nameless one squeaked, and his eyes widened.

"Why do you want to know?" Guard One asked, shoulders bunched.

"So I don't have to mentally refer to you as Guard One and Guard Two..." I pointed at them to make sure they knew who was who. "And nameless mute one and nameless mute two."

The tall mute hissed at me like a cat and stomped out of the room. *What was his problem?*

Chase, my mountain lion hissed back, but I ignored her.

"I'm Ben," Guard Two said before taking a deep swig of his beer.

"Matt," said Guard One.

"Patrick. You can call me Patty, though," the other Witch joined in. He jerked a thumb over his shoulder in the direction the other Witch went. "That's Chris. He doesn't...er...say much."

I nodded. Must've insulted him with the mute comment. "He's not in there brewing something really nasty for me is he? I'm not a fan of hexes."

"I wish," mumbled Ben. He probably didn't realize how good my hearing was. When my attention snapped to him, he grimaced.

"So…" Matt twisted his hands in the bottom of his stretched T-shirt. "The reason for your visit?"

"I'd like you to summon a Demon for me."

Saliva and beer hit my face with force as it sprayed out of Ben's mouth. "What?" he stammered.

The other two Witches looked like they'd wet themselves, the scent of fear rolled off them with such strength it brought out the predators in me. My feras screamed to attack the weak and take them down.

Hunt, my wolf growled.

Take, said my cat.

Relax, I ordered them both.

Underneath the salty, sweet sweat lurked something else…new crayons? How could they feel excitement at a time like this?

"Let me show you out." Ben stalked over as if he planned to physically haul me out the door. *Hah! Funny.* Maybe I should let him try.

"You're not going to apologize for spraying beer all over me? Cheap beer?"

Ben shook his head. He reached out to grab my arm, but hesitated. Thinking better of it, or seeing the best murderous expression I had in my arsenal, his arm dropped to his side. Apparently honey didn't catch more bees. I hated that saying anyway. No one would ever describe my disposition as sweet. *Time to stop playing nice and bring out the big guns.*

"Listen, bitches." I placed a hand on a cocked hip. "The way I figure it, you got even with the first practical joke. But didn't stop there. You owe me."

Ben grunted and tossed his empty beer bottle in a nearby recycling bin.

"We can't," Patty stammered. I sniffed the air. Truth.

"There's, like, four of you!" I paused and gave them a collective once-over. "Or do you all suck that much?"

Ben arched a brow. "I do not *suck*." Also truth.

Interesting.

I looked at the other two. Patty wouldn't meet my eye and Matt's cheeks flamed red. "Ben's apprenticing the three of you?" I waved my hand at the doorway Chris had walked through to include him in the conversation.

I turned to Ben. "So, what do you say, Master Witch? Will you summon a demon for me?"

Ben chuckled and twisted off the cap to another beer. "What's in it for me?"

I felt my eyes tingle as they partially shifted into those of my mountain lion. Patty and Matt scrambled back. "How 'bout I don't rip you to shreds?"

Ben didn't look impressed. "How 'bout I don't fling a curse at you?"

Curses tended to be particularly nasty and irreversible. Knowing the Witches incapable of scenting the spike in fear I gave off, I faked confidence and let a slow smile spread across my face. "You better hope you hit your target and it works quickly. I'm not your garden variety supe. And you have more to worry about than yourself."

Ben's confident veneer cracked for the first time. He faltered and glanced around the room. His apprentices, no matter how good, offered little in the way of support.

Fledglings, to him; amateurs to the supernatural community; prey to me.

"How 'bout we summon a Demon for you?" He conceded, coming to the same conclusion: his friends wouldn't be helpful in a fight, they'd be liabilities.

Mentally, I jumped up and down like a little girl, squealing in delight that I got my way. What I didn't expect was for Patty and Matt to do it physically. The grown men resembled first-year students at their first frat party, belly-bumping and all.

"We've been badgering him to summon the Demon again." Matt gushed before racing off. "I'll get the stuff!"

"What do you mean *again*?" I shouted after him.

"He finally showed us how a month ago," Patty explained before helping collect random items. Random to me. I hoped they meant something to the Witches.

"Why'd you make them wait?" I asked Ben, who downed the rest of his drink. Should I be concerned about drunk Witches summoning a Demon? Like impaired drivers making the road unsafe?

"First, the strength of summoning fluctuates with the phases of the moon, being the most powerful on the New Moon. Your timing is excellent. Second, I never call a Demon frivolously. There must be a purpose and payment made."

"What will we have to pay?"

Ben shrugged. "The Demon names the price. It depends if you're willing to pay it."

"Will he or she charge a consultation fee?"

Ben's lips twisted. "No."

Matt handed Ben a box of salt, while Patty encouraged Chris to come out of hiding. It didn't take much. Patty said, "Demon," and Chris jogged out of the room with an eager glint in his eye. Patty didn't have to say another word.

I rubbed my hands together. "So, who are we summoning?"

"Sidragasum." Ben didn't look up from sprinkling salt in a circle. The other's hung back watching his every move like dogs watching their master eat at the dinner table, confirming my suspicions that Ben knew more of what he was doing than the others.

"Who's that?" I asked, relieved the name didn't match the Demon I knew.

Patty tore his attention away from the circle and Ben's mumbling incantations. "He's one of Lucifer's assistants."

"We call him Sid," Matt added. "To avoid his unwanted attention when we talk about him."

"That..." Ben put the salt box down and brushed his hands off. "And it's a mouthful."

The other Witches gathered around Ben with expectant looks on their faces. Bubbles of excitement and hope floated in fragrant waves of crayons and clean lavender across the room. Ben shook his head and drew a knife across his own palm without ceremony. If I'd never seen a summoning before, I would've jumped up and yelled, "What the hell?" but this wasn't my first time. Been there, done that. When I'd freaked out at my first summoning, I'd embarrassed Dylan and had wanted to die from the shame. He'd cast me from the room and forbade me from future summonings. I'd never seen Bola's true form. Now, I was glad I'd caused my former Alpha to lose face in front of his fancy Witch friends.

The bitter scent of blood filled my nose as Ben clenched his fist and walked around the summoning circle. His blood splattered the lines and mixed with the salt. The scent of vanilla and honey of the Witches mingling with the blood and salt of the summoning created a potent mix and charged the room with energy. The Witches stood together and started chanting. "*Hekate. Si placet, ancora nobis ad orbis terrarium. Gratias tibi ago.*"

From what I could figure out with my limited experience, most of which I tried to suppress, Witches started their incantation calling upon their goddess Hekate, said their Ps and Qs, and somewhere in the middle made the actual request. It sounded like jacked up Latin to me. The more powerful Witches didn't have to vocalize the incantations, but they probably did anyway to appear more badass in front of norms.

In addition to knowing the proper words to incite, a Witch had to focus on what they wanted to accomplish, like extreme visualization. But above all, they had to anchor their spirit to the living world, the source of their power, orbis terrarum. If they weren't properly anchored during a Demon summoning, nothing prevented the Demon from taking them back through the portal, or from the Witches being pulled every which way and shredded from the streams of demonic power pulling through the open portal. An eternity as a Demon's servant or mincing of the body, mind and soul? No thank you.

Ben appeared confident. And bored. I bet he didn't need to recite out loud. He could probably summon this Demon all on his own.

"Hekate. Si placet, advoco Daemonium Sidragasum ad nobis. Gratias tibi ago."

The air in the room stirred, rushing around, flinging my hair like the wind. The portal snapped into place in the midst of a powerful maelstrom. A dark figure formed in the middle of the circle in a crouched position. When the air in the room settled down, the Demon straightened and turned to the group.

"Ah fuck," I breathed.

The sex Demon from the Vampire summit—wearing only a large grin—stood before me. Naked and proud, the Demon raked his eyes down my body. "Couldn't get enough?"

The Witches turned to me, questions in their gazes.

"Please. I'd no idea what your name was."

His lip quirked. "I don't believe in coincidences."

"Me neither. Fate likes to give me a hard time."

"I'd like to give you a hard time, too."

His almond scent drifted toward me. Like a siren song, it wrapped around my body, drawing me forward, catching me in its thrall.

I waved my hand in the air as if to clear smoke out of the kitchen after botching a roast. "Quit it with the sex mojo."

Sid sighed and stared at the ceiling. "As you wish." At least he didn't deny it. I hated supes who assumed I was stupid. They landed on the top of my Things-I-Hate-Most list.

I turned to the Witches and jerked my thumb at the Demon behind me. "Who did you say this guy was?"

"Satan's assistant." Matt winced.

"He seduces women for Satan and incites them to dance naked during the Sabbath," Patty mumbled and looked at his feet when I turned my death stare to him.

"I'm not all bad." Sid's voice slid around my shoulders like a satin sheet.

Pivoting to face the Demon, I crossed my arms. My face naturally scrunched up to show my doubt.

"I help create the illusion that the women are more beautiful than they are," Sid explained.

"Why would you do that?" I asked. "I'm sure you have a reason."

"To exacerbate the carnal desire in men." Sid sighed. "Isn't that the result every woman wants? Every heterosexual woman, that is."

"How magnanimous of you."

Sid stalked to the salt line and toed it. Little white electric lights flashed, revealing the invisible barrier that kept the Demon inside the summoning ring and protected us. "Let me have you for thirty minutes and I'll show you how giving I can be."

"No deal."

"What deal would you like to strike then, little Carus? Or did you have me summoned here to bask in the glory of my physical appearance?" He put both his hands on his hips and tilted his pelvis forward. I wanted to smash this guy's face against the kitchen counter, but even my eyes struggled not to roam his naked body. All seven feet of glorious muscles and his huge...

"I told you to stop it with the sex mojo."

"What's wrong? Don't like it when the tables are turned?"

"What are you talking about?"

"Don't you use your powers on men?"

I scowled at him. That was totally different.

He dropped his arms and he straightened. "Fine. What do you want?"

"I'd like to know who is behind the attacks on supes and how he or she is controlling humans to do it."

Sid tilted his head back and closed his eyes. Taking a deep breath in, it looked like he scented the air, savouring it and interring what he found to memory. "You seek information," he said finally.

"Yes," I hissed.

"There's a price to pay."

"Name it."

"Dance for me, little Carus."

My eyes narrowed. "Be more specific. What kind of dancing? And for how long?"

Sid leaned in. The scent of almonds rolled off him and encircled me like a lover's embrace. "I want you dancing naked before me."

Cringing, I asked, "For how long?"

A slow smile spread across Sid's face. "Until I finish... feeding."

I blanched and broke eye contact. "No deal. I won't add to your personal spank bank."

Sid chuckled. "You're the one in need of information."

"And you don't need to feed on my sexual energy. I'm sure you get plenty. Name another price."

Sid sighed and flipped a noncommittal hand in the air. "A little of your blood then."

The Witches gasped. "No," one of them breathed, too quietly for me to decipher which of them said it.

"Wouldn't that break the circle?"

Sid tilted his head, like a predator considering its prey's actions. I knew that look. I'd done it countless times to easy food in the wild.

Not prey, my cat hissed.

"You put it in a new circle and summon me again," Sid explained as if I was a five-year-old. The insulting tone would rub me the wrong way if I wasn't a baby in comparison to his age.

"What will my blood give you?"

Sid tsked and shook his head. "That information doesn't come free. Either you pay, or you don't."

"So naked dancing or my blood?"

Sid nodded. "Summon me when you decide. I grow tired of this conversation." After glancing at the huddle of Witches, he yawned to enforce his point.

The Witches moved closer to me. I peered at them and nodded.

"*Hekate. Si placet, expello Daemonium Sidragasum ad daemonum inferos. Gratias tibi ago,*" they chanted together.

"Little Carus, you *will* dance for me." Sid's eyes met mine before he disappeared.

Everyone stood silent in the room until the portal fully closed and the air settled.

"I feel dirty," Matt said, brushing his hands.

I agreed, and no amount of showering would clean the invisible grime coating my body. Why couldn't Demons request simpler things, like peanut butter or marshmallows?

"What are you going to do?" Ben asked me.

"I have no idea."

21

"**A**rgh!" Slamming down the phone on the charger with one of my favourite curse words, I stomped to my laptop. After my third failed attempt to contact Agent Joyce Booth's mother—Evelyn—I decided my only solution was to turn up unannounced tomorrow, manners be damned. I hoped Mrs. Booth wouldn't despise me enough to slam the door in my face.

I'll bring flowers.

Old people love flowers. Almost eighty, I'd know.

Between cold calls, I scavenged the internet for information on supernaturals with a connection to the water. Search engines could only tell me so much. The most successful search yielded ten thousand and four hundred results. One website listed seventy-five types of supernatural creatures from mythology including gods. Preter-Pedia listed sixty-two supernatural creatures associated with water. The SRD database had been equally unhelpful. I hated research and came to the conclusion that unless I wanted to pay Sid's price, I was screwed.

Now, how to tell Lucien...

My phone beeped. I glanced at the annoying object. How could one small electronic device instil so much fear? Taking a deep breath, I stalked to the phone and flicked it on, much like ripping off a bandage, I wanted the news fast. Maybe it was Mel.

Tapping the screen, I found a message from Allen instead.

Lucien's. Now.

Before I could reply another text came in from Wick.

Lucien's place was attacked last night. He's livid. Be careful. xo

Fuuuuuuuuuck.

I placed my coffee down on the counter and stripped as I headed to the nearest window to shift. How many times had I done this in the last few days? Too many! Too bad Lucien gave as little thought to my opinion as he did the dirt on the bottom of his designer shoes. I morphed into my falcon and took to the air, having to beat my wings extra hard to combat the sinking weight growing in my gut. When would this end?

Cuts that must've been deep at the time of infliction, faded to look more like kitten scratches on Lucien's face as he vibrated with fury in front of me. It was never good to read emotion on a master—it meant they were close to the breaking point. They rarely lost control, but when they did, it was an epic demolition derby of norm necks.

"I am angry," he stated.

As if I couldn't tell. Somehow hearing it vocalized made it worse.

Where's Wick? As much as I remained conflicted about my feelings for the Alpha Werewolf, I would've appreciated his solid presence by my side right now.

I stood with Allan, Clint, and a few other members of Lucien's inner circle in a line resembling those in an army movie where the new intakes got yelled at by an overzealous sergeant. Lucien emphasized each word like they comprised separate sentences. Every clipped note escalated the situation and created static electricity. The supe energy of the room amplified, causing me to flinch at the force behind each of Lucien's words.

"You're all making me so angry," Lucien continued.

The way Lucien spoke made me think of a man ripping through his clothes to become a supernatural green giant. I bit back the giggle bubbling up my throat. This wasn't the time.

Lucien's head snapped in my direction. His eyes narrowed, and his breathing grew shallow, like a seething hiss. "You find this humorous?"

Ah fuck. I forgot he could read my emotions through the blood bond. He wouldn't know exactly what I was thinking—a good thing—but he could tell I found something amusing.

Not waiting for an answer, the Master Vampire stalked toward me, his pupils dilating to the point where his eyeballs looked completely black. "My horde was attacked. My security compromised."

He reached out with Vampire speed and clutched my neck. Apparently, he didn't require a verbal response. He wanted something more physical. Squeezing my throat, he lifted me until my feet dangled like a recently hung outlaw in a bad western movie.

My feras screamed in my head. The beast stirred in my core and rumbled.

Lucien's eyes narrowed. *Still your feras,* he spoke in my head. *Now.*

Relax, I ordered my feras without thought. Fucking compulsion. My mountain lion hissed at me, but I repeated my demand and she settled down after pawing my brain. My wolf paced, but stayed quiet and my falcon fluttered her wings before snuggling into the side of the mountain lion. The beast, though silent, remained attentive, as if waiting for an opportunity.

Lucien shook me. "You make me look weak," he spat.

Seeing how he held me by the throat with one hand in the air, I would've argued the point if capable of speech. I flexed my neck muscles to fortify my windpipe and allow the much-needed air through.

"Incompetent." With a look of disgust, he threw me to the ground and returned to pacing back and forth beside my sprawled body.

My falcon screeched in my head like a deranged chicken.

Gasping for breath, I waited for my vision to clear and the blood to spread from my face to the rest of my body. I hated getting blamed for shit I didn't do. "How is any of this my fault?"

Whipping back to me, Lucien pointed a stiff finger at me. Instantly, I regretted the question. Lucien's teeth descended as he walked closer. "I told you to find me the person responsible! You haven't done your job."

A string of excuses ran through my mind, and I rejected one after another. It was time for the truth. "I've exhausted all avenues, Lucien."

"You failed me." Each word came out short and angry.

I nodded. What could I say to that? I refused to beg.

"And you've tried everything?"

"Yes." I climbed to my feet and faced him. If he was going to kill me, I wanted to put up a decent fight, and that wouldn't happen if I was collapsed on the ground.

"You lie." Allan's voice cut in. I'd forgotten he was in the room.

My attention snapped to Allan's in unison with

Lucien's. The master stopped pacing, and his attention on Allan caused the air to hum with power. Lucien's strength was formidable when released.

"What?" I asked.

Allan shrugged. "You haven't tried *everything*."

Under the hard gaze of the Master Vampire, my heart thundered in my chest as neurons raced a marathon to find the memory Allan plucked from my head. And then it clicked.

Sid.

"No." I shook my head and took a step back.

Sidragasum the Seducer? No way.

"What haven't you tried, little kitten?" Lucien's face flattened into a placid mask.

Probably not the time to correct him on using Allan's nickname for me. Nor the time to question why every single supernatural male butting into my life insisted on calling me, "little," when at five foot ten, I stood taller than most women. "I summoned a Demon to ask about the attacks, but wouldn't pay his price for the information. I still won't."

Lucien cocked his head. "What price did he name?"

"My blood."

The Master Vampire recoiled. After a long pause where he seemed to collect himself, he fixed me with a hard stare. "You will not give him this. You are *mine.* Your blood will give him access to me. *I forbid it.*" His last sentence a command. It rolled through my psyche and took root.

I nodded.

"Would he accept an alternative?" Lucien's voice calculating.

I cringed. "I won't pay that either."

Having read my thoughts the same time my brain processed them, Allan laughed. Not his normal chuckle, or his rich laugh when he was really amused, but something I'd never seen him do before. He bent over, supporting his weight with his elbows on his knees, and wheezed for breath between fits of gleeful laughter. His normally porcelain-pale skin flushed red. "That's priceless," he managed between the fits.

Lucien's arms folded and the corner of his lip twitched. "I can sense your humiliation, Shifter. This must be good. Tell me what the Demon requested." *Tell me,* he ordered.

Looking at the smooth granite tiles, I mumbled, "He wants me to dance naked for him so he can feed off my sexual energy."

Something flashed across Lucien's expression.

Oh no.

"You will do this," he said.

"Absolutely not!" I refolded my arms and my hip jutted out with attitude. A tangle of emotions swirled around me. Red hot boiling blood, squeezing ribs and a lack of energy didn't often go together, not with me, not since Dylan. My skin itched to shift and break away from Lucien's hold.

"You have done worse for your job with the SRD." Lucien's eyes narrowed. He stepped close. His smooth skin remained unwrinkled and impassive, his minuscule pores didn't need a mud mask. "You will do this. For me."

Or else? I didn't need to ask the question. It was implied by my defiant stare and answering silence.

"Or I will order Wick to shackle you to a chair and then I will gut your pretty Alpha boy over and over again between healings and make you watch."

Wick.

Just when I started to like my new master, he pulled out a big game changer. The taste of bitter blood filled my mouth as my fangs elongated, and I bit down on the inside of my cheek to prevent myself from doing something truly stupid, like lash out as a mountain lion and get killed. My gut clenched. No way would I allow my actions to cause Wick harm. Not when I could avoid it.

All this time I worried Lucien's orders would cause Wick to hurt me. I hadn't thought he'd reverse it. My stomach continued to churn and a dull ache started at the base of my skull.

"Be grateful I'm not insisting Clint watch," Lucien said.

Seeing the satisfied and calculating look in the Master Vampire's eyes, I knew he was well aware of what my decision would be. He smiled, his model lips unfurling like a red flag.

Time to dance for the Demon.

22

Once again I found myself sitting in a faux-leather chair across a desk from Agent Booth, wondering what the heck she was and why she wanted to see me. The woman seriously got off on stirring the psychological pot. She peered down her crooked nose at me in a silent staring match—which she'd won several times over, since I refused to play, and last time I checked, blinking still counted as defeat. Finally, she shattered the silence with her cheese-grater voice. "Any progress on your assignment?"

I leaned back and crossed my arms. "You could've asked me this on the phone. What gives, Booth? Why am I really here?"

The signs in the zoos saying "Don't Poke the Dangerous Animal" never applied to me either.

Booth's eyes narrowed and her lips thinned."You're right; your progress report is not why I requested your presence." She leaned in, lacing her fingers together on top of her desk. "But you can answer the question while you're here."

"I've made visual contact with the target, but wasn't able to contain him. The environment didn't allow for retrieval. Too public and too many unknown variables."

Booth tapped her pen on the desk. The air carried no scent of her emotions, and she gave nothing away with her expression. My skin itched.

"Do you have any leads?" she asked.

"Maybe."

"What are they?"

"Too soon to say. I'll be able to give you an update in a week," I lied through my teeth, banking on her not being able to tell.

Booth tilted her head, like an animal in the wild trying to figure out if something was edible. *Great.* "The reason I've asked you here is that some information has recently come to my attention."

A long heavy pause followed her announcement. "Okay, I'll bite. What information?"

"Lucien Delgatto and his horde were the most recent victims of an attack. Were you aware of this?" She studied my face as if looking for wrinkles. I didn't have any, yet. After this tête-à-tête finished, that might change.

I pretended to inspect my nail beds. "I heard something along the grapevine."

"Why don't we cut the bullshit?"

"You're the one scooping it." I shrugged. She knew something, and I'd prefer her to spit it out.

Booth's lips pursed. Taking a deep breath, and what

seemed like a moment to collect herself, a predatory smile spread across her face. "You were seen at Lucien's."

I forced my shoulders down from my ears. "By whom?"

"It doesn't matter."

"So I went to Lucien's. Big deal." The synthetic material of my seat started to heat under my thighs.

"Do you understand what Conflict of Interest means?" Booth leaned back in her chair.

My scalp prickled. "Of course. But I'm sure you're going to tell me anyway."

"On the contrary. I'm going to give you an example."

A weird fuzzy sensation encapsulated my brain as my scalp prickled and a sense of foreboding flittered across my skin.

"If an SRD agent were to become, say, *blood bonded*..." She spoke like the words soiled her in some way. "To a Master Vampire, it would be considered a Conflict of Interest because the agent would be torn between two different directives, and if they conflicted with one another, she or he would have *no choice* but to follow the orders of the Vampire over the SRD." She gave me a pointed look. "That is a Conflict of Interest. COI. And it is completely unacceptable."

I examined my fingernails again and tried to ignore the hammering of my heart. I didn't want to get fired. What would I do? I spent over thirty years living as a mountain lion in the forest. Feradea! The beast goddess might've blessed me with shifting abilities, but she neglected to give me stuff I could put on a résumé.

"What are you accusing me of?"

Booth let out a long breath with what resembled something between a laugh and a groan. "You have a Conflict of Interest."

"Prove it."

"I had a feeling you'd say that." She shoved back from her desk to open a drawer and fish out a tape recorder. Really? A tape recorder? Who still had those? Holding it in front of me, she pressed play.

"...and if that little tart thinks she can run from my blood bond, Agent McNeilly will have a hard lesson to learn..." Lucien's voice, though a bit scratchy and muffled.

Booth stopped the recording and glanced up at me. "And let's not forget all the news footage of the train incident placing you on public transportation with Lucien's human servant. Anything to say for yourself?"

"Ah fuck?"

"We have more evidence, of course. But I thought this clip neatly summarized it."

"How long have you known?"

"Me? The day after the blood bond happened."

A dull ache started to throb behind my eyes, and I pinched the bridge of my nose. The headache intensified. She'd known all along. "Why confront me now?"

"You have a task to complete for me." She tucked the recorder away in her desk. "And that hasn't changed."

So Agent Booth had her own agenda. It wouldn't serve her purpose to out me to the SRD while she had me running her personal errands. "What's changed then?"

Booth tapped the pen on her desk and pursed her lips. "The information leaked to people higher up in the chain. Agent Tucker demands something be done. He sounds like he's part parakeet, chirping COI every time he passes my office door. I've been ordered to deal with you."

I didn't want to ask how it leaked, because it didn't really matter—pretty sure Booth would've dealt with it anyway. "And how do you plan to do that?"

"Not the way they expect."

That sounded promising. "Are you going to kill me with anticipation?"

"I'm offering you the position of SRD Ambassador."

"What the hell's that?"

"You'll act as a liaison for the SRD with Lucien's court. I haven't spoken to him yet, but I'm sure the Master Vampire will agree to our conditions."

Of course, he'd agree. He'd have another claw dug into the side of the government agency with me as his representative. "Ambassador McNeilly..." I mumbled, trying it on. The title sounded nice to the ear.

"It means aside from your current assignment, you will no longer be an SRD agent. There will be no more assassinations or retrieval orders for you to complete. You will only be privy to information and resources as they apply to the Vampire court, and will be kept on a need to know basis. You will be paid as a contractor and will no longer receive benefits as you will not be considered an

SRD employee. Lucien will have to provide a top up salary and any extras you require."

"So my choices are to accept the new position or face unemployment?"

"Yes."

Not the most ideal situation, but pretty sweet given the alternatives, and much better than I could've hoped for. The tension in my shoulders eased. "Will Agent Tucker have to refer to me as Ambassador McNeilly?"

Booth's lips twitched. "Yes."

I stood up, mirrored by Booth and shook her hand. "Deal."

"Agent O'Donnell wants to see you before you go."

"Where is he?"

"Library."

"Of course." When I reached the door, I turned around to face her once more. "Hey, Booth?"

She looked over the rim of her glasses at me. "Yes?"

"The leak?" I didn't need to explain my question further.

"Will be dealt with."

"Good." I nodded. "You'll want to extract your agent from Lucien's horde."

"What makes you think I have only one?"

"Lucien will know there's a mole. And when he finds him or her, the penalty will be swift and severe. If you care for the agent's well-being at all, you'll pull them out and reassign them far, far away."

"If I had such an agent, Ambassador McNeilly, you can be assured I would do the right thing."

Booth's idea of the right thing probably varied widely from my own.

I FOUND THE OLD MAN IN THE SRD LIBRARY stooped over a gargantuan book many years his senior with Ma'ii curled around his feet. The coyote snored.

"Looks like you're off the hook, O'Donnell, you don't have to *handle* me anymore."

"So you accepted the Ambassador position." Donny smiled. "Good."

I slid into the seat opposite him and waved the settling dust out of the air. "You knew?"

"I know many things."

"Okay, Master Yoda. What else do you know?"

He turned another page and read in silence, ignoring me until, after a few minutes, I repeated my question. He sighed and looked up. "I know you haven't read the book yet."

Busted. "And why's that?"

"You haven't called me in hysterics demanding answers."

"Not exactly incentive to start reading."

Donny smirked and turned another large page, causing dust to float up and tickle my nose. I sneezed.

"Well, what could the *Encyclopedia of Mythical Creatures* possibly tell me?"

"The Carus can take on additional feras."

"Yes. We discussed this last time. What's the limit? How many feras could I potentially absorb into the cracks of my rocky soul and the…" I indicated my body with a flourishing wave. "Temple that is my body?"

"We don't know."

"Why is that?" Donny hesitated.

I gave him my best tell-me-or-I'll-punch-you-in-the-face stare. A complete bluff. I'd never harm this man.

"Our history has been passed down generation to generation orally. From what I've been told, the previous Caruses have all lost their minds."

"Come again?"

"Every Carus in the past were declared insane." When he saw me flinch, he tilted his head. "Does it make it easier for you to hear the truth when I rephrase it like that?"

"Not really. No. What about the beast? The luminol? Lumentos? Mentos?"

Donny shook his head.

"Lumpalumpas?"

"The lumentum. The Burden of the Beast. In the old stories, the more feras drawn into the Carus, the more at risk the Carus is to losing the struggle against the beast. When they draw too many in, they go crazy, lose control, and submit to the beast inside them."

"And how do they die?"

"In the past, it's been villages of farmers using their pitchforks." He peered at me over the book. "If you lose your struggle, at least you'll have a quicker, tidier death."

"Unless the SRD retrieves me."

"There is that. I wouldn't wish that on anyone."

"Why on earth would they do it then? The others. Why draw in more feras? It's hard enough with three. I couldn't imagine having more voices in my head."

"Because it's the key to learning control."

"You've completely lost me now."

"Just as you can absorb additional feras, you can expel them from your body as well."

"I can kick them out?" When I was younger, I had three horrific roommates that took advantage of my desire to be the ultimate people pleaser. They ate my food, ignored my requests for their share of the utilities, didn't clean up, stole my shoes and had massive raging parties where undoubtedly I'd walk in on someone doing the nasty in my bed. I never managed to kick them out. I avoided the entire confrontation by finding my own place.

"Yes. And it is said, once you have mastered this control, the beast is yours to command."

I squinted at the old man. "And how many of my Carus brethren have succeeded in this in the past?"

"None that I've heard of."

"Wonderful. So it's all conjecture?"

Donny shook his head. "No. It is known. Feradea spoke, so it is so."

"Spoke to you personally?"

Donny smiled more to himself than me and went back to reading the archaic book in front of him. I wanted to shake him for answers.

"Ouch!" I leapt out of my seat. Clutching my ankle, I glared down at Ma.

Leave the old man alone, he growled.

I did as he asked and limped out of the room, wondering how the heck I would juggle new and old feras with everything else already on my plate. Was I fated for the crazy house? Now it seemed more like a question of "when" instead of "if." Inevitable.

23

"Andrea," Clint crooned into the phone. "Have you finished your dirty dancing so soon? And here I thought you'd put it off as long as possible."

I shuddered. Not yet, and there had to be a way around it. "You have a mole in your horde." I trusted Clint wouldn't betray Lucien. As human servant number one, his life was tied tighter to the Master Vampire than mine.

A long heavy silence. "Who?"

"I don't know, but I've been outed. The SRD knows about the blood bond and they have tape recordings of Lucien. Has to be someone in his inner circle."

"How do you figure?"

"Lucien doesn't strike me as the suck and tell type."

"We'll deal with it."

"You'd better."

Another long pause. If I were a skilled surgeon and

opened Clint's mind, it would probably look something like the game Mouse Trap.

"What were the recordings?" he asked.

"They only played one, but claimed to have more. In the recording I heard, Lucien says something like, 'if that little tart thinks she can run from her blood bond, Agent McNeilly will have a hard lesson to learn.' For the record, I resent the tart comment."

Clint released a long breath with a chuckle. He paused before saying, "Were you fired?"

What the hell? He sounded concerned. Was something wrong with my phone? Interference, maybe? I examined my screen and discovered five bars—perfect reception. Huh.

"Nope," I said. "I've been promoted. You may refer to me as *Ambassador* McNeilly now." My mountain lion preened.

Clint grunted. "Ambassador of what?"

"SRD and Vampire relations. I'm the liaison between Lucien and the government. Agent Booth will contact Lucien to mete out the details and come to a finalized agreement. I want a raise. And benefits."

A pause. Pretty sure I heard the mouse traps snapping on the other end of the phone. "This is good."

"Well, I'm a bit bummed I don't get to kick ass anymore."

Clint's voice dropped. "I'm sure something can be arranged to meet your needs."

I shook my head. He was a walking innuendo. "What I need is a shower. Talking to you makes me feel dirty."

Realizing how he could take it, I quickly yelled into the phone. "And not in a good way!"

Clint laughed and hung up without saying goodbye.

IN THE PAST, BEFORE DYLAN, WHEN SOMETHING positive happened in my life, I'd go out, get drunk, find the hottest single man in the bar, and make out. Having animal magnetism had its advantages. Replaying my actions, I realized I would've been a certified slut if not for the pathetic reality good things didn't occur often in my life.

It didn't stop me from wanting certain things. My cat prowled in my head and my wolf paced. The falcon didn't do much. She screeched at really inappropriate times. All of them told me the same thing—it had been a long time since I'd been with a man, too long. All animals required physical release. I substituted my needs with SRD assignments, but now my role had changed.

So when I walked up to my building and saw Tristan leaning against the banister, he may as well have been chocolate with a bow wrapped around him.

Want, my cat purred. My own thoughts echoed hers. *Want.*

Tristan tilted his head, a slow smile spreading across his face. He strolled over to me. His hand flashed up, and he ran his fingertips down the side of my face. I wanted to turn my head and capture them with my mouth, but before I could, his head dipped into the crook of my neck and inhaled deeply. "I want you, too."

Oh god! I'd said that out loud.

The scent of arousal sprung up from both of us and mingled thick in the air like marble cake mix. Tristan slipped his hands into my hair and gently tugged my face to meet his. Soft lips pressed against mine. Too soft, too gentle. I answered his kiss with an aggressive one of my own, pushing him back against the railing.

As if my rough response gave the permission he wanted, Tristan gripped my hair, pulled my head to the side, and deepened the kiss. His tongue plunged in and stroked mine, sending lightning bolts down my body, pooling heat in every crevice.

He snatched the keys from my hand. I gave him enough time to unlock and open the building's front door before I attacked him again. We stumbled and fumbled our way down the hall, bouncing off the walls, before we staggered into my apartment.

Tristan gripped my ass and pulled me to him. His erection rubbed against me and tingling waves flooded to my body. Sweeping my feet from under me, in a move more martial arts than boudoir savvy, he had me pinned on the floor beneath his exquisite weight. I pulsated with need.

Off. These clothes need to be off. I ripped his shirt and encircled his torso with my legs, holding him tight. My hands glided over every inch of his exposed skin.

I licked his neck and bit his ear. He tasted of salt and

soap. A rising need overwhelmed me. Nerve endings sang with desire. I hadn't felt this good with a man since... since Wick.

The name, once remembered, acted like a cold wet cloth to the face. No, more like a bucket of ice water over the head. I pushed against Tristan's chest. "Stop."

He pulled back with wide eyes. "I thought you were with me."

"I was. I am. I just..."

Tristan tilted his head. His nose flared, and he sat back with a hiss, pulling me up with him. "Feel guilty?"

"I don't think it's right for me to let this go further when I haven't made a decision." *What the fuck is wrong with me?* Lucien could order Wick to do very bad things to me anytime he wanted. Was there really a decision left to be made?

My mind said no, but my heart said yes.

Gah!

Tristan nodded and then looked away. His jaw clenched and burnt cinnamon wafted off his skin. He said, "I thought from your...aggressiveness, you'd made your decision."

He stood up before I could read his expression and retrieved his shirt. But I didn't need to see his face. Bitter disappointment bogged down his usual citrus and sunshine scent. He fastened what buttons remained, but it fell open at his navel.

Lick, my cat demanded. God, how I wanted to.

I ran a hand through my hair and stood up. Where was my shirt? I glanced down at my exposed bra, breasts swelling and almost spilling out of the cups. Tristan followed my gaze and licked his lips.

"Better put this on before I rethink the whole gentleman angle." He tossed my shirt at me. No idea where he found it. I swiped it out of the air and slipped into it. It hung off my shoulders in rags. I glared at Tristan.

"Don't look at me." He smirked. "You were the one eager to get out of it."

I grunted and pulled the material across my chest. "Would you like some coffee?"

"Does it come with an explanation?"

"And an apology."

Tristan paused and scrutinized my face, as if he considered my apology and whether to accept it. I held my breath. Then his muscles relaxed, and a small smile creased his face. I released the pent-up air. He didn't run for the door; instead, he found his way to the couch.

"An apology isn't necessary," he said. "I'm disappointed, but I'm glad you stopped us. When I have you, there will be no regrets. No scent of guilt."

Heat rushed to my cheeks, making me super-duper-happy with a cherry on top. I made small talk until the coffee finished. As if sensing my need for space, or maybe in need of some himself, Tristan stayed in the living room, sprawled on my couch.

"I came to ask you about the Demon summoning. If you haven't done it yet, I wanted to offer to be there with you." Tristan accepted the coffee mug from me. "Thought you could use the support."

I squeezed my eyes shut, hoping it would dampen the need to jump him. Geez, my hormones had a mind of their own lately.

"You all right?"

"Yup." I sat down, unsure of my control. "Thanks for the offer, but I need to face this alone." I didn't tell him it would be the second time summoning Sid, or what I'd pay for the information. It probably wouldn't go over so well. Tristan might understand my predicament with him and Wick, but he was an Alpha, and my indecisiveness would be ripping him up inside. Add a horny Demon to the mix? Alphas could only rein back their dominant animals so much. I didn't want a rabid Wereleopard hauling me to his prowl for my safety. I needed information from Sid.

"You sure? I could watch from the sidelines."

"Thank you, but no." The less people who witnessed my humiliation, the better.

Tristan's eyes narrowed, but he didn't press the issue. We talked about the attack at Lucien's and the master's pissy mood. After Tristan finished his coffee, checked his watch, and left with a chaste kiss on my cheek. He promised to call.

It took every ounce of control not to pounce on him and drag his fine feline ass to my bedroom. But I could only hide my feelings about the Demon summoning for so long, and if Wick or Tristan ever found out about my plans to strip and jiggle for one of the damned, my decision might be made for me—instead of two men, I'd have none.

24

Whenever I envisioned a life or death situation where the heroine fought against all odds to save her loved ones, my thoughts filled with guns, hordes of enemies, blood, guts, and some badass combat moves. Never a bedazzled thong.

"Are you sure you want to do this?" Ben asked while sprinkling the salt line. I'd been right. He was strong enough to summon a Demon on his own and didn't need his coven of Witch Novices to help. Score one for me. I didn't want an audience for this.

No longer able to vocalize assent for what I was about to do, I nodded and clutched my robe closer to my body. "You know the drill?" I managed to croak.

Ben glanced up through his plain blond hair. "Summon and get lost? Yeah. You only repeated yourself a dozen times or so."

I waited.

Ben rolled his eyes. "And tell no one."

"If I ever hear about this..." My voice trailed off in a threat.

"Yeah, yeah. Bodily harm and dismemberment. I remember."

Nodding more to myself, I looked around my living room.

"Andy, look." Ben straightened his lean frame. "It's about an hour until dawn. The sun will automatically banish him to the demonic realm when it rises. Make sure you specify the length of time. You will dance for him until he's fully fed from your energy or fifteen minutes before dawn, whichever comes...I mean, occurs...first. The remaining time is for him to answer your question."

Ben walked over and clasped my hands in his. Though I was often naked around other supes, if I extended my arms, my robe would open. Ben was uncomfortable enough. He'd asked if I'd wear something for the summoning, three times. He also thought Demon feeding involved masturbation, despite telling him it didn't, three times. So I kept my arms stiff and bent, like a deformed T-rex, as Ben grasped my hands.

"Remember to make him take a blood oath to make good on your agreement."

My body trembled against my will.

The air stirred as the portal drew power from the energies around us and started to form. A current circulated the room and whipped my hair around and brushed over my exposed skin.

"I knew you were good enough to say all that crap in your head," I said.

"I am." Ben turned and gave me an I'm-the-big-dawg look. "The chanting is for show."

The portal snapped in place. The tiny hairs on my forearms sprung up as the Demon's portal snapped open and the large imposing figure of Sidragasum appeared in the centre of the circle.

"I'll be outside if you need me. The circle is strong enough to hold him." Ben cast a wary look my way. "Don't get caught up in the moment and step over it. At least not until he swears a blood oath to do you no harm." Even if he did, another supe's idea of harm could vary greatly from my own. Something I learned from Lucien.

I growled over my shoulder at Ben's retreating back. It looked a little shaky, as if he chuckled on his way out. I might have to beat him up anyway.

Sid coughed lightly to get my attention.

I turned slowly to the Demon waiting patiently in the summoning circle.

"Little Carus." The Demon's sly grin greeted me. "I had a feeling we'd meet again."

Biting my bottom lip, I examined Sid's naked form, all seven feet of tanned olive skin, unsure of how to continue. At least he was hot; it would be harder to strip for a Frankenstein doppelgänger.

"I take it from the lack of a blood offering in the circle, you've chosen option A?" he said.

Taking a deep breath, I spoke the agreement parameters Ben made me memorize. It sounded more like a business agreement, words strategically placed to allow no wiggle room, misinterpretation, or deliberate evasion. Sid looked amused, but when I finished, he nodded and without any comment, slit his palm open by drawing one long yellowed claw along it.

"By my blood, I agree to these terms and swear to uphold my end of the bargain." His blood pooled on his upturned hand until it slid off and fell to the floor in large thick drops. If tonight didn't go well, the forensics team would have a hard time with the blood spatter analysis.

I shifted one fingernail into a long mountain lion claw and repeated the process. Sid's nose flared as the scent of my blood reached him. He licked his lips.

"And I thought it would be my dancing to give you a hard-on." I evaded Sid's gaze and decided the safest place to look was the ceiling.

"Little Carus," Sid crooned. "You have no idea what a treat a dance from one of the gods' chosen is to me, to all Demons. The very idea makes me hard." He reached down to emphasize his point.

Refusing to look to where Sid's hand drifted, I clicked the docking station remote and turned on the music I'd selected. Heavy bass filled the room as I dropped the robe and started to move.

"Oh yes, little Carus." Sid's smile spread slowly. His eyes twinkled. The scent of almond swirled around as the music consumed me. The animal magnetism I usually kept tightly reined in released, flooding the air with potent pheromones. I planned to use all my talents to my advantage so this would end sooner than later. My feras took control, swaying and gyrating to the rhythm in a dance as old as time. I tried to forget I had an audience, and tried not to notice how Sid's body tensed and his head fell back as he fed off my sexual energy. His voice laced through the notes of the song. "Dance for me."

25

As it turned out, the appetite of a Demon was not a thing of legends—it was very, very genuine. Or my dancing really, really sucked. Being the dancer in question, I preferred to think the former more fitting. I couldn't be *that* bad. It took Sid the Demon a long time to finish feeding.

"Does none of this embarrass you?" I asked after he'd moaned and proclaimed himself full.

"Why would it? We're sexual beings. This is as natural as ice caps on the mountain melting to cold spring water or birds migrating south for the winter. Why soil the experience with such negative emotions?"

Huh. A poetic Demon?

"You have a question, little Carus, and your time runs short. Ask."

I pulled my gaze away from the naked Demon. "There have been a number of attacks by humans on supes these last couple of weeks. The attackers don't have red eyes like those typically possessed. Their irises are their regular colour, but they glow. I want to know what Demon is responsible, how they are controlling the humans, and why they're doing it."

Sid tsked and shook his head. "The humans are not possessed."

The Demon's hand shot up and stopped me from launching into a tirade.

"A Demon is not responsible. And since I'm feeling benevolent, I will elaborate, although under normal circumstances that would require a renegotiation of terms. What you describe is subconscious control by someone with psionic abilities."

The air became too thin to breathe properly, and I needed to sit down. My body took the shortest path; with a loud thud, my ass hit the floor. "Can you tell me something to help me find the person responsible, or did I dance and lose what little remained of my dignity for nothing?"

"Not for nothing, little Carus." Sid leaned down to meet my glare. "And I have fulfilled my end of the bargain and more."

My vision blurred. My mouth filled with the taste of my last meal. *For nothing*.

"But..." Sid's voice interrupted my psychotic break. "I know of a man..."

I glanced at the tightly draw Venetian window shades, predawn light sneaking through. "Talk fast, Demon. We're running out of time."

"A Witch survived an attack and caught one of the humans responsible. I know where he's being held."

"Alive? One of the possessed humans has been captured alive?" My ears tingled as if they perked up. There'd been no survivors until this point, and the VPD and SRD had yet to track down the identities of the bodies found. Had they, I would've visited each and every one of the victims' homes, questioned their loved ones, and combed the areas they were last seen. But like the investigators for the VPD and SRD, I had little to go on. This survivor was important.

"The Witch's name is Lucus Klug. German for clever or smart. Aptly named, that one," Sid said. "Keep that in mind."

I committed the name to memory and then observed the Demon. He stared back, waiting expectantly.

If he waited for me to shower him with praise and gratitude, despite his going "above and beyond" to help me, it wasn't going to happen. I scrambled to my feet. "Why are you being so nice? What's in it for you?"

"It serves a purpose."

"And what's that?"

"It's in my best interest to be *nice* to you. After the performance you gave me tonight, I'm hopeful for a repeat. If you have any further questions, you know how to contact me."

The room brightened as the sun continued to rise. The early morning chatter of birds filled the room. Sid's body started to waver, like a mirage in an X-rated desert movie.

"And my price."

Without any further warning, Sid disappeared. No gaping portal opened. He simply vanished. Deteriorating like a biodegradable garbage bag, only quicker.

26

As I talked to Lucus Klug on the phone, I envisioned a slight man waving a wand in the air for emphasis while he described his ordeal. What was it about Witches that regardless of age, gender identity or sexual orientation, they all came across as drama queens in their early twenties? After getting to know them, Ben and his coven of male apprentices appeared an exception to the rule.

"Has he told you anything?" I asked.

"Sugar, he don't remember nothing. Fishing one moment and handcuffed in my love den the next. No idea of the damages he did. Not a clue."

Love den? A comment bubbled up in my throat, but I swallowed it down. *Keep it professional, McNeilly.* I took a deep breath before continuing. "Would it be possible for me to come over to your…er…love den and question him?"

"What could you possibly do that I can't?"

"I can be very persuasive."

"So can I, sweet cheeks. Ain't nothing you can do to this boy that I haven't already done. I'm a Witch, you know."

"I'm aware."

"I threw a truth spell at him. That boy's mind is blank. Doesn't even know his own name."

I clutched my cell phone and took a deep breath. No name? No memory? I still had nothing to go on. "Is there anything you can tell me of interest?"

"Unless you're interested in cleaning up puke, sugar, ain't nothing here for you."

"Damn. Side effect of your spell?"

"You know it. The man sure does love his vegetables."

There was such a thing as too much information—the nameless man's dietary habits definitely fell into this category. "What are you going to do with him?"

"Well, seeing how he's innocent and all. I'm going to keep him until this Supe Slayer nonsense blows over."

"To keep him safe?"

"Mmhmm."

Before I could think of some witty response or muster up a pathetic argument for the man's freedom, the Witch hung up on me. Imagine that.

I flipped my hair up into a ponytail before heading to my bedroom. Lucien and his horde didn't know I spoke with Sid last night. It would buy me a little time to pursue my other assignment. Today, I planned an unannounced visit to Booth's mom.

Dressed in skinny jeans and a light blue cashmere sweater that brought out my gray eyes, and naturally tanned skin tone, I picked up my purse and headed for the door.

My phone beeped, telling me I had an unread message. It must've come in while I was in the shower. Tapping my phone screen, I punched in my password and read the message. It was from Clint.

> Progress, little dancer?

Balancing my purse and keys in one hand, I texted back.

> Tonight.

> Can I watch?

> You can fuck off.

I could hear his laughter in the silent response to my last text.

AGENT BOOTH'S MOM LIVED IN A TIDY TUDOR-style cottage house with a white picket fence, which somehow managed to scream crazy cat woman with chained gimps in the basement despite the wholesome appearance. I knocked on the door for the third time. No answer.

The home sat on a corner lot, nestled between two quiet streets in a sleepy neighbourhood. Sniffing around the perimeter revealed no supe scents, but Herman didn't have one.

The fully fenced back yard represented a minor obstacle, but I scaled it with the agility of a house cat and flipped over to the other side with skills worthy of a military combat soldier. Freshly cut green grass gave the space a lush appearance. Red roses, lilacs, and japonicas lined the inside of the fence and created a fragrant oasis. None of the other houses could look into the yard, but despite the privacy, I refrained from shifting to my wolf form for an even stronger sense of smell—no point. If Herman lurked around, stealing more of Mrs. Booth's stuff, I wouldn't smell him anyway. Besides, if he happened to be here, I wanted to be in human form to confront him. At least at first.

I opened the screen door and sniffed the gap between the solid wood door and its frame. And recoiled.

Death.

The doorknob stared back at me. I slowly turned it and the door clicked open. Decay slammed through the space and smacked me in the face, hacking at my nasal passages like an inexperienced Do-It-Yourself renovator.

Pulling my sweater over my nose, I stepped inside the house.

I should have brought one of my guns. The thought flittered through my mind. Who knew what weapon would be most effective against a scentless, lab-escapee supe. The more, the better at this point. I had an arsenal of semiautomatic handguns and assault rifles in my apartment's safe, but I tended not to use them. I *was* a weapon in my own right. Plus, if I shifted, I left whatever I brought with me behind. For that reason alone, I liked to travel light. It went against my personal beliefs to leave loaded firearms where anyone could stumble upon them.

Still, my Sig would feel pretty nice in my hand right now.

The first room contained an assortment of old woman shoes. There were multiple pairs of plain white runners with extra thick soles. The room had a bench with hooks above it for jackets. A mudroom to a realtor.

Kick-ass shoe room to me. I'd love to have one of these. I hated bending over to pull knee-high boots off in my narrow hallway.

The mudroom led to a neat kitchen. Crumbs and a dirty butter knife sat on the counter where ants scurried in paths to the food. I'd sniff harder to figure out what was on the knife, but the overbearing smell of death stopped me. Looked like peanut butter.

When I walked through the kitchen to the dining room, I found the body of whom I could only assume was Agent Booth's mom. She lay sprawled on the floor, her face smushed into the carpet, expression unreadable. One arm was trapped under her body, as if covering her heart. Covering or clutching?

Sniffing around the room revealed no new scents. Only old lady and old dead lady. One and the same. No one had been here. Except perhaps Agent Booth or Herman...or both.

I knelt beside the body, careful not to disturb it. Despite undergoing several stages of decomposition, nothing indicated a violent death. No obvious fractures or breaks. No sprayed blood. It looked like she stood from her armchair three to four weeks ago and fell, clutching her heart.

Natural causes?

Didn't see many of those in my line of work. No wonder the crime scene creeped me out.

Leaving the body, I walked up the carpeted staircase to the second floor. Who mowed the lawns then? Herman? A kid from down the street?

The main bedroom remained vacant and looked undisturbed. Holding my breath, I moved to door number two.

When the door swung open, I gasped. Hundreds of photos plastered the walls, all of Agent Booth. Discarded albums were strewn across the floor, pages flipped open, pictures ripped out. Around the pictures, someone had scrawled "Joyce," "Agent Booth," and "Who are you?" I stared at a shrine. Three candles stood unlit by the unmade bed. Sniffing the air revealed no new scents, but I'd bet my booty Herman slept here.

Where was he now?

Probably hocking more of old lady Booth's stuff.

I closed the door on the disturbing scene and retraced my steps. I'd have to come back later. Not wanting to disturb it and scare Herman off, I skirted around Evelyn's body, and let myself out the back door. Hopefully Herman didn't have a heightened sense of smell or he'd know I'd visited, regardless of what I did or didn't move.

As I drove away from the house, I sent a silent apology to Agent Booth's mother. Her body should be laid to rest or given the appropriate respects of the dead, not left to decay in her living room.

How should I tell Agent Booth?

27

I couldn't tell Booth what I'd discovered. Not yet. I had to nab Herman first, so she wouldn't have the chance to interfere with the retrieval. In an attempt to distract my guilt-ridden brain from thoughts of Booth's mom rotting away in her house, I pulled out the *Encyclopedia of Mythical Creatures*, looked up Carus and started reading. My fingers barely registered the sting from the cover. The book did little to lighten my mood.

> *"Carus: Feradea's Chosen One. Gifted with the ability to have multiple feras, the Shifter can take on multiple forms, including an animal hybrid referred to as the Ualida, the amalgamation of all feras resembling a demonic being. Each of the Carus' feras is a spiritual guide and representation of part of the Carus's soul. To be complete, the Carus must possess all his or her spiritual feras. Also see Lumentum."*

Holding my breath, I flipped to the appropriate page.

"Lumentum: The beast of burden living deep inside Feradea's Chosen One. The beast, also referred to as the Ualida, is the divine form of the Carus and a spiritual amalgamation of all feras associated with the Carus. If the Carus loses control of the beast, it may escape, transforming the Carus to a nexus of evil that will reap devastation to all. It requires great control to keep the Ualida caged and any shortcoming can result in catastrophic events, hence "beast of burden." To date, no Carus has successfully controlled the beast. Most Ualida were executed by local authorities after causing mass destruction. Also see Carus and Ualida."

Ah fuck.

The sound of someone knocking on my door interrupted me before I could look up Ualida. The citrus and sunshine scent slid in from the building's hallway before I opened the door. Tristan waited on the other side. I checked my appearance in the mirror and smoothed my hair.

When I opened the door, I nearly staggered at the beaming smile on his face. As it was, the shock of seeing his angelic beauty caused me to suck my breath in. "Tristan."

"Andy." He moved into the entranceway, slipped a hand through my hair to clasp my neck and leaned down for a kiss.

"Hi," I mumbled into his warm supple lips.

A hand glided down my body, grazing my breasts before grasping my right hip. He pulled me closer. "Hi."

"To what do I owe this pleasure?" I pushed him away so I could breathe.

"Andy, the pleasure is all mine...but I'll share." He stole a quick kiss before stepping out of my personal space. The air felt cold on my skin in his absence. We stood in the entrance hall of my apartment and studied one another.

"Am I interrupting?" A husky voice growled.

Pleasure and panic shot through my body simultaneously.

"Wick!" My voice sounded high pitched as I craned my neck to see over Tristan's shoulder. "Hi!"

After a long awkward pause, Tristan stepped to the side. He probably didn't like Wick at his back.

"Um. Why don't you both come in? Coffee?" My voice squeaked.

They both nodded without taking their eyes off each other. Caught in a battle for dominance neither wanted to lose, it meant they'd keep staring at each other in order to not break eye contact first.

"This is ridiculous." I grabbed a jacket from the closet and held it up between the two. "Now neither of you submitted." I looked over to Tristan's side, still clutching the jacket in shaking hands. "Tristan. You were here first, so please come in and make yourself comfortable."

Tristan chuckled and shook his head. After he shucked his runners, using his toes on one foot to pull his heel out of the other, he sauntered down the hall and turned the corner.

"Wick?" I let the jacket fall. He turned his wolf eyes on me and blinked a few times before the yellow cleared to their beautiful deep espresso. "Join us?"

Wick saluted and stalked to the living room. But not before he smacked me on the ass. When it looked like they were content to give each other the hairy eyeball, I left them sitting in the living room to make coffee, but before I could put three mugs on the counter, I knew I'd made a mistake.

A deep growl radiated from the other room. I abandoned the coffee grounds and ran over to find the two Weres—thankfully both still in human form—nose to nose. Wick, slightly bent over Tristan, used his height as a seven-inch advantage. His growling grew deeper. "She is mine."

Tristan bared long canines in response, and a deep rumble vibrated from his chest through the air. His eyes shifted to cat slits. "She's unclaimed. The choice is hers."

The energy in the room crackled with power as the Weres took a few steps back and circled each other. Their emotion thick and heavy in the air. I struggled to breathe. It reminded me of vacationing in Ontario during the summer when the humidity index flew off the charts. At least my shirt wasn't stuck to my skin from excessive sweating. Not yet, anyway.

"Guys." I waved my hands. They ignored me. Their stare-down continued. They took a step toward each other. I bit my lip.

All supes gave off more energy compared to humans. Each preternatural being possessed a unique signature, but regardless of type, whenever supes congregated, the energies fed off one another, heightening the power in the room. With two alphas facing off, the effect grew exponentially, crackling the air with potency. Goosebumps spread across my arms, the tiny hairs raised, the energy lathed my skin, one cold lick at a time.

One step closer, and the static electricity generating from their bodies would electrocute us all.

"That's it!" I exclaimed, right before I smacked my palm on my forehead, again and again.

Both Tristan and Wick's eyes slanted in my direction. Something about seeing their potential mate repeatedly bashing her forehead with her hand must've jarred them from their pissing match. The next thing I knew, they both stood beside me.

"What is it?" Wick asked at the same time Tristan reached out to smooth my arm and say, "Are you okay?"

Wick snarled at Tristan. Tristan turned and hissed at Wick. Practically besties.

"The Supe Slayer attacks groups of us because we give off more energy. He or she must detect the elevated power somehow."

"And feeds off it." Wick finished the thought process for me. "The supes are being dragged to the Slayer alive so he can feed on them before discarding their bodies."

"Do you know what preternatural being does that?" Wick shook his head. I turned to Tristan.

"No idea." The Wereleopard looked thoughtful. "But I'll ask around. Someone must know."

"A water supe with psionic skills that feeds off energy. That narrows it down a bit, but I have a feeling we're still missing an important clue," I said. *The Encyclopedia of Mythical Creatures* sat on the table and glared back at me. *Looks like the big book of monsters and I have a hot reading date tonight.*

A beeping sound emitted from Tristan's pocket. He pulled his phone out and tapped the screen. His brow furrowed. "I have to go. Work." He glanced up at me and hesitated. His gaze flicked to Wick, and I knew, just knew, he didn't want to leave me alone with the competition. He exhaled deeply. "I hate my job right now."

He leaned in to kiss me goodbye, but a growl from Wick stopped him short. Tristan's gaze slid to the Werewolf again, and he arched a brow before he returned his full attention back to me. "I'll call you."

Before Wick could do any bodily harm, Tristan planted a solid smack of a kiss on my lips, winked, and walked out the door.

When I turned to the Werewolf in the room, his yellow wolf eyes bore a hole in my head, and I quickly looked away. Avoiding the vibrating ball of anger, also known as Wick, I skirted around him, sat down and guzzled some water.

"Have you already decided then?" Wick asked. His despair slammed into me fractions of a second after his voice.

I choked on my water. "Why would you think that?"

"You seem very close to Tristan. And he did not have the luxury of having you under house arrest for weeks. And he did not spend a week with you in his arms, taking it slow." His phone vibrated in his pocket, but he kept his attention locked on me.

I hiccupped. My cheeks heated, and I slapped a hand over my mouth. It didn't help. I hiccupped again.

Wick shook his head and walked over to me as I sat up and draped myself over my knees. "I hate hiccups." My voice immediately followed by another involuntary reaction.

"I never understood why they exist. Seems like a rather useless reaction for the body to have." He sat down beside me and rubbed my back. His phone vibrated against my thigh.

"I favour the Phylogenetic Hypothesis, which proposes hiccups are remnants of the neural mechanism from when our amphibian ancestors frequently switched between breathing in air and water."

Wick's eyebrows rose into his blond hairline.

"I um..." My eyes shifted for the nearest exit.

"You are a closet geek." Wick sat back and crossed his arms. A slow smile spread across his face. "Admit it."

"Not exactly in the closet anymore, am I?" My hiccups subsided—a perk of being a Shifter, my diaphragm recovered quicker than a norm's.

He tucked a loose strand of hair behind my ear. "How did you get so knowledgeable?"

Exhaling deeply, I sagged into the couch. He draped an arm around me and pulled my body toward him so my head rested on his shoulder. I took a moment to enjoy the simple gesture before speaking. "In my pursuit to find relevant information to what I am, I came across a lot of random biological facts. I sort of collected them, still do, as if they'll somehow become useful if there's ever an apocalypse. Even now that I know more about myself and my abilities, I still read *Scientific American* and *Preternatural Science*."

The muscles in his shoulder twitched as his fingers caressed my skin. "Cannot break the habit?"

"It's more like a compulsive disorder than a habit, but yeah. I can't stop accumulating useless factoids."

We sat in companionable silence. He pulled his phone and tapped the screen. "I have to go," he said, but remained seated. The air darkened with the laden scent of Wick's sadness. His mind had wandered back to his question about making a decision.

"My cat has always been more dominant than my wolf, Wick." I explained in a hushed voice. "Even before Dylan. But then after..."

Wick started to speak, but I turned to him and placed my finger over his lush lips.

"But after, I retreated into my cat and lived as one for many years in the wild. It's even more dominant now, and there's an inherent trust. My wolf..."

"You do not trust your wolf," Wick whispered against my finger.

"I don't." *And I can't trust you either*. I choked on the unspoken words "I'm so sorry."

"Is that it, then? You have decided?"

My wolf growled. I swallowed a couple times before I could answer. "No."

Wick's brows furrowed.

"I haven't made a decision. I feel like I'm being split in two with these feras of mine, but I'm not going to let them make this decision for me." I met Wick's yellow wolf eyes. "I'm going to make it. Me." I thumbed my chest a little too hard. *That's going to bruise.*

Wick's eyes blazed. "Good."

He leaned in for a kiss, but halted a fraction of an inch from my lips. His nose flared. "You smell of him."

"Um." Didn't know how to respond to that. He said it matter-of-fact, but somehow I couldn't shake the feeling of guilty gnawing at my belly.

Wick stood and pulled me up with him. I walked him to the door, unsure of what to say. Awkward, didn't quite cover it.

"I will call you." He drew my hands up and kissed my knuckles. Beyond awkward.

28

The sauna-like conditions inside my A-to-B car had sweat running down my back in less than three minutes. I'd pulled to the side of the road to set up a phone call, and without air-conditioning, the sweltering heat decided to try and cook me.

Deep thrumming echoed through my chest and demanded I walk into the forest. I ignored the urge, and tapped Donny's number on my phone's screen instead. Now, a series of rings filled my ears as I monitored the cars on the road. As a space in traffic opened, I stepped on the gas and maneuvered the car into the lane.

Donny picked up and answered with a grizzly, "hello."

I spoke quickly into my hands-free device. "I need to pick your brain."

"I thought you hated zombies?" Donny's craggy voice rattled my headset.

"What? Oh yeah, I despise them. So stupid." I paused. "Wait. What?"

Donny laughed.

Picking brains, zombies, got it. I glared at the phone. "Listen old man, I don't have time for your jokes."

That made him laugh harder. "To what do I owe the pleasure of your telephonic communications then?" he asked. Amusement rang like bells in his voice and his formal question irritated me. He did it on purpose. I could tell.

"I need to know what water supes have psionic powers and feed off supe energy."

A long pause.

"Donny?" The light ahead turned orange, and I eased the brakes on. A loud metal-on-metal sound punched the air as my brakes struggled to stop the vehicle. Sweat trickled down my face.

"Carus, what makes you think I would have an answer for you?"

"You're ancient. You should know everything."

Donny grunted. "Why don't you read the—"

"If you tell me to read that stupid encyclopedia one more time, I'm going to tell you what to do with it. Or more precisely, where you can shove it." The light changed, and I prodded my dilapidated car onward.

"Well now. Your attitude has changed since becoming an ambassador." His tone teased. "All high and mighty now."

I sighed. "Can you help me?"

"There's too many, Andy. I can't narrow it down for you with two pieces of information."

"Four." I flicked my fingers out as I counted them, even though Donny couldn't see the action. "One: water supe, two: psionic, three: feeds off energy, and four: prefers supe energy."

"No. Two."

"Donny," my voice threatened.

"One: water supe and two: psionic. All preternatural beings with psionic skills require feeding off energy. And all beings, supernatural or otherwise have the same type of energy; it's just higher or increased in supes. So as you can see, your last two facts are already accounted for by psionic."

"So you can't help me."

"Not with that, no. But I wanted to ask you how things were going. I promised not to inquire about whether you've read *the book*, but have you thought about going for a walk in the forest?"

I drummed my fingers on the steering wheel and continued toward Mrs. Booth Senior. "I did read it, and no. Why would I walk in the forest? I'm running around like a headless chicken, I don't have time for nature walks to *find myself*."

"Not to find yourself, you silly girl. You need to open your mind and your heart. Find another fera, another part of yourself, a part you need."

A bike courier darted out from two parked cars. *Crap!* I swerved to avoid him, and narrowly missed colliding with the van in the next lane. The car behind me honked, and the cyclist yelled profanities. I flipped them both off.

"What about going crazy?" I asked.

"What about it?"

"Are you pushing me to do this, so I go nuts and the SRD can lock me up and prod me with lab instruments?

"Carus, if I wanted that, I wouldn't have to wait. They butcher anything unique and beautiful, regardless of their state of mind."

I glanced in my rearview mirror. The angry driver in the car behind me turned off on Cambie. Good riddance.

"Awww, Donny. You think I'm beautiful."

"And unique," he replied without pause. "You need to learn about yourself. A Carus is a gift to us all, and I don't want to lose you because you're too stubborn to try a life lesson."

"I've had plenty of life lessons, thank you very much."

"There's no quota on learning, Carus. If there is, the moment you reach it, you die." Donny's voice drifted off.

Not liking the static silence on the other end of the phone, I thanked Donny and said goodbye. The car's steering wheel squished under my tightening grip while I made a decision. "I can't believe I'm doing this!"

I ripped off the hands-free headset and chucked it on the passenger seat. Instead of continuing straight through the next intersection, a direction that would lead me to Agent Booth's mother's house, I turned right and headed for a patch of nature.

Open my heart and my mind.

My phone beeped. Easier said than done. I glanced at my cell's screen to see a message from Officer Stan Stevens. Turning it on silent, I made a mental note to call him back as soon as I finished finding my inherent awesomeness.

The nearest green spaces had probably been Stanley park or the nearby university, but both felt too cultured and definitely too populated for the privacy I wanted. Instead, I drove to the mountains in North Vancouver. It felt right.

Never being to this particular location before, I parked the car on the side of a rural road and walked into the forest. I found an old dirt trail used more often by deer and bears than humans. I had the oddest sensation while I walked that I knew where I was going, as if I'd been here before. The path opened up to a small clearing in the deep woods. I sat cross-legged in the centre.

And waited. And waited.

My eyes pinged open. I checked the time on my cell phone. How long was I going to give this? If it took any longer, I was going to get stuck in rush hour over the bridge.

Argh!

Inhale. Exhale. I concentrated on my breathing to

relax my muscles and mind, like the karate exercise my old sensei repeatedly made me do to focus my chi. The sun broke through the clouds sporadically, trickling down to illuminate the grass below and warm my chilled skin. I closed my eyes. *Breathe.*

The soft patter of tiny feet and the rustle of bushes ahead to the right caught my attention. Keeping my eyes closed, I focused on the approaching sound. *Pitter, patter. Stop. Sniff. Pitter, patter. Stop. Sniff.*

The urge to leap to my feet and rush to the animal overwhelmed my senses, but I remained still. I needed to stay calm and wait for this fera to come to me. When a cold, wet nose pressed against my bare arm, I nearly yelped in surprise.

I opened my eyes and turned my head to see a beautiful red fox sitting a foot away from me.

Are you my new fera? I asked.

The fox's voice was a playful rasp in my head, but her words confused me: *I am you. You are me. We are one.*

The other three feras in my head repeated the line as if it were a chorus in a popular song. They'd each said the same thing to me that night almost sixty-six years ago. It didn't make sense then, and it didn't make sense now. *Not helpful.*

Not like other feras. Less, but more.

Can you explain using full sentences? I asked.

No.

Groaning, I flopped back to lie on the forest floor. The fox trotted up to me and leaned in to lick my face. I swatted her away like a fly, but she dodged my hand. I froze with my arm stretched out. If I touched her, would the same thing happen? I shuddered and blocked the memory of my first contact with a fera before it could bubble up.

I am you. You are me. We are one, she repeated.

The meaning of the encyclopedia hit me like a wrecking ball bashing into the side of a dilapidated building. It said each fera was a "*spiritual guide and representation of part of the Carus's soul.*" As a part of me, I needed this fox to be complete. Sand to my rocky soul, and whatnot. She wasn't like the feras of other Shifters who had a personality and identity of their own. She was me. I was her. We were one. A light bulb went on. It flickered a bit, but the meaning sank in anyway.

How do we do this? My first time had been so traumatic; I had no idea if it would go down the same way.

The fox cocked her head. *One touch.*

I nodded. That's all it took with the others as well. I'd had this compulsion to pet them, and the instant my hand made contact, I drew them into my very being. Guess I hadn't messed up the bonding as badly as I thought.

I hesitated to extend my arm. *Are you sad? You're giving up your life.*

If a fox could snort, that's what she did. A short blast of air rebounded across my dendrites. *Not life, until we're one.*

Before I lost the courage, I reached out to run my hand down the flaming fur, but the instant my fingers made contact, the fox shimmered and wavered. She lost colour, as if my finger somehow sucked it out of her. The transparent, black and white fox smiled before she disappeared, drawn into my body like dust suctioned into a vacuum. *I am you. You are me. We are one.*

The impact of my new fox fera was immediate. She slammed into my essence. Like one shot of tequila too many. My mind over-filled. My head hurt, sending sheering pain to the back of my eyeballs. My skull ached as if my brain doubled in size to accommodate the extra animal.

I moved my hands to gently press my temples, patting down my hair. Nothing had changed. Not on the outside at least.

Inside, a full-out battle for dominance reigned. My mountain lion immediately set to establishing her superiority, and my wolf followed suit. The falcon, never interested in shows of dominance, screeched loudly, sending more lancing pain through my head. I dropped to my hands and knees, and waited for the throbbing to stop.

And then I felt it. The beast within. She stirred. As if sensing my weakness, the Ualida pushed, and rose, wanting control. The desire to give in and let her rule coated my tongue with a bitter taste. One shift, and I'd be strong, powerful, and invincible. Nobody could hurt me.

Wait! This is wrong.

The words from the encyclopedia floated through my head as I fought to contain the rising danger: *If the Carus loses control of the beast, it will escape, transforming the Carus to a nexus of evil that will reap devastation to all.*

The only time the Ualida wrested control, she

destroyed the Werewolf pack responsible for nearly obliterating my will to live. Lately, she'd become more *present*. But she tended to awaken when danger came to kick my ass. She had no cause to defend me now.

I'm safe.

I repeated this line and pushed her down.

My feras halted their infighting and joined the struggle, working together to shackle the beast back to the centre of my core.

It worked.

With the Ualida settled into her resting place, the feras established their hierarchy—same order as before with the poor little fox at the bottom. That's what she wanted anyway.

Something trickled down my upper lip. I reached up to wipe it away, and when I held my fingers back, they were coated with blood. Nosebleed. I used my shirt to blot the rest of it off and stalked back to my car. The blood soaked into my shirt.

After jumping into my car and slamming the door shut, I rested my head on the seat and closed my eyes. My brain throbbed and every muscle in my body ached. Apparently I had masochist tendencies. Adding a new fera? That shit hurt.

My feras sang in my head, now content: *I am you. You are me. We are one.*

29

When I opened my apartment's front door, Stan barged in with a scrunched-up face, knocking me out of the way without so much as a "hi."

"Why didn't you return my calls?" he demanded.

"Nice to see you too, Stan. Please, come in. Make yourself welcome." I didn't waste one of my megawatt smiles on his back.

"I've no time for your sass." He stalked into my living room and halted, as if surprised to find it normal.

"Sass?" I squinted at him. "You're too young to use pre-Purge slang like that."

He grunted and resumed studying my place as if he expected circus animals to leap out any second.

I cleared my throat. "Not what you expected?"

Stan returned my glare, and I waved my arm in a grand gesture to indicate he sit on the couch.

"What's so urgent?" I asked. "Did you find out something about the Supe Slayer?"

"Not exactly. But it's related, and we might've closed another case," he said, finally taking a seat. He kept his back upright and his weight forward.

"Oh yeah?"

"We caught one of the possessed humans running away from a grocery store. Stole a bunch of cucumbers. Turns out, she owns a chain of grocery stores herself—none of which have been robbed. Think she might be the thief behind the recent vegetable thefts."

Cucumbers, vegetables, possessed humans. The dendrites in my brain clicked into place. I held up my index finger to Stan and pulled my phone out. After quickly tapping the screen, I found the number I wanted and hit call. Stan ignored the power of my finger and started speaking. I shoved it against his lips. He sputtered, but stopped talking, seconds before the Witch picked up the phone.

"Hello?" Lucus's voice snapped.

"Hi Lucus. It's Andy McNeilly. We spoke earlier."

"What do you want?"

"Quick question."

A pause. "Shoot."

"You said your man puked up a lot of vegetables."

"Mmhmm."

"Were they cucumbers by any chance?"

"Well now, how'd you know that? Yes, they were. Thought the boy had a hankering for them, but he won't go near them now."

Now? "Is he still handcuffed in your love den?"

Lucus chuckled softly. I envisioned him shaking his head. "Now sweet cheeks, that ain't none of your business."

I didn't bother correcting him on the use of double negatives. "You're right. Thanks for the information."

"Mmhmm." He hung up on me again, thwarting an awkward goodbye.

I whirled around and ran to my office.

"Andy?" Stan called out after me.

"Shhh. Not now. In the zone." I flicked my laptop open and after I logged in, pulled up my favourite search engine on the screen. Doing a search for "supernatural + water + cucumbers" yielded many results. I clicked on the first link, read a few lines and gasped. The Kappa: a Japanese water supe capable of psionic mind control with a diet consisting of energy sucked from its victims and cucumbers.

Stan entered the office and folded his arms. He was a smart cop and remained silent as I pulled books off the shelf until I could get to the one I wanted.

Encyclopedia of Mythical Creatures zapped my fingers, but I ignored the insignificant pain to look up the Kappa. The short paragraph confirmed the Internet site, but the information presented made the Kappa seem harmless, relatively passive, and almost ridiculous. I needed more information before I acted.

And I knew just who to ask about Japanese supes.

THE LARGEST JAPANESE VAMPIRE I KNEW IN existence slipped on his tailored jacket and cast a what's-wrong-with-you face in my direction as if he hadn't dropped the biggest knowledge bomb of the day on me.

"So the Kappa's real?" I asked, again. The little pink satin robe Lucien had lent me to visit Allan's chambers barely covered my crotch. From the draft my backside kept getting, it failed to conceal my ass. But that's not what made me uncomfortable.

Allan's "chambers" included a main sitting room and lounge area, but instead of being stocked full of BDSM paraphernalia like handcuffs, chains, or a rack, it appeared shockingly *normal*, almost like grandma's house. Soft brown leather sofas, a cream carpet devoid of blood stains, beautiful enlarged photos of Japanese land-scapes. No subs running around serving us. No stench of fear clogging my nose. Just Allan's vampy scent and rose petals. He must have space in the dungeons for his playroom.

Allan tilted his head, probably reading every thought as it flittered through my head. "You're a post-Purge supe. Are you honestly questioning the possibility that Kappas exist?"

I didn't bother correcting him. I was born in the first

year of the Purge, so technically the prefixes post and pre, didn't apply to me. "The encyclopedia mentioned flying cucumbers. It's a bit hard to swallow."

Yes, the Purge had revealed the existence of the supernatural, but if vegetables started flying about like magic fucking carpets, I'd lose it. Stan had looked at me sideways when I'd told him my suspicions.

Allan laughed. "That was a part of the children's bedtime stories. To soften the harsh reality. The Kappa is more powerful and deadlier than that."

"Great..."

Allan's lip quirked. And then he stilled. His nose flared, and his fangs elongated. "Do you fear the unknown, little girl?"

Any fear I had dissipated. "Down boy. It takes more than a little water sprite to scare me."

He looked thoughtful. "Noted."

I groaned.

He smiled.

"How much more badass is the Kappa compared to what I've read? Give me the basics."

Allan wrapped his tie around his collar and deftly tied it in place. "I've never met one."

I folded my arms and dug my toes into the plush carpet. "Postulate."

"They're human sized. Their backs are hardened with a material like a tortoise shell. They're green, scaly, and have a beak for a mouth. They lure children to the water and drown them."

"Why?"

"Why not?"

My eyes narrowed.

"They absorb energy through physical contact, much like Vampires gain life through drinking blood. I'm assuming they target children because they're easier to lure and control."

"Yet this Kappa is now targeting supes—not exactly helpless or vulnerable."

"Maybe this Kappa is more...what's the phrase you like so much? Badass?"

I pursed my lips. "What kind of water?"

Allan frowned.

"Where does a Kappa live? Fresh water like rivers and lakes. Oceans?"

"I'm not sure."

"We're on the West Coast. I can't walk five fucking kilometres without falling into a body of water." I flung my hands up in the air.

"Then it looks like you will be doing a lot of walking and falling, kitten."

Our eyes met and the gleam in his eyes read, "No help here."

"So I'm looking for a humanoid turtle in a body of water?"

Allan moved with Vampire grace to one of his couches and sat down. "Yes."

"Anything else?"

"It has incredibly strong psionic abilities. Your

Shifter mind should be harder for it to penetrate, but I would keep your animals close." He waved his hand at the other couch.

"How do I defeat it?" I flopped down on the soft cushions, tugged down my robe and pinned my knees together.

"The Kappa is said to be incredibly courteous," Allan said.

"It drowns children."

Allan shrugged. Not seeing the contradiction.

"So kill it with kindness?"

"In the bedtime stories, the hero defeated the Kappa by bowing to it. Obsessed with being polite, the Kappa bowed back. The water in the bowl spilled out and with an empty bowl, it could no longer move." He gave me a pointed look. "That would be the time to strike."

"What bowl? I read nothing about a bowl, only that they looked something like a mutant turtle."

Allan grunted and leaned back. "The *sara*. It's an indentation on the top of their head that resembles a bowl. It's the source of their power and contains water from their habitat. It needs to be full in order for the Kappa to travel on land. If it drains or spills out, the Kappa can't move. It is said if a human refills the bowl, the Kappa will serve them for all eternity."

"So I have to find it, lure it out of the water, and get it to bow to me?" I snapped my fingers. "Easy peasy."

Allan dipped his head in acknowledgment and adjusted his jacket.

"Do you sleep in your suit?"

"Interested in my sleeping habits?" Allan's lips twitched. "Clint will be jealous."

"Ugh." I threw my hands up. "You two are insufferable. Not everything is an innuendo."

"Ah, but when faced with a curvy female, it's hard not to take it as such."

"Not your type." The urge to tug at my skimpy robe again gnawed at me, but I bit the inside of my lip and ignored it.

"I merely like to play your strings. You rise to the bait so easily, little kitten."

A big whoosh of air escaped my lungs. Bantering with Allan could only distract me from my problems so long. "What am I going to do?"

Lure it, my fox whispered. *Use a norm.*

My cat hissed, but I wasn't sure if it was in agreement or agitation. The fox spoke out of turn.

"Lucien only tasked you to find out who was behind the attacks."

My head snapped up. "You're right. Will you pass the message to him? I'm going to get the heck out of here before he orders me to do more."

"He'll call you back."

"I know. But I could use the time off. And I'm not sure I'm the best candidate for taking the Kappa down."

"You do need to work on your ground game," Allan agreed.

I imagined punching him in the kidneys, which elicited a bark of laughter from him.

"Good night, kitten."

"Night." I stood, dropped the robe and shifted into my falcon. The cool night air, my one constant companion, refreshing and calming, met me as I flew out Allan's window. Mentally ticking items off my to-do list, I realized how much I had left to do.

30

"You've been avoiding my calls." Booth's craggy voice rattled the speakers on my phone. "Why?"

The small window of reprieve from Lucien would be used to close my Herman Assignment. I couldn't avoid it any longer, but it didn't make what I would say to Booth any easier. Taking a deep breath, I whispered into the phone. "I know where he is."

"Where?"

"Why don't I take you there? We can retrieve him together." I crossed my fingers, hoping he'd be at the house this time.

"I'm at the office. Pick me up."

"Be there in fifteen minutes." No need to tell her I was already on my way. I made it in ten to find Booth already waiting for me in front of the building. She wrung her hands together, but as soon as she saw me pull up with my car, she untangled them and let them fall to her sides.

Booth nodded, opened the door and slid in without a word. Not even a comment on the squeaking hinges or dented side panels. I glanced at her out of the corner of my eye, but she stared straight ahead. If only I could read her scent. Her eyes had a glazed sheen to them. Anxious? Nervous? Hard to tell.

She didn't initiate conversation and we rode in the car in absolute silence. Thank fuck. I didn't have to dodge or evade awkward questions like: *Where is he?* Or, *where are we going?*

When I pulled up to the house, Agent Booth frowned. "This is my mother's house."

I placed a hand on Booth's arm. "Were you close to your mom?"

Booth shook off my hand. "I visit her for Christmas and on her birthday. We have little in common."

I nodded. My mind raced to find a gentler way of breaking the news to Booth.

Booth's gaze slid to mine. "What do you mean *were*?"

The breath I'd been holding escaped in one big whoosh of air. "She's dead."

Booth sat silently for what seemed like hours, but in reality only amounted to a few minutes. Her fingers tapped on the armrest. "Herman?"

I shook my head. "No. Appeared to be natural causes, but I think Herman's been using her place as a hideout. I had to leave your mom so he wouldn't know I'd found him. I'm sorry. It's been weeks. You may not want to see her."

Booth's eyebrows pinched in the middle, giving her

an even sterner appearance. After a few minutes, her face smoothed out and she sighed. "I've seen bodies in decomp before. Like I said, we weren't close. Let's get Herman."

She wrenched the door open and hopped out with an almost energetic bounce, as if she was a ten-year-old arriving at an amusement park instead of a middle-aged woman about to see her mother's decomposing body.

I clasped the door handle, muscles tense. Booth's cold reaction to her mother's passing didn't sit well. Even if they weren't close, I expected...more. Maybe not hysterics or tears, but something to indicate Booth had a soul. Her behaviour was odd.

I narrowed my eyes at her back. No scent. No feelings. *What are you?*

More than one fera growled in my head. My skin prickled and my muscles coiled. I staggered and braced against the car, pressing my forehead against the hot metal. My mountain lion pushed, and the beast stirred. I took a few deep breaths, preventing the shift.

When I looked up, Booth glared back. She waited for me with crossed arms and a tapping foot. Without words, I joined her, and we walked to the house, not bothering to hide our approach. Booth seemed unaffected by my reaction to her odd behaviour.

"Should we sneak around back?" I asked.

Booth scoffed and held up a gold key. "Unnecessary."

I followed her lead. We entered the home without knocking and paused briefly for Booth to study her dead mother from a few feet away. The smell of decay hit me like a wall and I shuddered. Booth pursed her lips and carried on.

What the fuck? My skin shivered, and my falcon pecked at the inside of my skull. She wanted out. She wanted to fly away from this creepy moment.

My feet weighed a ton as I lugged them up the stairs behind Booth, now moving faster and with a spring in her step. We found Herman in the bedroom that doubled as a shrine to Booth.

He spun around at our entrance, eyes wide. I crouched and readied for an attack.

The air, hot and rank with the smells of death, stifled my breath as we waited. Waited for what? I took a step forward, then hesitated. Booth stood relaxed, with her lips curled into an almost timid smile. No look of concern marred her middle-aged face. I straightened up and took a step to the side. Whatever was going on here, it didn't involve me.

"Ren," Herman breathed, gaze settled on Booth. His forehead wrinkled, and he shook his head back and forth. Why was he calling Booth that name? Ren? It looked like he was asking himself the same question.

"Sobek." Booth waved her hands, indicating for him to come to her.

He tilted his head. "My name's Herman."

"Sobek," Booth repeated. "Come here."

Herman stumbled toward her, arms flopping at his sides, gaze still transfixed on her face, almost trance-like.

His eyes remained wide, yet soft. When he stopped a foot in front of her, she took off her glasses.

Herman staggered. "Ren?" he whispered. "I don't...I don't understand."

That made two of us.

"You will, Sobek. You will." She did something weird with her hands—the thumb of her right hand pressed against the centre of his forehead as she gripped his head. The thumb of her other hand poked the centre of his chest while her hand rested against his pectoral muscle.

Huh?

She mumbled something, repeating herself, over and over again.

I leaned closer.

"Remember," she said. "Remember."

Herman's glazed eyes cleared, and he looked at Booth, really looked at her, as if seeing her for the first time. "Renenutet," he whispered. "My love."

Before I could say, "get a room," the two were making out like a couple of high school students at their first dance, with me awkwardly standing to the side.

"I...umm...I'll give you some space." I backed out of the room. They didn't notice.

From my car, I texted Booth the information about the Kappa. I'd forgotten to tell her about the Supe Slayer when I first saw her because, well, I didn't want to initiate conversation in the car and somehow later...it seemed a bit inappropriate for the moment. And now, I knew she was indisposed. I hoped the text would fulfill my agreement to her.

I scrolled through my messages and bit my lip. I'd texted Wick and Tristan the information about the Kappa as soon as I found out, but hadn't heard back from either of them. Had the Kappa already gotten to them? Was I too late?

I picked up my phone and paused. Who did I call first? Tristan or Wick? Or should I stop by and check up on them? But which one first? They didn't exactly live on the same block. They were both powerful Alphas. They should be all right. Maybe I could send another group text to them and ask if they were okay.

Coward.

I blew air out of my lungs and stared at my stupid cell phone as if it should give me the answers.

It vibrated, and then started chirping. Tristan's name popped up on the screen.

My heart caught in my throat. I fumbled the phone, but somehow managed to hit the right button. "Hello?" I answered, my voice hitting several octaves above natural.

"Where are you?" he asked.

"About to drive home. Why?"

"I want to make sure you're safe. This Kappa...if it has psionic abilities, it could pick up from others that you're onto him, or her. I don't like the idea of you being alone."

"Being alone is probably the safest thing for me right now. The thing is drawn to groups of supernaturals. No way am I having a party."

Tristan paused. "Will you let me check in on you?"

"Promise to behave?"

"Absolutely not," he said.

"I have some research to do. Give me a couple hours."

His voice was all purr. "So you can anticipate my visit? Deal."

I groaned, knowing I'd made a mistake somehow and said goodbye.

At the next stoplight, I checked my phone—still no reply from Wick. My chest hollowed out. I dialled his number, and it went straight to voicemail. Instead of turning at the next intersection, which would take me home, I kept straight and headed for Wick's, my heart hammering in my chest.

CARS LINED THE STREET, AND I HAD TO PARK two blocks from Wick's. What the hell? I slammed my car door in frustration and trekked to the house. I heard voices, laughter, and music from a distance and knew what brought everyone to his home. *Idiot!* He was having a pack meeting? Now, of all times? Sure, tonight was a full moon, but still...

When I stomped into the living room, anger prevented me from tossing my purse on the counter like I normally did. Most of Wick's inner circle, including Wick, sat on the couches. And Christine. She sprawled across Wick's lap, straddling him. Her head twisted around like a possessed Chucky doll to cast me a smug smile. The she-bitch had challenged me for dominance a few weeks ago and lost in front of her entire pack. She hated my guts because she wanted to be at Wick's side, and he wanted me. Or so I thought.

Maybe Wick preferred a sure thing to the unknown challenge I represented. His hand on her ass definitely attested to that.

Bite, my wolf demanded

Bite all of them, my fox twitched.

"Wow." I eyed Christine and a now frozen Wick. "Typical."

"Hi, Andy." A shy voice had me turning to see Jess, one of the shewolves in Wick's pack, right before she enveloped me in a hug. "It's good to see you."

"Um...thanks." I patted her back a bit awkwardly until she let me go. Everyone else remained frozen. Wick struggled to get Christine off. She clung to him like an octopus, but he peeled off her limbs, picked her up, and dumped her on the cushion beside him. When he turned to face me, I stilled.

"It's not—"

I held my hand up and interrupted him. "What it looks like? Spare me. You didn't answer your phone, so I came to tell you the Supe Slayer is a Kappa—a water supe capable of psionic mind control. Loves cucumbers and is attracted to large amounts of energy, which we already knew. Pretty stupid to have a pack meeting, if you ask me." I gave Wick my best death stare. "Pretty stupid in general."

"It's a full moon tonight." Wick's voice was quiet. Full moon was the only time of the month Weres had no choice but to shift. They also tended to be the horniest at this time. I knew from experience with Dylan's pack. A sharp pang stabbed my chest, and it became difficult to breathe. I wheezed in to fill my lungs.

Wick's hands hung at his sides. With round eyes and a partly opened mouth, he walked a few steps toward me.

"Ah." I turned my gaze to Christine, who glared back at me. Wick froze. "That explains a lot."

"Did you want to join us, Andy?" Christine's voice was snide.

"Not at all." I spun on my heel and left a sputtering Alpha behind me. Not even the scent of how he felt could catch up to me, and for that, I thanked the beast goddess.

Wick didn't chase after me. He didn't call out.

Confirmation of his guilt.

My heart shrivelled up into nothing, and my eyes stung. I blinked and blinked, refusing to let the tears fall.

He wasn't worth it. Was he? No. No, I wouldn't let a man make me feel like this again.

My mom had always told me, "No man is worth your tears and the one who is, won't make you cry."

I didn't know who she quoted. I didn't try too hard to find out. For some reason, I liked that it came from her.

31

Was it unreasonable to expect a grown virile male to stay nookie-free when women threw their bodies at him? Especially when I kept him at arm's length? True, I hadn't committed to either Were. Technically, Wick and I didn't have an exclusive relationship. We hadn't had *the* conversation, hadn't slept together. Not like him and Christine.

My heart spasmed when another stabbing pain unleashed.

Well, okay. I only knew Christine wanted Wick, not if he reciprocated the feelings, or whether they'd had a physical relationship. I squeezed my eyes shut, but the scene kept replaying in my mind. Her body draped over his. They hadn't been making out, but his hand...his large calloused hand...had spanned to cup her ass and hold her in place.

More could've happened after I left. Or might've happened had I not shown up and ruined the mood.

Maybe something had already occurred and I witnessed post-coital cuddling instead of the preamble to foreplay. I'd been naïve enough to believe Wick remained abstinent while pursuing me, but seeing Christine all over him ripped off the blinders. I wouldn't assume good behaviour from anyone anymore.

Cynical? You bet.

Maybe I acted unreasonable. After all, Tristan's hand had been on my ass the way Wick's had been on Christine's. Didn't that make me as bad as Wick?

No.

Not in my opinion. And that's what hurt. I'd been upfront and honest with Wick. My animals pulled me in two different directions to two different mates. When things got hot and heavy with Tristan, I'd stopped him from having his wonderful way with me out of respect for Wick. But then, to find Wick in the arms of Christine, not affording me the same respect or transparency... If blood could boil in a living body, mine did.

The plastic steering wheel squeaked under my hands as I clutched it tightly and banged my forehead against it. A few honks sounded behind me, and I looked up to find a green light. I couldn't get home fast enough. When I finally slammed the door to my apartment behind me, I locked it and went straight for the Canadian Club. Nothing like the burn of whiskey to wipe away the image of Wick and Christine sitting in a tree.

After a few swigs and some embarrassing coughing, I enjoyed the fleeting dizziness of inebriation. My high metabolism quickly demolished the floating feeling, and the cold stark fall back to sobriety followed. I couldn't even get drunk right.

One more group remained to warn about the Kappa. I capped the bottle and promised CC I'd be back soon. Deep down, I knew it was for the best that my speedy metabolic rate prevented more than a moment of drunkenness. I couldn't drown my sorrows in a bottle. Nobody could. It only made it worse in the end.

Dragging my feet, I made my way down the hall and pounded on my neighbour's door. When it was finally flung open, I had a second to register Christopher's angry face before he blew a fine white dust into my face.

"What the hell?" I batted at the air in front of me. I started sneezing. The powder flew into my nose and stuck there, clogging my lungs. My mouth gaped open, sucking back long dregs of air, only to take in more of the vile powder. I stumbled and sank to the floor. Christopher stood over me with a smug look on his face, unaffected by my suffocation.

The beast rose. I squashed her back down. *Not needed*. My mind sought the mountain lion and I willed the change. The process dislodged the powder as my feline form flowed forth and wiped out the more fragile human one. I gathered my strength, belly low and stared down my enemy, my prey.

Christopher's eyes widened as I hissed and stalked forward. He staggered backward, tripped on the carpet and caught himself from falling by latching onto the door frame. He mouthed the word, "No."

Too late, I hissed. Muscles tense, ears back, I prepared to pounce.

"What the hell?" Ben bellowed, running up behind Christopher. "What's going on?"

I blinked. Then, I stopped snarling. Realizing how close I came to leaping and tearing the Witch apart, I sat down and waited to hear the full story. My tail twitched.

Christopher turned his mute stare to Ben. He didn't say anything—wouldn't or couldn't—I didn't care. One false move and I'd detach his head from his shoulders. He tried to kill me and I wasn't in a forgiving mood.

Christopher jammed a bottle of white powder into Ben's hand. It had a label. Ben quickly read it and started sputtering. "Why would you do that? Do you have any idea how dangerous she is?"

I purred at the compliment, and they both glanced in my direction. Ben cast me a nervous smile and Christopher gave me a death stare. *That's it. Off with his head.* My purring stopped, replaced with a deeper, more volatile rumble. I shunted my weight to my hind limbs.

"No!" Ben threw his arms wide and stood in front of Christopher. "Andy, stop. Please. He's sensitive about not speaking, and you insulted him."

I yowled.

Ben cringed and moved his hands up and down in a frantic effort to get me to calm down. "I know! I know! He shouldn't have tried to kill you. He should be punished, and he will. But please, not death. He's a victim here as much as you."

Christopher twitched, and my attention snapped to him.

"Matt! Patty!" Ben called out over his shoulder. "Get Chris out of here."

I tilted my head and listened to the other two Witches scurry over to haul Christopher out of my line of sight. My eyes narrowed at Ben. He took away my prey.

"Please. Shift back. Let's talk."

If anyone understood emotional damage, it was me.

It took me over thirty-three years to get over the majority of my past, and it still came back to kick my ass from time to time. Christopher obviously had Demons to fight like me. Did that make his actions okay? No. But dammit, I liked these Witches.

I huffed and shifted back. My limbs tingled from the quick, successive transformations. To hide the shaking of my body, I placed a hand on my hip and glared at Ben.

Ben's eyes rounded and did an up and down dance until he trained them on the ceiling. "You're naked!"

"Of course, I'm naked. Clothes don't shift with me." I pointed to my shredded clothes, but the gesture was lost on him. He made an effort to look anywhere but at me, so he missed it. "You owe me a new outfit."

"Yeah, of course, whatever. Can you go put some clothes on?"

I folded my arms over my boobs and cocked a hip. "Now why would I want to do that? I've got nothing to be ashamed of, and I like that this makes you uncomfortable. You need to put a leash on your friend, or I will kill him." My falcon screeched her approval in my head.

Ben nodded, gaze still averted. "Understood."

"I also came to warn you."

Ben glanced at me. His eyes quickly travelled down before he caught himself and looked up at the ceiling again. "What about?"

"The Supe Slayer is a Kappa. It uses psionic powers to control humans to attack groups of supernaturals. He gets the humans to drag them to the nearest body of water so he can feed off their energy. We're pretty close to the river, and you live with a bunch of other Witches. I thought you should know. Maybe mix up some potions and fortify yourselves against an attack or something."

"Thanks, Andy. We owe you." His gaze flicked to my face.

I gave him a pointed stare. "You have no idea."

AFTER GETTING ALL THE LOCATIONS OF HUMAN attacks, supe bodies and human bodies suspected of being involved with the Supe Slayer from Stan over the phone, I started mapping the incidences to determine the location of the Kappa. Stan hadn't been too supportive, claiming if an entire division of cops couldn't find a link from the data, there was no way I would. Silently, I agreed with him, but my pride wouldn't let my mouth stay shut. I'd cursed and told him where to stick his support, and he'd muttered a half-assed good luck before hanging up.

By far my favourite cop.

Looking at my map, riddled with dots, I came up with nothing and regretted my strong words to Stan. The incidences were scattered throughout the Lower Mainland of British Columbia—rivers, streams, ocean. Nothing consistent...unless...unless they all came from the same source. I set my coffee mug back down and stumbled closer to the large map I'd pulled out and frantically pinned to my living room wall. Nope. That didn't work. Different feeder lakes—Pitt, Steve, Harrison. If backtracking didn't work, maybe looking forward would. The Fraser River was the biggest river that spliced through the area, but there were too many clusters that couldn't be linked to it for the Kappa to operate from there.

All water runs to the sea.

Gah! It was as obvious as a boner in sweatpants. Now I had an answer if anyone ever asked me what it felt like to be struck by lightning. The Kappa originated from Japan. How did it get here? Duh! The most direct route for a water supe to get to the west coast was to swim across the Pacific Ocean.

No point in getting my panties twisted trying to figure out *why* a Kappa would take such an exorbitant step to remove itself from its natural habitat, but if I extrapolated the exits of all the streams and rivers, I could find out if anything intersected. The cops wouldn't have known the origin of the supe until now. No wonder they missed it.

Tapping on my door interrupted my ruler and pencil work. I put them down and stretched my neck out as I made my way to the front door. If Christopher stood out there with another batch of magical pixie dust, I was going to—

A pile of humans burst through the door. I heard glass breaking and bodies entering through the sliding doors behind me. Spinning around, I shifted quickly to a mountain lion. Nausea slammed my body from the speed of the transformation. If I could make it to open sky, I had a chance of flying out of here.

The bright-eyed humans piled onto me, grabbing at my legs and tail and fur. I lashed out, swiping them away, but they kept coming back in waves. I tried not to hurt them too much because I knew they were victims as well, but I wasn't willing to be Kappa food to protect them.

I yowled and bucked out of the grasp of two strong men. Whipping around, I flung three people off my back, but more replaced them. Panic started to seep into my consciousness as I kept spinning and trying for the exits.

Someone shoved a burlap bag smelling of onions over my head. Snarling, I bit at it and shook violently. I couldn't get the material loose. Rope slid over my body and I barrelled away from the sensation only to meet a wall of human bodies.

The beast stirred.

No. I squeezed my eyes shut.

Let it, my fox whispered, a little red devil on my shoulder. *Embrace it.*

They managed to bind my hind limbs. I kept kicking the humans away, but the ropes dug into my fur, tightening with every movement. They'd come prepared. My front claws sank into the sack and yanked hard, but tiny human hands kept pulling the material back.

The beast started to rise.

No!

Embrace it like a fera, but keep your mind, keep it separate. The fox nudged my mind with her nose.

Keep control, my cat hissed.

We help, my wolf growled.

If my falcon said anything, the cacophony of voices in my head along with the successful binding of my front legs drowned her out and shrivelled any remaining resolve to keep the beast chained.

Instead of letting the beast overwhelm me, I embraced it, as I would any of my feras, and willed the change. Skin stretched, bones snapped.

It hurts. I'd forgotten about the pain.

Teeth elongated, claws protracted, scales replaced fur. My insides sent waves of sheering pain through my body as they expanded. Ribs cracked, my heart swelled, limbs stretched. As I grew in size, the ropes snapped free and the burlap onion bag ripped off. Some of the humans cried out and fell back. Rage filled every fibre of my being down to the cellular level. My body swayed as the fading pain drained from my essence and left me high on adrenaline. I hummed with energy.

I opened my eyes and squinted at the bright light. Possessed humans surrounded me with wide eyes and gaping mouths. Their limbs hung useless at their sides.

I *roared*.

32

Three unexpected things happened at once. My neighbours barged through what remained of my front door armed with all sorts of Witch paraphernalia and looking more like the kids from *The Goonies* than characters from Modern Warfare; Wick and Tristan dove into my living room from the busted bay window, both in human form but snarling; and all the possessed human's lost the brightness in their eyes and dropped to the ground like limp sacks of potatoes.

The beast roared again, straining against my control, wanting to mete justice. *I wanted justice.* The beast represented the darkest side of me. I saw that now. With my head tipped back, hands clenched, and wings stretched out behind me, I bellowed my anger, shaking the whole building. A car alarm went off outside.

"What the hell is that?" Tristan hissed.

"I think it's Andy," Wick replied.

"Um...looks like everything's good here," Ben

mumbled. "We'll uh...We'll just go back next door." He turned to the exit, catching my attention. My eyes narrowed, my body instinctively moved to track his. *Prey*, the beast's voice chilled my blood down to the very marrow.

"Stop!" Tristan barked out.

Ben froze as if he'd stepped on a land mine and realized he couldn't step off or he'd blow up. Not far off. I tensed. My predator eyes watched every movement, waiting for an opening, waiting for weakness.

Tristan held up his hand. "Back out of the room slowly. Don't give her your back."

Wick nodded. "We don't know how much control Andy has."

I narrowed my eyes at Ben, retreating backward with his arms up. He tripped on his own feet and stumbled. *Prey*, the beast growled. I surged forward and Ben scurried out the door in a crab walk. I stood and considered going after him. My stomach rumbled. *Hungry.*

"Andy." Wick's whiskey and cream voice interrupted my thoughts and I whirled around. He stood in the middle of the room, with his hands out to the sides in a non-threatening gesture. "I am sorry about earlier."

Tristan glanced over to the Werewolf. "Probably not the time to remind her why she's pissed at you."

Wick waved him off and turned back to me. "It was not what you think."

My attention pinned down on Wick's face. *The betrayer*. Anger rose up from within like a bubble of stomach acid. I barred my teeth, and hissed.

"Those are some large fangs," Tristan mumbled.

"Can you talk, Andy?" Wick's eyes widened as I took another menacing step toward him.

"*Betrayer*," I growled, my voice ricocheted off the walls. Wick cringed and Tristan looked wary.

"That's the beast talking, Andy," Wick said.

Was it? The emotion zinging through my body felt right. Images of Christine fawning over him while she sat in his lap replayed in my mind. Then, images of their naked bodies entwined, with her straddling him while he guided her gyrating hips with his large calloused hands. They moaned together in pleasure. My attention zoned in to his palms, held out in a supplicating gesture.

"Do not let the beast use your anger to consume you." Tristan poured power into his words."It's okay to be pissed at Wick, but you don't want to kill him."

Didn't I? Emotion swirled within me before it settled a little, like dust after being disturbed. No, I didn't want to kill him. I sucked a deep breath in, while the beast, still agitated, paced in my head.

"You're safe now," Wick said.

My eyes snapped to his face, and my body turned. The fury I'd swallowed earlier rose back up and burned my throat. *Christine.*

"I have never slept with Christine. Hear the truth in my words."

Kill him, the beast growled.

No. I squashed the anger down, knowing it was ill-placed, and straightened from my threatening stance. He hadn't slept with her. *Yet.* Even if he had, that didn't justify ripping off his head. This beast wouldn't control me. My body vibrated as the beast made another attempt at a coup before withdrawing, recessing beneath the surface, simmering and waiting. I let a long breath out and my muscles relaxed.

Wick and Tristan exhaled in unison.

"I'm better now," I said. My voice didn't sound as rough or omnipotent as before, but it still sounded like it had been warped for a scary movie. "I think."

Tristan tilted his head. "You're quite breathtaking in this form. Scary, but beautiful."

I snorted, and my nostrils burned. *Ouch!* Smoke fizzled up and stung my eyes. I could breathe fire? No way.

"You should look in the mirror. See what we see." Wick nodded to the wall behind me.

Still wanting to punch him in the junk, I turned instead to catch my reflection in the hallway full-length mirror—the one I used to check out my outfits before heading out.

A deep chuckle escaped my throat. *Are you kidding me?* I looked like a dragon-human hybrid that would give a comic book geek a hard on. Dark and scaly, my body still held a vaguely human figure, only larger—at least eight feet tall—but my hands and feet, distinctly demonic, resembled those found on dragons with scaly long digits ending with talons. The obsidian scales that covered the majority of my body receded to give way to my stomach and breasts, which were lined with a dark, fine fur. My breasts were huge and round, and my nipples a bright cherry red. *Wow... just, wow.*

My back itched and wings stretched out behind me, using unfamiliar muscles. Bird wings essentially acted as front limbs, but with the Ualida, they were an extra appendage. Large and black, the skin connecting the bone and muscle tissue appeared almost translucent, letting in light from behind. *Could I fly with them?*

The face reflecting back in the mirror, however, snagged my attention. The facial features appeared familiar, mine, yet different, more extreme and reptilian with eyes slit like a dragon. My skin tone had darkened from its regular tan to match the obsidian scales and fur. Two small black horns protruded from my forehead and extended up. Large, pointed ears made it look as if I wore the fake elf prosthetics sold at Halloween. My black hair, oddly, remained the same and fell long and straight.

Then my tailbone twitched and a long spaded tail swished around my legs.

"Do you think you can shift back to human, Andy?" Wick asked. The smell of his anxiety hung sour in the air. The beast delighted in his discomfort, but I didn't like the Alpha Werewolf unsure of himself. It was wrong. Weak.

"I think so." I lied.

Tristan and Wick exchanged glances. Guess they caught that, too. I wished I could mask the scent of my emotions.

The beast didn't want to rescind her control over my body when I tried to change back. She dug her claws in and brought up all my nastiest thoughts and emotions to wear as armour. Not nice. Instead of changing back to human, I wanted to turn around and swipe Wick's head off from his shoulders. *No.* I gritted my teeth and pushed back. Next I saw Angie doing porn star worthy activities with Tristan, causing smoke to barrel out of my nose and fangs to protrude from my lips. I could not allow the beast to use my anger and insecurities against me. *No, no, no.*

All four feras rose up within my mind. Together they tackled the beast and I pushed her down, out of my head and away from the master control centre of my brain. This time, when I willed the change, it came easily.

Lying in an exhausted, naked heap on the human splattered floor, I decided I preferred not to repeat the experience for a long time, or at least not until I had a larger supply of energy drinks. My bones felt like cereal left in milk for too long.

"Andy?" Tristan asked, kneeling beside me.

Wick brushed a strand of hair away from my face. "Are you okay?"

I groaned and rolled over. "Yes," I muttered. "What are you both doing here?"

"I came to explain." Wick cast Tristan a wary look, but went on. "Christine must have heard you approach before I did. She took advantage of my distraction and pounced on me. When you came in, you shocked the hell out of me. I was trying to untangle myself from her."

My nose flared. His words, all true, but his hand had clutched her ass and he hadn't looked like a struggling victim until after he saw me. *Did I have any right to be angry? And even if I didn't, would his pretty words make this pain go away?*

Tristan watched us both, eyelids lowered to hide his thoughts, but burnt cinnamon wafted off his skin and gave his emotions away. Anger...on my behalf?

Not ready to deal with All-Things-Wick, I turned to the Wereleopard and ignored Wick's hurt expression. "And you?"

Tristan gave me a half smile and shrugged. "Came to seduce you." He jerked his thumb in Wick's direction. "Then I saw this one lurking outside."

"Lurking?" His low growl provided a small warning before he dove over my body and slammed into Tristan.

atching two strong men grapple, slinging curses, and trading blows, I felt no motivation to break it up. They weren't trying to kill each other, not really, or they would've sustained more damage by now. I sat back amongst the passed out humans and watched as the men alleviated pent up tension.

One of the norms beside me moaned and rolled over, rubbing her temples. Her eyes fluttered open and then widened as they took in my appearance.

I looked down. *Oh right.* No clothes. Grunting, I got up, ignored the cry of my stiff muscles, and shuffled into the bedroom. The closest sweatpants and T-shirt would have to do. I hoped they were clean.

Didn't smell like it.

When I came back out, Tristan and Wick still tumbled around on the floor with their hands around each other's throats, disregarding the norms they steamrolled. I put my hands on my hips and trained my face to look more serious. Inwardly, I found it kind of funny. Their faces turned redder by the minute.

"When you two are done whatever pissing contest you're participating in, I need your help. The humans are waking up, and I'd like to escort them out of my home."

I didn't wait to see them untangle; instead, I turned and found my cell phone and called Stan.

He picked up after the first ring. "Officer Stevens."

"I have about twenty Kappa victims passed out in my living room. Alive." I prattled off my location in case he forgot the time he'd barged through my door. "Please come and collect them. They might have retained helpful information."

"You live out of my jurisdiction."

"Then send someone else. I'm sure you have contacts." I jabbed the off button before he could issue another excuse. Cops! I might like the guy, but right now I wanted to tell Stan exactly where to shove his *jurisdictions*.

My phone beeped with a text message from Stan:

20 Minutes.

I deduced from the lack of a happy face that he was a bit pissed at me. *Whatever.* He didn't turn into an eight-foot scaly monster tonight, so I'm pretty sure I won the "Shitty Night" contest.

True to his word, Stan arrived twenty minutes later

with several transport vans to haul the humans away. Most of them were too groggy to walk unassisted, which worked for me. I didn't want them to remember me or where I lived. Talk about an uncomfortable intercom conversation. *Why was I at your place unconscious? A Kappa brainwashed you to abduct me. Thanks for visiting. You can go now.*

I watched them load up the last of the wobbly humans into one of the vans and crossed my arms over my shirt. It was cold out tonight, and in my haste to clothe myself, I hadn't bothered with a bra. Even if I couldn't feel it, the cops staring at my chest and stumbling up and down the stairs as they carted around the Kappa victims, told me my nipples stuck out like the knobs of a game controller, begging for someone to start playing.

"What are you going to do?" Wick walked to stand beside me.

My body stiffened. I still didn't know how to respond to him. Part of me wanted to jump his bones and the other part wanted to slap him.

"Are you still angry with me?" he asked. His right eye was swollen and he had a large scratch down his cheek. Tristan had given him a few good ones.

Yes. No. "I don't know."

Wick's lips pursed. "Andy, I am sorry you are upset, but you have no reason to be."

"Maybe. But that doesn't mean I can forget. You didn't look horrified to have Christine all over you."

"I am a man, Andy."

"What's that supposed to mean? How does having a dick make it okay?"

"Having a d—No! That's not what I..." He took a deep breath. His cheeks rippled as he clenched his jaw. "It is the full moon. And when a woman rubs herself all over me, it's hard to ignore. It doesn't help that you are not mine. Not yet."

I puffed my cheeks out, unsure of how to react.

"You have no right to be angry at me for this," he said.

An unpleasant prickling ran up my spine. "You can't tell me how I can or cannot feel, *Brandon*."

Wick recoiled. His lips flattened out and his muscles tensed. "You have been running around with another man, letting him put his hands all over you, put his mouth all over you, and *you* are going to get upset at *me* because I did not automatically throw Christine on her ass when she pounced on me? Because it took me by surprise and I did not react right away?"

"You seemed to have no problem *reacting*."

Wick closed his eyes and clenched his offending hands. "The moon madness had already sunk in. It is stronger for an Alpha than anyone else, I feel it coursing through everyone in my pack. My thoughts are always on you. When a womanly shape started rubbing against me, I believed it was you at first. So, yeah, I reacted. That is why I did not fling her off me right away."

"Oh."

"That's it? That is all you have to say to me?" Wick inhaled deeply again. "Are you not being hypocritical?

Or, are you looking for an excuse to give up on us and run the other way?" He glanced over his shoulder at Tristan, who stood about twenty feet away with the cops.

The hollow feeling in my gut didn't close up with Wick's confession. The heavy sadness still tugged my heart deep into my chest and I kept picturing him with Christine. Did he want an apology? Probably. Did I owe him one? Probably. Maybe I was being hypocritical.

Wait a fucking minute. How'd he turn this around to be my fault?

Wick watched my face and the smell of burnt cinnamon grew heavier in the air around us. "Fine," he bit out, coming to some conclusion. "What are you going to do about the Kappa?"

I swallowed, not liking Wick's anger or the emotional distance growing between us. I didn't know how to fix it. Did I want to? His tie with Lucien meant an unsure future for our relationship anyway, especially if I managed to find a way out of my bond to the Master Vampire. Maybe distance was for the best.

And maybe I was sabotaging this relationship to make the choice easier.

"Not sure," I said, answering his question about the Kappa. "Don't think I can sit back and let someone else handle it though. Feels like the Kappa sent those humans after me personally. His habits are evolving."

Tristan, who'd been saying goodbye to Stan, walked up to us with a blank expression. He didn't have a black eye like Wick, but he sported a bruised jaw and he walked with a slight limp. He probably heard my entire conversation with Wick. He definitely caught the last part because he commented. "If the Kappa's psionic skills are so strong, he might've read from a human mind that you were onto him."

"Not that many people know."

"Besides Lucien's horde, my pack and I'm assuming Tristan's prowl?" Wick's face darkened when he spoke of Tristan and more burnt cinnamon wafted off of him. I guess he didn't like that I'd warned the Wereleopards. He didn't like a lot of things about me right now.

"Andy!" Stan shouted.

I looked up at the officer and we exchanged nods before he hopped in a cruiser and drove off. A convoy of police cars and vans followed him and left me on the empty sidewalk with two hot Alphas. Wick's statement teased my neurons. Sure the Vampires, Werewolves and Wereleopards knew, but...

"They're all supes, though," I said. "The Kappa can't mess with our minds easily, or so I'm told. Not a lot of norms know," I said.

"Besides the entire Vancouver Police Department?" Tristan pointed out. "And whatever vamp tramps are milling around Lucien's court."

I grunted. Trust a security expert to point out the details. "Point taken."

My phone pinged at the same time as Wick's. I didn't need to check it to know it was a summons to Lucien.

"Lucien," Wick confirmed, tucking his phone back in his front pocket. "He wants us at his place right away."

"I'd like to come," Tristan said. His request surprised me.

Wick whirled around and narrowed his eyes at the Wereleopard. His body vibrated.

"Why would you voluntarily place yourself in the demesne of a Master Vampire again?" I asked.

"His animal to call is a wolf, not a leopard. He'll have no control over me that way, and he's already bonded two servants. That's a pretty rare feat, and I doubt he could bind a third."

"But your bloo—" I started.

He held a hand up at my objection before I could stammer it out. "This concerns your safety, so it concerns me too. I'd like to help take this Kappa down. Besides, it will eventually turn to my leopards again."

"You could leave." Wick grunted.

Tristan sapphire irises turned cold as he gave Wick a dark look.

Wick shrugged. "You don't have to stay. You are not under Lucien's control. Not yet anyway."

Tristan turned back to me, ignoring Wick. "Please ask Lucien if I can participate with the planning and have safe passage."

I tapped the message out on my phone.

Lucien's response was immediate. *Bring the pussy cat.*

34

Lucien sat like a fucking stone on his throne-like chair. His face showed no emotion, and with the room reeking of vampire death and decay, I couldn't sniff for any clues. I'd give Clint's left nut to know what thoughts hid behind his dead eyes. His stillness creeped me out. Should I run? Did he contemplate something nasty for me to do, like lick his shoes? I glanced down at his feet. He wore some sort of reptile footwear tonight.

It had been five minutes since I unloaded all the information I'd gained—everything I knew, thought and guessed about the current Kappa situation. He'd interrupted a couple of times to ask some questions for clarification, but otherwise he remained silent. When I finished, his eyes went vacant and his muscles relaxed as if he withdrew to the recesses of his mind. He sat like that for five long minutes.

"So." Lucien's voice shattered the silence like a kid's baseball through a window. He blinked a couple of times, seeming to focus his eyes. His muscles tightened to give him his usual controlled demeanour, every movement efficient and intended. "He's tapping into the norms in order to spy and keep tabs on us," Lucien summarized, propping his chin up with his fist while he sat forward on his throne, looking like Auguste Rodin's *Thinker*.

Everyone stood at attention, waiting.

"Thoughts?" Lucien might've spoken softly, but he may as well have barked out a command, because power flowed through his words.

"We need to pinpoint the Kappa's location," Allan replied. "Andy's narrowed it to somewhere along the coast."

Lucien barked out a short laugh. Obviously, not impressed.

"Better than what we had before," Allan muttered. "But..." He broke off and his brows bunched together like two bighorn sheep butting heads. He turned away and started pacing.

"Allan?" Lucien's face twitched. "Any thoughts on how to locate the Kappa?"

Allan shook his head and continued stalking back and forth.

"Can you pinpoint where on the coast?" Lucien turned me.

"I was in the process of doing that when the humans attacked me. It would take some time and if I do find a common point of interest, it wouldn't necessarily mean that's where we'll find the Kappa."

Lucien smirked. "We need to find some way to locate this creature before it acquires more humans."

Use someone, my fox whispered. *Use bait.*

"We could use someone." I cleared my throat, uncomfortable that I acted on the fox's suggestion without thinking it through. "Use someone as bait. Then follow to find his little hidey-hole."

Silence met my suggestion. Lucien showed nothing, of course, and the two Weres looked pissed I'd spoken up. Their scents and clenched fists gave them away. It didn't take much to figure out why they weren't pleased. Over-protective, much?

"No." Allan's voice caused everyone to jump except Lucien. He spun in our direction. "We don't want to meet the Kappa on his own turf. It's his or her power base, and we'd have no way to stop it." Allan took a deep breath. "We'd play right into its hands."

I let out an exasperated groan. This is why I'd hated working in groups at school—everyone shot my ideas down and nothing got done. It annoyed the hell out of me.

"We need to get the Kappa to come to us." Allan tapped his chin.

"We'll need some tasty bait for that," Clint said.

Then silence fell over the room like fresh snow blanketing grass fields at night.

"Use me," I said. All eyes turned to me. I held my hand up against whatever protest Wick was about to give and ignored Tristan's deep growl. "We feed false information to some humans about the big, bad Carus, being alone somewhere. Maybe more than one norm and then set them loose. With his psionic skills, he'll read the information straight from their minds. He'll know by now his possessed norms weren't successful in capturing me. So if he wants to feed on the buffet that is my supe energy..." I waved to indicate my body in a way that would make Vana White proud. "...he'll have to come himself."

"Did you just refer to your energy as a buffet?" Clint asked.

"Don't be jealous. Doesn't suit you."

Clint grunted.

"What if he doesn't come and sends a hundred humans instead of twenty to capture you?" Tristan asked.

I shrugged. "I doubt he will, not when his first group failed, but if he did, we'd take care of it."

"They're only *humans*." Lucien flicked his fingers up in the air.

I wasn't going to touch that comment. Some supes were technically *human*, too, just not normal. Some said Shifters descended from the beast goddess, Feradea.

"Why would he risk coming after you?" Wick asked.

"Um...hello? Energy buffet?" I waved my hands around my body again.

Wick cleared his throat. "I meant, why would he think he'd get you when his humans could not?"

"He doesn't need to drag me anywhere. He could feed off me on-site."

Tristan and Wick growled at the same time, then glanced at each other and stopped. Tristan folded his arms. "He'll have to think he can best you in some way."

"We could tie her up in an abandoned warehouse near the ocean," Clint suggested. Somehow I didn't think he was interested in capturing the Kappa anymore.

"He will send more humans," Wick grumbled.

"No," Allan objected. "He wouldn't. The humans wouldn't be able to transport her. Once they undid the restraints, Andy would best them all over again. But if she was tied up, and we told the humans we drugged her or Lucien commanded her to stay, the Kappa could gain entry into the warehouse and feed off her without any struggle and minimal expended effort."

Tristan and Wick exchanged a glance. They wore almost identical grim expressions. If they banded together, I might lose my resolve.

"Use me," Tristan said.

"Can you mind speak to the others?" I asked. "We'd have to bring in your prowl and I know you don't want to risk them. Let me do this. It will work."

"Whatever lifts your skirt," Clint said.

Tristan and Wick looked less convinced. Unease radiated off them and swirled in a heady mix that stuck in my nose and made me sneeze. Allan handed me a tissue.

Wick clenched his jaw and refused to make eye contact.

Tristan's mouth turned down and his calculating gaze darted around the room. "Is this what you want to do?" he asked.

"No. But I don't hear any better ideas."

"Perfect." Lucien clapped his hands, making us jerk and look in his direction. "We need to select humans. Allan—make arrangements for the warehouse. Clint—bring in the girls." He snapped his fingers, slipping right into the Vampire Master stereotype.

35

Some girls might actually fantasize about being strapped and chained to a large table in the middle of nowhere with a quartet of handsome males—Vampire, human servant, Wereleopard and Werewolf—looking down at them. I was definitely not one of those girls. First, with such a variety of supes, there had to be a joke in there somewhere and it bothered me that I couldn't figure it out; and second, it was way too reminiscent of my previous experience with a smelly Werehyena named Mark. He'd strapped me to an operating table to play knives with my skin.

I shivered. At least this time I was clothed and no one planned to rape me. There'd been nothing sexual in the Kappa's attacks.

"Are you okay with this?" Wick asked, his face full of concern. "It's a bit like..."

"Mark? Yeah, I'm aware." His expression touched me, but not as much as I thought it would. Part of me liked that he hurt a little. Because the "Christine" incident still stung. The petty, ugly part of me, of course.

"Who's Mark?" Tristan demanded.

I turned to the Wereleopard. "I'll tell you all about it after this mess is over."

"I'm holding you to that," he said, smoothing down my hair.

Wick snarled at Tristan.

Clint rolled his eyes and exchanged a glance with Allan before speaking. "The straps and chains aren't secure. You can pull out of them anytime. When he gets here..."

"Yeah, yeah, I'll try the bowing thing and if that doesn't work we move to Plan B."

Clint nodded, trailed a finger down my face and spun to stalk out of the room. My skin crawled. There was no need to go over Plan B. It was simple annihilation.

"Be good, kitten. Be strong. We have your back." Allan pinched my cheek before glided with vampire grace out of the room behind Clint, leaving me with Wick and Tristan. My heart fluttered. I always made fun of heroines in books who managed to fall for two guys at once, and now I found myself in a similar predicament. In my defence, my feras were as much at fault for tearing me in two directions as my heart.

Tristan leaned down to kiss me goodbye, but a loud, very unsubtle growl, stopped him. He glanced up at Wick. "Could you turn around?"

"No," Wick said with a flat voice. He might be a little pissed at me for not falling over myself to offer an apology, but he hadn't relinquished his claim on me yet.

Tristan grunted and pulled back. He pushed his forefinger along my lips. "We'll be close." He straightened and looked across the table at the Werewolf, who vibrated with anger.

Wick shifted his weight, and gestured with his hands for Tristan to get a move on. When Tristan didn't move, Wick glared at him, narrowing his eyes. They'd gone yellow, wolf angry. "I'd like to speak to Andy alone."

I didn't want to speak with Wick alone. Not until I could figure out what the hell I felt. I didn't want to make things worse between us.

The Wereleopard smiled. "What makes you think I'll give you privacy when you gave us none?" He crossed his arms.

Thank you, Tristan. Then two sets of yellow Were eyes focused on me. Uh oh. I squirmed in my...seat? Table bed? "Come on, guys. You're making me uncomfortable. Could we continue this later?"

Wick huffed and leaned down to plant a chaste kiss on my cheek. "Use your internal voice to call us. We won't allow anything to happen to you."

"For once we agree on something." Tristan nodded at him. They exchanged another look, but one less malicious. They stalked out of the room, making sure to keep more than an arm length between them.

They wouldn't go far; instead, they would stay within telepathic range. It was handy being able to communicate to the group without raising a vocal alarm.

I only hoped the Kappa wouldn't be able to eavesdrop with his formidable psionic skills.

When I participated in high school volleyball, we often played late in the evening or in all-weekend tournaments, meaning we had to catch sleep where and when we could, generally in cramped seats, bleacher stands, or on the sidelines curled up to the ball bags. I became renowned for developing this skill into an art form.

For some reason, my old expertise failed me on this occasion. Not that I wanted to sleep while waiting for a Kappa to come suck out my energy, but at least relax. Instead, I stared at the dilapidated warehouse ceiling with its exposed pipes and rusted metal with my rapidly beating heart as a musical backbeat. Cold and stagnant air carried a faint smell of fish, this place probably used as a cannery at one time. The coastal winds gusted against the ocean-side wall of the warehouse, making its presence known, but not growing in strength; no storm tonight. Aside from the wind and the occasional drip of water, the warehouse provided an eerie silence.

I adjusted my position on the table, trying to find something more comfortable. My legs and butt went numb within twenty minutes, and my back prickled, indicating it would soon follow. If the Kappa showed up right now, I couldn't slip my shackles and jump off the table quickly. I'd more likely fall on my face in a crumpled tangle of sleeping limbs.

Wiggling my toes and fingers, I worked to get blood flow back to my extremities. With no way to track time, I guessed it had been at least an hour since the boys left me. *How long is this going to take?*

I didn't dare call out and ask. Not when a maniacal Kappa with psionic skills lurked about.

Team Lucien hadn't thought this part through. What if I needed to go to the bathroom? *Oh no!* I squeezed my eyes shut. The very thought evoked the need. I flexed my thighs and tried to squeeze my knees together. Now that the thought occurred, I'd think of nothing else unless I found something to distract me.

I had no more than fifteen minutes before I either had to admit defeat and call the guys for a bathroom break or pee myself. Obviously, I'd prefer the former option, but if the Kappa was watching, it would tip him off. We needed him to believe Lucien had confined me as punishment. If Lucien's minions let me powder my nose, it would look suspicious. Lucien had a reputation of humiliating those he punished. He made them suffer.

Looks like I'll have to pee myself. And I wore my nice Brazilian thong today, too.

A scraping sound echoed from the far corner of the room. It startled me and dispelled any further bathroom thoughts. Why couldn't I smell anything? The scraping got closer, inch by inch, echoing off the wall. A deep breath dragged in from across the room, raspy and shallow. The faint scent of ocean water finally wafted to me as confirmation. The Kappa had come to play.

"Carus..." Its voice slithered around me, sounding distinctly male, but that might be too big of an assumption. "So nice to meet you."

I lifted my head off the table and looked at what could only be described as a humanoid turtle, slicked with a sheen of slime. Standing around the same height as Tristan, I'd put him at six feet, and almost the same in width; not fat, but muscular and broad with a circular body shape. The brown outline of his shell peeked around his body. His feet and hands appeared the same shape as a turtles, only man-sized. Did walking upright come natural to him?

"Wish I could say the same," I said. "You have me at a bit of a disadvantage."

A wheezing sound emitted from the Kappa.

Laughter? "Just the way I like it."

I didn't even want to entertain what else the Kappa liked.

"So which one are you?"

"Pardon me?" The scraping got closer.

"Well, you're not wearing your colour-coded headband, so I have to guess which mutant turtle you are— Donatello? You look like the bō staff type."

The wheezing sound grew louder, vibrating against my ear drums. "You joke at my expense. Not very nice."

I frowned. There something odd about this whole situation. Didn't feel right. Maybe I wasn't used to polite targets. They usually slung curses at me. "And why are you here?" I threw back at him.

Without commenting, the Kappa drew up closer, now only a few feet from the end of the table. *Close enough*. I twisted my wrists and in one fluid motion jerked my hands out of the restraints and hopped off the table. The Kappa's eyes widened.

"My name is Andy." I bowed. "Pleased to meet you."

The Kappa grunted and bent in a stiff bow to mirror my own. It looked forced, as if he struggled against a compulsion. Maybe he did. "Tamotsu," he said, grinding his teeth.

The water sloshed out of the weird bowl-shaped construction on the top of his head and splattered against the concrete floor. When Tamotsu straightened, he eyed the watery mess with a deep frown.

Set me free, Tamotsu's jarring voice rung in my head and I felt my body move forward without conscious thought. *Hand me the water.*

There was a bottle of water under the table. If plan A worked, I had to fill the bowl so the Kappa would be under my control. If I gave the water to the Kappa and he refilled his own bowl, he would remain free. Free to rampage the Lower Mainland and cause more innocent deaths.

Forget what you know, Carus. Set me free.

The compulsion to do what he asked burned my muscles; a bitter flavour coated my mouth like stomach acid. I chose not to fight it; instead, I'd use the momentum to approach the Kappa without raising his suspicions. Picking up the water bottle, I moved toward Tamotsu.

That's it, he said. *Free me.*

I nodded, like a brainwashed norm and stumbled toward him, maintaining the act as his voice curled around me. Tamotsu made another wheezing sound and motioned me closer with his hands, but instead of gifting him with the bottle, I avoided his clutching grasp and reached up to empty it in the bowl.

STOP!

His voice sank into me like claws digging into soft flesh. My hand with the bottle froze midway to the bowl on his head, suspended in the air like an offering on an altar. *What the fuck?* The compulsion was stronger than before...before I went along with it...before I gave him access to my will. I'd played right into his hands.

Help! I tried to call out to the guys, but my thoughts bounced back at me, as if an invisible shield surrounded my head blocked the outgoing message. *Help me!*

My cries echoed in my brain.

Fuck.

The Kappa's mouth twitched and he snatched the bottle from my hand. His fist swung out from nowhere and smashed into my right temple. My body whipped around in a clumsy pirouette. Then something solid impacted with the underside of my jaw. I flew through the air. Skin stuck to metal and ripped as I skidded to a stop on the commercial flooring.

The cold metal urged me to stay down and enjoy its refreshing touch, but the wheezing supe behind me had other plans. I staggered to my feet, swayed, lurched to the side and then turned around to face the Kappa. My feras screeched in defiance and the beast awoke. My vision wavered. I caught myself from falling and blinked rapidly until only one Kappa existed in front of me.

The Kappa twisted the cap off and filled the bowl on his head. He tossed the bottle to the floor at my feet, where it bounced off my shins and rolled, coming to rest against the spares I'd brought.

"Now, my sweet, I feed." His eyelids drooped, hooding his eyes, as he sniffed the air. He moaned and shuffled closer. A scaly hand clutched my arm, one clawed finger at a time enclosing around my exposed skin. "So potent. So strong." His forked tongue slithered out, tasting the air before caressing my shoulder, and then I felt it, his pull on my energy, as if he sucked me dry like a Vampire overcome with blood lust.

No! I screamed inside my mind.

Tamotsu pulled harder at my energy as I remained frozen and incapacitated by his compulsion. With each passing second, my essence drained through his contact with my skin.

"That's it," Tamotsu's slithering voice continued to roll over me and reinforced the compulsion. "Give me more. Give me all." He reached forward and gripped my other arm.

The beast inside me stirred, and instead of suppressing her, I let her rise up. Shaking the grogginess from Tamotsu's drain, she surged for dominance, breaking her chains, breaking my control, and with it the

Kappa's. My skin folded in on itself, bones cracked, pain lanced, and I watched as Tamotsu shrank in size before me.

Stop! The Kappa ordered.

I twisted my wrists around and grasped his arms as I continued to grow and stretch, skin peeling back to reveal my demonic appearance. Tamotsu lost his smug reptilian expression and his eyes widened as he drooped immobile under my grip. He still held onto my arms as they changed, thickened and lengthened, beneath his hands.

My wings spread out as the transformation completed and I roared.

The Kappa screamed.

I dropped my head and focused on his face, wondering if I could bite off his head and then spit it out.

No! Tamotsu's compulsion brushed like butterfly wings against my fortified brain. I shook it off and laughed, a deep rumbling sound. I stilled when my monstrous bellow filled the room and shook the building. Pleased with the sound and its effect, I laughed again. Fear wafted off the Kappa in heavy clumps of sweat-laden air, sickly sweet and delicious.

I inhaled deeply and licked my lips. My claws dug into his flesh, puncturing his scaly skin—so frail. With a bit of extra pressure, I could snap his bones. The sudden burst of blood in the air filled my nostrils and I tightened my grip.

Break his bones and pick them dry.

Tempting, so tempting. Raising Tamotsu up, I held him at eye level. "Give it back."

The Kappa's eyes widened. He nodded and energy flowed into my body, at first in hesitant trickles, then, as if some dam broke, it flooded my senses, pounding into my brain like storm waved against a rocky shore. I staggered back, but kept a firm grip on the Kappa with my claws. *If I fall, he's coming down with me.*

My head cleared and I straightened up to look at the now drained Kappa, appearing older somehow and more wrinkled. Shrivelled. Weak.

Prey.

Kill, my beast shrieked. When Tamotsu cringed, I realized I'd said it out loud, echoing the beast. Control slipped in and out of my grasp. I spun the Kappa upside down in my hands and shook him like a rag doll. The water plummeted from his head bowl and splashed onto the floor against my dragonesque feet. His stench of fear mixed with pain tasted succulent on my tongue. The Kappa stiffened in my arms, and I threw him to the ground.

When I pressed my right foot down, the talons of my feet slid off his shell, but pierced the scaly hide of Tamotsu's legs. *Good enough.* The sound of bones cracking rang in my ears like delightful carols. I reached down and sank my claws into his shoulders before hauling him up to throw him against the wall. He bounced off it and lay limp on the ground.

My tongue, with a mind of its own, licked my lips.

Kill.

In the back of my mind, a small fox voice screamed this wasn't me. I might've been a killer, but I was never cruel. Drawing out death never brought me joy before. I halted in my tracks, fingertips inches from Tamotsu's shivering, sprawled body. *Not me.*

Not me.

I took a deep breath and a step back. My feras leapt up inside my mind and snuggled in close to my awareness, to where they could help and lend support.

Not me. I took another step back and clung to my feras until the rage inside my mind died down.

Where were the guys? Surely they'd know something had gone wrong by now. Should I call out to them? The Kappa's control had been obliterated. A shiver raced up my spine and punched my brain. No! They couldn't see me like this again. I'd been lucky not to hurt them last time. Besides, they couldn't help with an internal battle. Drawing in a laboured breath, I turned my attention inward, calling for my feras. *Help me.*

They jumped in response and tackled the beast, bringing her down from her blood vengeance. Her desire to kill receded. My muscles strained and condensed as I half-transformed, sweat broke out on my face and trickled into my eyes, stinging them like droplets of acid. I pushed the beast inside her cage.

I staggered across the room to the spare bottles. When I reached for one, I snatched my hand back, realizing it remained clawed and beastly. Drawing in a shaky breath, I refocused and completed the change.

I collapsed to the ground in a sweaty heap, my

breathing ragged, my body humming with pain. My limbs hung limp by my sides, as heavy as cinderblocks and as malleable as noodles. I forced my eyes open and met the hard gaze of the Kappa. His body twitched as he struggled to move. I'd broken his legs.

Crap! I scrambled to my feet, snatched a water bottle and hurried to Tamotsu's side before anything else could go wrong. Who knew how fast he healed.

"Get up," I hissed, yanking hard on his arm. Pain lanced through my body.

He stumbled to straighten, groggy and incoherent. His legs oozed blood onto the industrial flooring and shook to support his weight. Twisting the cap off and tossing it to the side, I poured the water into the bowl on top of the Kappa's swaying head.

Tamotsu howled and dropped to his knees, seizing his face with both hands. He rocked back and forth, muttering in Japanese.

"Stay and obey," I said, and tried to hide my shock when he did exactly what I asked.

"As you command, Master," he croaked.

Well, I'll be damned. It worked. Now what?

36

It's done, I sent via mind speech to the guys using my best gangsta impersonation. For some reason, I felt more badass staring down at my now captive Kappa. Most of my aches and pains had dulled thanks to Lucien's blood bond, which promoted quicker healing. Within minutes, the men barged into the warehouse, moving around Tamotsu and giving him a wide berth.

Clint pulled up short. "What the hell happened to you?"

Wick stumbled to a stop a few feet from me and growled. He turned toward the Kappa, but Tristan placed a hand on his arm as if to hold him back. Wick stopped, but the sounds of his rumbling chest filled the warehouse.

Tristan's sapphire eyes remained glued to me, taking in my sweaty, naked appearance and bruised face with a quick glance up and down my body. "Are you okay?"

"I'm fine." I waved them off.

The men stiffened and glanced at Tamotsu. Did he try to order them around like he had me? Was he feeding off them? I turned to the mutant turtle. "You will do no harm, you will not put anyone under compulsion, and you will not feed, unless you have my leave." I mentally reviewed what I said to make sure I covered all my bases. Just because he was mine to control, didn't mean he couldn't act on his own. He could probably slip around orders as well as Shifters and Weres could avoid the truth without outright lying.

Allan stood in front of Tamotsu and prattled off a slew of Japanese words.

"There is no need to translate, Akihiko. I speak English. I understood her orders."

I mouthed Allan's Japanese name and made a silent note to research it later—if we all survived.

"How is that possible?" I asked.

The Kappa's reptilian eyes cut to me. "My psionic skills allow me to absorb languages easily."

Another thought crossed my mind. I snapped my fingers. "You are not to dispel the water on your head by bowing to anyone else or shaking it from your head."

Tamotsu wheezed. "My compulsion prevents me from actively pursuing freedom once bound. You need not worry. The water can only be removed by unfair means of a third party. Or..." He paused to give me a weird look. "You can, of course, order me free."

I snorted.

"What is your name?" Allan asked the Kappa.

"Tamotsu."

Allan's eyebrows furrowed above his nose, like two mice burrowing in for the winter. "Of what?" he asked.

The question made no sense to me, but apparently it did to the Kappa. He sagged in on himself as if he'd received an MMA body shot and couldn't breathe.

"Nothing," he said. "Not anymore."

"Explain." My hands flew to my hips.

The Kappa turned to me. "Tamotsu is a Japanese name for protector or defender. Akihiko has reminded me of my biggest failure. My biggest shame."

"What did you defend?"

"My nation. I defended the coast and fed only on those wishing ill to the inhabitants. I can read minds and would pluck out the evil ones from their thoughts."

"How did you end up in Canada?" I asked.

"A giant wave sent from the depths of hell. The next thing I knew, I washed up on your shore along with debris and carcasses from my homeland." Tamotsu's head dropped. "I failed. I failed them all."

I fought the instinctive urge to place a consoling hand on his shoulder when I remembered what this one creature was responsible for. "So you tried to redeem yourself by feeding off supernaturals and using humans? You're responsible for so many deaths."

"I fed off humans at first. For months. And the local authorities had no idea. It wasn't until I fed off a supe, by chance, that I realized a better food source existed. There's a higher density of paranormals in this region. It's like a buffet." The Kappa licked his lips. "I never fed off the Japanese living in the area, supe or otherwise."

"Kind of you to racially profile your victims. What happened to only feeding on evil?"

Tamotsu shrugged. "You're all evil here."

We stood in silence as we observed one another.

What was I going to do with him? I wanted to punch him in the throat for his last comment, but that was only a temporary solution. I had orders to deliver him to Lucien, but he'd just add Tamotsu to his collection of unique underlings. I risked the possibility of running across the Kappa in a future confrontation from opposite sides. The idea did not thrill me. Right now, he belonged to me. I had control. Could I send him back to Japan? He'd probably revert right back to his evil supe-slaying self the moment he got his freedom. Kill him? That was the simplest solution.

I cursed.

"That language is not attractive on a lady's tongue. It is quite unbecoming," Tamotsu said.

"Good thing I'm not a lady," I said.

"What are you going to do?" Wick leaned in and asked.

I wish I knew.

37

My mind raced through possibilities faster than I could chug down the only three water bottles I could find. The transformation to the beast and back had left me thirsty and shaken, my skin a fragile protective layer to numb bones and drained flesh. Wick and Tristan had remained in the warehouse, probably to hiss and howl at one another, but also to allow room for the Kappa in the vehicle. Once we arrived at Lucien's mansion, Allan and Clint abandoned me in the car with Tamotsu so I could recuperate while they ran inside to brief their master. The leather seats creaked, and the whole car reeked of Vampires. I found Tamotsu's ocean scent refreshing, even with its tang of seaweed.

I met the Kappa's disturbing reptilian gaze and said, "Okay, listen up, Donatello—"

"It's Tamotsu," the Kappa interrupted.

I waved him off. "Whatever. You serve me and will do

as I say. You will follow Lucien's orders, as if you served him. The only time you will not follow his directives is if they will cause me or mine harm in any way. Mine include all Werewolves from Wick's pack, including Wick, all Wereleopards in Tristan's prowl including Tristan, my four Witch neighbours—Ben, Matt, Patty and Christopher, and the police officer, Stan Stevens. If Lucien's orders will bring harm to any of the aforementioned parties or he orders you to empty your bowl, you will decline and flee to me as soon as possible. If Lucien asks you who you serve, you will tell him it's him. Is that clear?"

Tamotsu's sharp turtle mouth flicked up at the corner in what I could only assume was a smile. "Perfectly," he said, before the wheezing laugh erupted from his mouth. "Anything else, master?"

I had a sinking suspicion I'd left something out, but I couldn't figure out what. I'd never make it as a lawyer. Something niggled at my brain. All the fine print stuff gave me a headache. At least Wick and Tristan would be safe. "Am I leaving anything out?"

Tamotsu stilled. His reptilian eyes closed and a weird buzzing sound filled the room. Was he humming? "You may wish to limit who I feed on."

I snapped my fingers. "You will not feed on me or mine. You may feed on any humans or supes Lucien provides, but not to the point of death. You may not kill your food."

The Kappa nodded. "That will suffice."

"Oh." My sharp voice caused the Kappa to flinch.

"And you may not disclose any of this information to anyone, including Lucien."

The Kappa wheezed. "As you wish."

Tamotsu withdrew into himself, slouching and shoulders rounded. His eyes glazed over in a closed-off kind of way. When I hopped out of the car and walked toward the house, he took his time getting out to join me. His shuffle looked more lopsided than before. Even with his supernatural quick healing, he still hurt from our fight.

"You killed a lot of innocent people," I said, trying to assuage the guilt broiling in my gut by reminding myself what this supe was capable of when untethered.

Tamotsu nodded. "Serving a Vampire is a worthy punishment for my transgressions. I will make you proud and bring honour to your house." He straightened as the guards opened the front doors of the house. Lucien and Allan walked out.

"And shield your thoughts, and mine, if possible, when Allan is around," I leaned over and whispered into the Kappa's ear.

Tamotsu's eyes slid sideways. "Akihiko can read minds?" He sounded thoughtful. "It will be nice to have someone to speak to in my native tongue."

I grunted and watched Lucien and Allan stop at the top of the stairs, expecting us to come to them. How typical.

"Rest assured, Carus. I will keep your thoughts protected."

Well, that was a relief. I fought to hide my satisfied

grin as I climbed the stairs beside the Kappa to stand before Lucien and Allan.

"Little Carus." Lucien's voice was more condescending than usual. Must be because of the audience. "You've done well."

"The Kappa is yours," I said. "He will obey your orders."

"Will he now?"

I nodded.

Allan narrowed his eyes at me, and it took every ounce of effort not to hold my breath—Lucien would notice that. But Allan remained silent. Did he sense the shield around my mind? Did that give away Tamotsu's ownership? Allan said nothing, keeping his thoughts to himself. What were his motivations? He wasn't against Lucien...but he wasn't for him either, at least not all the time.

"Akihiko," the Kappa said, interrupting my internal musings. "I look forward to conversing with you regarding our shared homeland."

Allan turned his attention from me to the reptile with a small smile. "As do I," he said.

"Will you join us for a drink?" Lucien asked me.

"Um...no thank you. Don't think I'd enjoy your particular vintage."

Lucien laughed. "Ah, but I enjoy yours."

Thoroughly creeped out, I managed to say goodbye and extract myself from the situation without any bloodletting and with as much grace as I could muster, which is to say, very little.

ooth wasn't at the downtown SRD headquarters, which I was fairly certain she lived at. Her office had been cleared out, and Angie hadn't seen or heard from her. Apparently, her unexplained absence pissed off the big boys at the top, almost as much as the missing files. She'd taken a number of confidential folders; mine among them. With no love lost between Booth and her overly curvy Wereleopard receptionist, Angie took great joy in telling me the latest SRD gossip.

Only one other place existed where she might be. Pulling up to Booth's mother's house, I slammed the car in park, jumped out, and jogged up to the front door. I didn't knock, opting to barge in.

Booth and Herman curled into one another on the loveseat in the living room where Booth's mom had died. They sipped tea. I sniffed the air. Chamomile tea. No lingering scent of the body meant they'd called in a Witch for cleanup.

Booth and Herman didn't react to my dramatic entrance. Once I took in the living room and returned my gaze to her, Booth waved her arm at the armchair across from them. A third cup of tea waited on the coffee table in front of it. Herbal scented steam rose from the dainty cup.

"We've been expecting you." Booth's gravelly voice sounded different than before, fuller, as if she'd held something back before.

"You owe me some answers." I plopped down on the floral cushion.

"I owe you nothing."

"I did you a favour."

"Will you waste it on a silly question?"

That stopped me. More went on here than met the eye. I could never read Booth, and now was no exception. "No. You're right. I should save the favour. How do I get a hold of you?"

Booth reached over the coffee table and handed me an ugly figurine with a cobra-headed Egyptian goddess. At least, I assumed it was Egyptian. "Hold this and say my name."

"Agent Joyce Booth?"

Booth shook her head. "Renenutet."

I sat down and watched the two of them sip their drinks as if they entertained like this every day. They looked so domestic and so wrong at the same time. Their otherness clashed with the floral sofa pattern and excessive use of doilies.

Yet, something about seeing the two of them together stirred my heart. I wanted that. Companionship.

"You've gained more, since we first met." Booth's intense gaze penetrated my soul. I squinted at her face and realized why she looked different—she no longer wore her trendy glasses. There was something odd about her eyes, too. Not quite human.

I frowned at her statement. "What do you mean?"

Herman leaned forward and analyzed me; his regard sent a cold sheet of ice over my body. Despite the harshness of the sensation, it didn't feel malicious. "Ah," he croaked. "I see it now. The Carus."

I sat back and sipped my tea. The herbs coated my tongue and tingled my nasal passage. Why did everyone seem to know more about me than I did? My ignorance pricked me like a thorn in the ass. Good ol' Donny was getting a visit very soon.

"You have four guides now. Before you had three," Booth said.

"One too many. I feel like my head is going to explode."

Booth nodded. "You need to dispel some."

"But how do I choose which one, and how can I dispel something that is a part of me? They make up *my soul*." I patted my chest with the palm on my hand, in case they didn't realize how much my soul meant to me. I was pretty sure the soul wasn't housed in my heart, but that's what hurt every time I thought about the prospects of losing my soul, so it seemed appropriate.

"Dispelling does not mean losing. Your guides will always walk with you, once found and bonded." Herman's voice raked the air, interrupting my disparaging thoughts.

"Could you be any more cryptic?"

"You fear something you shouldn't. I merely want to assuage that," he said.

"Can you elaborate?"

Herman blinked, his slit eyes refocused on my face. "The Carus must walk this journey alone."

"Well, can you tell me what's up with the two of you? Without me having to cash in on my favour? Did someone brainwash Herman? Or why—"

"Sobek," Booth interrupted. "His name is Sobek."

Herman turned his head and the two of them stared into each other's eyes, in what I'd like to say was a dreamy way, but it was too still, too cold, too...different. And creepy.

Booth broke the eye contact first and glanced over at me. "To answer your two questions—we're husband and wife, and yes, something like that."

"I wish I could tell if you spoke the truth or not."

A small smile appeared on Booth's face. "Not the first time you've wished that, I bet."

"Without me using my favour, will you tell me what you are?"

Herman, or Sobek, or whatever, stood up slowly,

pulling Booth up beside him. "We must leave, Carus. We will give Feradea your regards."

Huh? "Huh?"

Before I could demand some answers, the two clasped hands and disappeared. No puff of smoke, no lingering scents, nothing. Just disappeared. If the two empty tea cups didn't sit on the coffee table in front of me, I'd consider committing myself to the nearest mental health institute.

Somehow, I managed to leave the house feeling more confused than when I entered.

39

T he sun filtered through the forest canopy, lighting the way down the path. I came to the same clearing where I'd met my fox fera and sat down cross legged in the centre. I tried to clear my mind. *I am you. You are me. We are one.*

All my feras perked up from their resting places within me, and repeated the mantra. A breeze of deep love surrounded and warmed me. For once, the absence of Wick and Tristan, the domineering Alphas, came as a relief.

Little fox, I started. And then stopped, unable to go on. A tear streaked down my face.

Why sad, Carus? she asked.

I don't want to lose you.

You cannot lose what has been found.

It was pretty close to what Herman had said earlier, but I still felt unsure and nervous. The little fox nudged me. *Be strong.* She grinned.

Strong, like predator, my cat hissed.

It still sat wrong. I wasn't ready. Standing up, I shucked off my clothes and concentrated on the fox before willing the change. It came fast and ready. My bones shrank into themselves, and I felt more than saw my red hair shoot out. Shaking off the last shudders of the shift, I stood in the clearing as a fox, vibrating with energy. Everything seemed larger, brighter, and fuller. I sniffed the pine-laced air and suppressed the urge to race off into the bush.

A helicopter flew over the area. I ducked and sprinted to the tall grass that lined the clearing to cower. The fox might be intelligent and perceptive, but the small size left me with an overwhelming feeling of vulnerability. As a falcon, I might be small, but spending most of the time in the air, I was virtually untouchable.

Run, the fox whispered. *Be free*.

Despite my nerves and my common sense telling me not to, I obeyed and took off into the woods. I leapt over logs, sprinted down deer trails, and weaved between the trees until eventually I found my way back to the clearing. The sun, lying low, was no longer visible from the break in the canopy. Time to go home. I had to do this now, or I'd lose my resolve.

Running in the fox's shape lent me strength and clarity. Taking a deep breath, I shifted back to human form and focused on the fox's energy. *Please leave my mind. I... dispel you.*

A warm heat spread and covered my body as if I lay on some tropical beach basking in the sun. Somehow I knew it was the fox's love for me. Maybe she said so, I don't know. I was too consumed by the warmth. And then...nothing.

Cold and alone. Barren.

I bent forward, resting my arms on the ground and cried. The fox in my head was too much, but with her gone, I felt empty.

Something brushed my leg. *Why sad?*

I screamed and jumped up. A ghost version of the fox grinned at me. I reached down and touched her—soft and smooth as the first day we met. She wagged her tail.

Now I walk beside you like a normal fera. Not in your head. But no one can see. No one can hurt. Stronger. Safer.

The other feras vibrated with excitement. They rushed back to my mind, and the feeling of emptiness lessened. I searched within for the fox and found nothing. I held the image of the fox and tried to shift again, but nothing happened. My eyes pinged open.

I can't take your shape, I said to the ghost fox.

No, Carus. You need to reabsorb me for that.

The idea of taking in the fox again, and the pain and chaos that followed stopped me from reaching out. I didn't even know if I could do that. But if the fox remained "outside" my body, what purpose did she serve now? Feras never answered questions straight-up, but it didn't mean I wouldn't try. *So, I can see you?*

She nodded

And I can touch you?

She nodded again.

But nobody else can? Every fera was a Shifters greatest strength and greatest vulnerability, because the death of the fera meant the death of the Shifter.

I exist only for you.

EPILOGUE

The walk out of the forest had been long and lonely; my other feras wise enough to remain silent and leave me to sort out my thoughts. My Witch neighbours had invited me over by text message, and I'd accepted, not wanting to sit by myself tonight.

When I opened my door to go down the hall, Tristan's presence surprised me. With his hand half-raised to knock on the door, he paused.

"Hi," I said.

"Hi." He shoved his hands in his pockets and rocked back on his heels. "I came to check on you."

"Well, I—"

Tristan's lips on mine stopped my words. His arms came around to hold me tightly against his chest. My hands had a mind of their own—one snuck up to run through his silky black hair and the other drifted down to grip his tight ass. He answered by deepening the kiss and pushing me into my apartment and against the wall. Citrus and sunshine curled around me with invisible, caressing fingers, sucking the air out of my lungs and replacing it with delicious heat. Tristan's tongue stroked mine and warmth spread from my chest, sending tingles down my arms and legs. As much as I wanted to haul him to my bed, this wasn't about the lust racing through my veins and aching between my legs. I needed this reassurance. I needed his presence. I needed him.

Tristan pulled back and touched his forehead to mine. "I've missed you."

"I missed you, too."

My apartment grew heavy with unspoken words of who else I might miss.

"You were heading out?" Tristan's normal purr held a gruff edge.

"Yeah." I cleared my throat and straightened his shirt, running my hands down his chiseled abs. "Going over to my neighbours for some karaoke."

Tristan took a step back and smoothed my shirt, tugging it back to my waist before gripping my hips. "Another hobby you forgot to mention?"

"No. I can't sing and neither can they. I just..."

"Didn't want to be alone?"

"No," I whispered.

"Can I join you?"

I hesitated.

"I can't sing either," he said. "No judgment."

I laughed and nodded. Tristan took my hand and led me out of my apartment. The Witches opened their door with smiles and hugs. I had no idea what they'd planned, but it had to be better than watching reruns. They accepted Tristan's presence easily and invited him to join us.

The little fox trotted beside us like a devoted puppy, giving me strength and comfort. *I'll never walk alone again.* She also gave me a lot to think about. If I could dispel her, it meant that I could dispel any or all of my feras.

Maybe I could even dispel Lucien and rid myself of the blood bond shackling me to him. He'd said it himself —I should think of him as a "blood-sucking fera." If I could remove his control, I would be free.

Free to choose whatever life I wanted...with whichever mate I chose. I glanced over at Tristan. He listened to Ben talk about the crazy gnome elder who'd come into headquarters. Matt passed me a beer, and Christopher, thankfully, kept away.

I could dispel my mountain lion or wolf and no longer be torn between two mating calls. But which one would I choose?

Right now, Wick's unavoidable obedience to Lucien was enough for me to keep my distance, as much as it pained my wolf and my heart.

Tristan looked over and flashed a smile.

The sight warmed my chest and strengthened my resolve. I wanted to know more about Tristan. Right now, he didn't appear to have any faults. The very thought sent warning bells ringing in my head, like an impending tsunami headed my way. Nobody was perfect. Everyone had cracks in their veneers.

I watched Tristan accept a carrot "microphone" from Patty. What secrets did Tristan hold close?

I planned to find out.

"Ready, Andy?" Ben looked over at me and raised his beer bottle as the opening notes to Milli Vanilli's *Blame it on the Rain* blasted through the stereo speakers. "Ready, Tristan?"

I brought my beer bottle up and used it as a microphone as I belted out the first verse. Tristan joined in, not at all ashamed he sung slightly off key. Not a bad fault to have, in my book.

The Witches joined in for the chorus, and Patty took over for the next verse, crooning into his fake microphone. I looked over the group and realized these Witch bitches weren't so bad after all. Then my attention snagged on mute Christopher banging on the drums—empty bulk coffee tins—glaring at me as if he contemplated my death.

Well, maybe some of them were.

They call me DEMONIC...

As an ambassador with the Supernatural Regulatory Division, I need to be calm, respectful, and diplomatic.

But no one has ever accused me of possessing these skills.

I equally detest the Vampire Master of Vancouver and the SRD, and if the latter discovers the beast I keep locked inside, I could end up in the government labs. When a menacing demon throws an important vampire summit into chaos, though, all my secrets could get exposed, and I'll have more than job security to worry about.

I'm willing to sacrifice my pride, my career, and possibly my life to neutralize the demonic threat and protect my loved ones, but can I make a choice that will break someone's heart?

And complete another's?

Don't miss this fast-paced, addictive urban fantasy with sugar and spice and everything not-nice by international bestselling author, J. C. McKenzie.

Previously published as *Carpe Demon* by the Wild Rose Press.

Acknowledgments

I'd like to thank mt critique partners and beta readers—Jo-Ann Carson, Charlotte Copper, Kelly Atkins, J.A. Garland and Anna Kearie.

Thank you to my editor Lara Parker and cover designer Olga Sauchenia.

I'd also like to thank my readers for continuing to support me and enjoy the worlds I create.

I hope you enjoyed the story.

J. C.

About the Author

J. C. McKenzie is a book loving, gumboot-wearing, unapologetic science geek. She predominantly writes urban fantasy and post-apocalyptic dystopian fantasy with strong romantic elements. When she's not spinning tales, she's in the classroom sharing her passion for science and mathematics while secretly warping the young, impressionable minds of our future to carry out her evil plans for world domination. She lives in the Pacific Northwest with her family.

Visit her at jcmckenzie.ca

facebook.com/j.c.mckenzie.author

instagram.com/j.c.mckenzie

tiktok.com/@jcmckenzie0

bookbub.com/authors/j-c-mckenzie